1959 Rome, Vatican City

*The Secret of Fatima has be
in one of those archives wh... are like a very deep,
dark well, to the bottom of which papers fall and
are never seen again.*

THE HOLY INQUISITION PREFECT,
CARDINAL ALFREDO OTTAVIANI

1915 England

*And both that morning equally lay
In leaves no step had trodden black.
Oh, I kept the first for another day!
Yet knowing how way leads on to way,
I doubted if I should ever come back.*

ROBERT FROST - THE ROAD NOT TAKEN

THE

HIDING GAME

SAGA

TIGER

ROMEO

METAPOX

#2

raechel sands

Tiger Romeo is an imprint of Goldheart Ltd a UK company - www.goldheart.gold

Published by Tiger Romeo 2017
First published in paperback and ebook in 2017 by Tiger Romeo
First published in Great Britain, the USA and Australia in 2017 by Tiger Romeo

THE FATIMA SECRET - CENTENARY EDITION

Raechel Sands is represented by Nancy Owen Barton Agency - nowenb@aol.com

Raechel Sands asserts the moral right to be identified as the author of this work
Cover and book design by Keith Sheridan
Cover photograph by Paolo De Faveri
Layout by Sarahjane Jackson

A catalogue record of this book is available at the British Library

ISBN 978 1 912148 00 4 - paperback
ISBN 978 1 912148 40 0 - ebook

JULY 13, 1917

THE THREE
SHEPHERD CHILDREN

JACINTA AGE 7, FRANCISCO, 9 AND
LUCIA, 10 — RECEIVED *THE FATIMA SECRET*

Jacinta & Francisco died after World War One in the great influenza epidemic.
On May 13, 2017 Pope Francis made history by making them the first (non-martyred)
child saints in the 2,000-year history of the church. Sister Lucia, a Carmelite nun, died in 2005.

THE FATIMA SECRET
1917 – 2017

⭐

www.goldheart.gold/Fatima

1959 Cape Cod, USA

*No names have been changed to protect the innocent,
since God Almighty protects the innocent
as a matter of Heavenly routine.*

KURT VONNEGUT JR.

Genghis Khan's army

*physically slaughtered some 40 million people, but his
invasion of the Crimea should be recognized as
the most spectacular incident of germ warfare in history,
with the Black Death as its disastrous
consequence. The world population did not recover to
pre-plague levels for over three hundred years.*

CENTERS FOR DISEASE CONTROL AND PREVENTION (CDC)
EMERGING INFECTIOUS DISEASES, VOLUME 8, NO.9

Book 2 of the Hiding Game Saga

No one knows what it's like
To be hated
To be fated
To telling only lies.

No one bites back as hard
On their anger.

None of my pain and woe
Can show through.

PETE TOWNSHEND - BEHIND BLUE EYES

HG

CONTENTS

PART ONE

THE DOGS OF WAR

We stand now where two roads diverge.
But unlike the roads in Robert Frost's familiar poem,
they are not equally fair.
The road we have long been traveling
is deceptively easy, a smooth superhighway
on which we progress with great speed,
but at its end lies disaster.

1962, RACHEL CARSON - SILENT SPRING

Trouble in Wonderland

Who killed Cock Robin?
I, said the Sparrow,
with my bow and arrow,
I killed Cock Robin.

Who saw him die?
I, said the Fly,
with my little eye,
I saw him die.

Who caught his blood?
I, said the Fish,
with my little dish,
I caught his blood.

All the birds of the air
fell a-sighing and a-sobbing,
when they heard the bell toll
for poor Cock Robin.

ROUD FOLK SONG INDEX - NUMBER 494

1.0

Wednesday, March 18, 2015
235 West 32nd Street, New York, NY 10011, United States
11:40 a.m. New York / 4:40 p.m. London Time

*I*n the Garment District of Manhattan, Blanka's fifteen-year-old half brother, William P. Hart, walked along the parapet of the rooftop above his father's loft. Will liked heights, he liked to take risks. What his teachers called a vivid imagination, his father Professor Max Hart, dismissed as wild flights of fancy.

Will was born eleven years after his father and Drox (his collaborator, the African-American doctor, Ray Oxberry) had raised The Goldheart, and the seventy tons of solid gold had completed its arduous journey through the Mediterranean, across the Atlantic and into the jurisdiction of the Port Authority of New York and New Jersey. Will's birth was something of a miracle and, for Max Hart the boy represented everything that his murdered wife – Kitty Maguire – had meant to him.

The night before, Will had turned up unexpectedly at his father's loft, having run away from school. Hart's greatest fear was that he would lose his son to the same forces that had killed his wife. This unspoken fear went a long way towards explaining why his father even bothered to listen to his son's lame excuse – that he had seen dead bodies in his dreams the previous night – before resolving to run him back to school the next day.

As Will looked down the several floors to Sixth Avenue below and then up at the towering Empire State Building, he took in the light, the clouds scudding through the city sky, the flock of European starlings. He could almost see angels flying. Will and Blanka had different fathers, but given Kitty's genes, they were definitely full siblings in spirit.

The loft's landline started to ring. His father was still out at Bellevue psychiatric facility where he consulted, so Will jumped down, ran to the stairs and answered it.
'Will, what are you doing there?' It was Drox from Paris.
'Hi Drox.' Will was happy to hear from 'the mad-scientist guy who worked with his sister' (as he called him). 'I'm just home for a day. When are we doing the 3D scan of The Goldheart like you promised?'
'Later,' Drox said. 'Right now I must speak to Max. He's not answering his cell.'
'He probably forgot to turn the ringer back on. Have you tried the Scanner?'
'They're being jammed, when is he —
'Jammed?' Will knew enough to realize that was serious. At that moment Hart marched up the stairs onto the roof terrace and glared at Will.
'What are you doing out here?' Hart demanded.
'It's Drox, urgent. Scanners are jammed, your ringer's off.'

'Jesus,' said Hart, grabbing the receiver.

Drox spoke quickly and clearly. 'SOS from Grinin on his CIA-Blue. Crusoe and Blanka are at the scene.'

'London protocol?' asked Hart

'London protocol,' said Drox and hung up.

★

*A*s Drox set the burner on the seat of the Paris taxi bound for Charles de Gaulle airport, it rang. It was Farringdon (an MI6 techie working for Blanka).

'GCHQ's jamming the full spectrum of our Scanner frequencies,' he said. 'Can you retune everything to OhZone's next higher octave?'

'Six minutes,' said Drox, opening the master retuning protocol on the gold-colored ℧Scanner on his lap. 'Tell Blanka: jet and bird, thirty minutes.'

'Wilco,' said Farringdon.

1.1

The Grinin's Penthouse, River Heights,
35 Victoria Embankment, London S.W.1, United Kingdom

*I*t was said that Grigori Rasputin, the mad and powerful holy man of Tsarist Russia, always had tricks up his sleeve, but Grigori Grinin, our one-armed Rasputin, had no tricks left. The lights had gone out and he was dead.

Grigori Rasputin had been tortured by MI6 agents at the bidding of Mansfield Cumming – the original C of Britain's MI6 – then mutilated and castrated in an effort to make him divulge the state secrets of his mistress, the Russian tsarina. As the song said

> *Ra – Ra – Rasputin lover of the Russian Queen*
> *They didn't quit, they wanted his head*
> *Ra – Ra – Rasputin Russia's greatest love machine*
> *And so they shot him 'til he was dead*

Of course, during the First World War, history tells us, Britain had strategic interests in having Russia stay in the war on Britain's side – against Rasputin's advice.

In 2015 Britain also had strategic interests in securing Grigori Grinin's weapon, Metapox, for itself. To stop Grinin making a vaccine against Metapox, the current C had ordered Felicity, his protégé, to murder him. Sans mutilation and castration, he'd got off lightly compared to the tsarist Rasputin. But Felicity, having killed Grinin, hadn't finished. She had additional plans.

Yet there are more worlds than our histories record, and there are forces at work outside our world that have tricks of their own. At 4:42 p.m. on March 18, 2015 Major Grigori Grinin suddenly became aware that he was seeing his body as it floated face down in the aquarium of his lounge. The thought

> *I'm a ghost*

came from the back of his mind but, strangely enough, didn't disturb him at all. He had been a life-long atheist until his contact with Kitty Maguire and the Fatima Secret. His return to the religion of his birth had been a great comfort to him, but he had only explored the afterlife as a theoretical conjecture, not any sort of expectation. Like many of his other preoccupations, he had not discussed it with his wife, Diana.

Grinin felt strangely at ease with himself, as if a weight had been lifted. His body had finally stopped struggling. But what exactly am I? He saw his aura suspended near the ceiling. He had two arms and hands again! 'Splendid,' he chuckled to himself, 'God is now my surgeon!'
The water in the aquarium, darkened with his blood, was curiously inviting. Grinin saw the fish frantically swimming away from his body to the corners of the tank. My poor fish, I've made quite a mess of your little world.
He could hear music and his attention shifted to the turntable with the Deutsche Grammophon record still playing the last movement of *Pictures at the Exhibition*. When the music ended there was a jarring return to the other noises around him, and it was then he saw a woman in a little-black-dress stood next to his aquarium, reaching over and examining his dead brown eyes with cold medical objectivity.

He remembered the last moments of his life with a shock. She had been disguised as the Nanny – but had removed her disguise, her mousy wig and the prosthetic appliance over her face – he hadn't had his glasses on. But he didn't need glasses any more, his soul could see clearly now! She was the exact likeness of Blanka's Russia Desk girl, *Nearby*! But at the same time he realized it wasn't Nearby. There was a sinister blankness in the face, a total lack of compassion. The woman in the little-black-dress had come to kill him, and had indeed killed him. She was the killer. She had wanted to do it while she was fucking him! A thoroughly nasty piece of work. Insane and vicious. Had she given her name? There was no memory there.

Grinin now remembered his body's last act of will before he left the world of the living and came to this other place – a transformation the Greeks had called, 'crossing the River Styx.'

Sinking to the bottom of the aquarium, he had willed his body to turn over and resurface, face up. He wanted her to see his face; he wanted her to know he was still looking at her, even though his eyes were dead.
Then he had felt her fear. It was the last thing he was aware of as the lights went out. Her very strong fear. The fear every murderer, every assassin feels for an instant. The irrational thought: what if the victim comes back to life on me? comes back to haunt me?

Out of that fear he learnt his killer's identity. Pure evil, he reflected. The reincarnation of possibly the most wicked child killer the world has ever known. Dear God. He felt thousands of pairs of eyes coming on like lamps in the dark around him. Mothers, children. Many, many children. 'Well, Herr doctor Felicity,' he said. 'There are a lot of souls waiting to turn up the gas burners of hell for you. Let me introduce myself – I'm the late Grigori Grinin and I'll be making you my *special project...*'

Suddenly his thoughts changed. My children! Diana 's at work! They're in danger! Diana!

A couple of seconds later, his cell phone lit up with an incoming call. The caller ID said

Diana. Accept or decline.

An electrical energy in the ether was rising and falling like surfing waves.

Grinin recognized it from the power cut at the Jericho Café. Another outage was beginning, but these waves were stronger. From his new vantage point he knew it would help, this mysterious force.

He could see far below, in the basement, Blanka and Nearby trying to override the disabled elevator controls. Jude was with them. The MI5 officers had sealed the lobby and called in the police. On Victoria Embankment, he could see his former KGB colleague Lara setting her men into play. Thousands of feet above, over south London, his fellow defector Sokol Comarova flew towards River Heights in the OhZone helicopter. Grinin could pick out the first Met police arriving, only yards from what would become their new headquarters in two years' time.

Felicity Robinson had been agent OhZone 7 just ten days.

When she limped quickly down the hall, away from Grinin's garotted corpse, his ghost concentrated all his energy on her. Felicity turned, spooked, and knocked into the antique table, sending the Toby jug of the Queen crashing to the floor; while the tranquillizer syringes landed amidst the jagged chunks of china.

When Nearby's voice came from the intercom – Grinin's ghost could feel Felicity's fear *peak*. Ah, he thought. Nearby is one of your former victims is she?

Harnessing the surge of energy waves, he projected them with intense anger into the fire alarm system and heat sensor above Felicity's head. At 60°C (140°F) the bulb released – inundating Felicity with water. As she reached up to stem the flood, her hand touched the wet outside of the electrical sensor which gave her a mighty jolt. She stumbled and her injured bare foot crunched down on jagged pieces of Toby jug. She grimaced in pain and lifted her foot, slivers of Queen's head impaled in it. Blood ran freely from the bullet hole through her foot onto the Turkish carpet as the fire siren went off a few inches from her. Grinin watched as Felicity's hands shot to cover her sensitive AI ears and she slipped in the downpour, landing in the broken china and cutting her hands and face. But the effort had been too much for Grinin's ghost, and he felt a sudden bewilderment...

Weightless, he felt himself drifting away from the Earth.

1.2

As Felicity scrabbled among the broken pieces of china for the dimethohexital syringes, the landline on the table started ringing, further distracting her.

The twins peered around the edge of the doorway of the playroom through the shower of water. Olga Grinin pointed at Felicity, whose back was facing them, and asked, 'Nearby?!' Her sister, Emma, in the blue football shirt Blanka had given her at the party, signalled, No! then grabbed Emma's hand and bolted across the hall into their bedroom. Olga slammed the door shut, turned the key and removed it from the lock (as their father had taught them for such an emergency).

The twins caught their breath and clutched each other. Olga started to cry, and Emma, despite her own trembling, took on the role of the responsible one. 'She's not Nanny, not Nearby. She's bad.'
'Where's Daddy? said Olga.
Emma shrugged, 'Let's do what he said…'

'The closet,' gulped Olga with a sob, as she followed her sister inside their closet. The twins looked at each other and repeated:
'Push Mr Punch.'
Each placed their hands on the twelve-inch high smiling figure of Punch in a toy theatre. They pushed, and watched as four solenoids clicked, securing the bedroom door to its frame with bolts.

★

Felicity had just gotten back on her bare feet when the power surge plunged the hall into darkness. The siren stopped dead, but the sprinklers kept going. Her nut brown hair wet and clinging to her face, she raised her hands to stop the stinging spray from going in the cuts on her face, even as it washed the blood from her right leg, bathing the carpet in red. At first Felicity thought Blanka and her team had taken out the power, but when her AI vision was affected, she realized it was no ordinary power outage. She could see in the dark hall, but not clearly; there were fuzzy lines all over her AI sight. Then she heard the sound of Blanka's zip line embedding itself at the top of the elevator shaft. 'Buggering bitch,' she said.

Drenched, her leg throbbing, Felicity tried to look through the twins' door, but her AI vision failed her. She quietly pushed down the handle, and sighed as she found the door locked.
'Emma? Olga? Let me in,' called Felicity sweetly. 'We'll play such lovely games.'

Olga opened her mouth to shout back, but Emma pressed her hand over it. 'Quiet as mice. It's the hiding game. Shh!'
'I have badges for you… and candy,' shouted Felicity.
'I'm scared,' Olga whispered. 'Want Daddy and Mama.'
'It's okay,' said Emma holding her sister's hands tight. 'Blanka and real Nearby are coming.'
Frustrated with calling through the door, Felicity dropped to her knees but gasped in pain – as her injured right knee took her weight – letting go the candy which fell into a puddle. 'Bugger,' she said. 'Bugger, bugger, bugger!'

Dropping the badges and syringes into her bag, she took out her MI6 lock-picking kit. She picked the door lock with ease, climbed to her feet and pushed the handle down again. But the bedroom door wouldn't open.
Stepping back, Felicity shoulder charged the door. The frame shuddered but the door refused to budge. It was obviously firmly anchored. A stab of pain from her knee summoned her attention to the blood running down her right leg.

A feature of the AI allowed OhZones to monitor their own medical 'Obs,' internally, and Felicity did this. An OhZone's pulse and temperature were lower than humans; and Felicity's read NFO (Normal for OhZone). Oxygen level was higher than humans: NFO. Blood volume should be a third higher (it was also thicker and clotted quicker), but the reading was in the red: she had lost 1.4 liters.

Stringing her bag around her back, Felicity grabbed some of Diana's head scarves from a hook, made them into a tourniquet and tied it above the leg wound. There was no question of kicking in the door.
Her anger turned cold and she took her 321 from her bag, stepped back

and crouched down on the floor. She aimed the pistol, and pulled the trigger. The extreme recoil from the cartridge threw Felicity back into the wall, her dense Lutetium-enhanced 245lbs leaving a woman-shaped depression.

The round took out the door frame and the reinforced wall around it, sending the door flying into the bedroom in a cloud of smoke. The depleted uranium bullet had embedded in the far wall, its intense heat melting the plaster.

*I*n the silence before Felicity pulled the trigger, Emma told her sister. 'We have to play the game for real now. The secret carpet will hide us.'
Olga nodded, but her face suddenly showed anguish, 'My tiger!' she cried, pointing at her toy lying in the bottom of two bunk beds. Before Emma could stop her, she dashed to the bunk and grabbed the tiger.

Just as the wall exploded and the bedroom door came crashing in, Olga reached the closet and Emma shut and locked the lead-lined door safely behind her.
'The hiding game,' the twins whispered. 'First Mr Punch then Mrs Judy.' But when they pushed the figure of Judy, nothing happened. Then there was the roar – from outside – of a huge wind battering their building.

As suddenly as it had begun, the power outage ended – the fire siren started ringing accompanied by a cacophony of car alarms from the streets below – and a motor whirred above the children. As they had been drilled by Grinin dozens of times, they gripped each other tightly. Four cables connected to a 'dumb-waiter' mechanism raised the carpeted floor of the closet, and hoisted them to safety in the crawl space of the roof!

*A*s Felicity walked in over the top of the bedroom door, holding the badges and syringes, the siren restarted and her AI hearing returned, deafening her. She covered her ears and spun around, disoriented by her AI vision. She couldn't see the twins anywhere. Through the window she saw snow and hail batter against the glass. When a seagull smashed into the pane with a bang, she jumped.

Pulling herself together, she remembered her on-board computer, which had been described in an OhZone training session she had attended. Internally, she addressed this back-up AI: 'Hera, locate Emma and Olga Grinin.'

From the AI portion of her brain came the reply, 'The Grinin twins are inside the closet, rising in a dumb-waiter to a crawl space approximately ten feet above.'

Felicity dashed to the closet and ripped open its lead-lined door just as the bottom of the dumb-waiter was disappearing. She grabbed the corner of the mechanism, pulled the carpet from under the twins' feet and jammed the motor. Olga, clutching the tiger, tumbled to the edge. As Felicity continued to pull, the dumb-waiter tipped over more and Emma reached out to grab Olga, but caught hold of the tiger instead, while Olga fell head first into the waiting arms of Felicity.

Emma screamed. Olga kicked Felicity and sank her teeth deeply into her arm, biting for all she was worth, drawing blood.
'Little bitch,' said Felicity.
Pulling her arm away, Felicity flicked the cap off a tranquillizer syringe and injected all 2mls of dimethohexital into Olga's arm.
Still kicking, Olga twitched a few times and then went limp in Felicity's arms.

Felicity checked Olga's neck for a pulse. Finding none, she rolled her body over and stared at the little girl's expressionless face. Her brown eyes were open, staring at nothing. Felicity touched them gently – tenderly even.

As if from another world, Felicity heard the howling of car alarms and the wailing of police sirens on Victoria Embankment. Those noises mixed with voices calling out from the CIA-Blue radio in the penthouse lounge, as well as the sounds of Blanka coming up the elevator shaft.
With Olga in her arms, Felicity looked up past the dumb-waiter to the crawl space.
'Emma,' Felicity pleaded. 'You have to help me. Olga's hurt. I didn't mean to hurt her. But she's hurt. I just need your help, my darling, and she'll be fine.'

With tears in her eyes, Emma held her tongue. She's not going to be fine! You just killed her. She stood up in the crawlspace and took a couple of small steps – opened the portal exactly as her father had taught her – and ran out onto the rooftop of River Heights.

1.3

*C*rusoe Robinson, agent OhZone 3, pulled himself up over the roof parapet just as Emma bolted from the portal, dragging Olga's tiger by one paw. Her blue football shirt immediately told him it was one of Grinin's twin daughters. Emma recognized Crusoe, in his body armor and helmet, as one of the officers who guarded her father. Crusoe walked towards Emma and opened his arms in a 'Which direction is the danger in?' gesture.
Emma pointed at the penthouse and Crusoe drew his Sig 321 and aimed it in that direction.

With Olga slung over her shoulder, Felicity climbed the ladder from the penthouse hall into the fire escape to the roof.
There, where she had left them the day before, were her Jimmy Choo Myren flat over-the-knee boots (which C and everyone else called her C.F.Ms).
They will reduce the bleeding, she thought, wincing in pain as she shoe-horned a boot onto her leg. Then she pulled on the other boot, picked up Olga's body, and pushed a hatch open onto the roof.

Felicity's appearance on the roof sent Emma scrambling behind an air conditioning plant.
Felicity knew Olga was dead, but continued to use her as a ploy.
She shouted to Crusoe, who was her husband Jude's elder brother. 'Crusoe! Thank God! Help me with Olga.'
He looked at Olga limp over Felicity's shoulder and then at Emma hiding behind the plant. The three year-old, tears streaming down her face, shook her head frantically. Crusoe focused on Felicity 'What have you done?' he shouted.
'A hit man's killed Grinin,' Felicity shouted back, looking down at her blood soaked leg. 'I was shot giving close protection.'

Crusoe hesitated; with so many sides contending for Grinin, it *was just plausible.*

Felicity moved Olga off her shoulder and into her arms to conceal her 321.

From behind the air conditioning unit Emma jumped up and pointed, 'she did it!'

The two OhZones looked up at the same time, their AI hearing detecting the approaching OhZone helicopter long before it could be seen.

'She killed Olga!' Emma screamed. 'I saw her do it!'

Crusoe aimed his pistol at Felicity and ran towards her, weaving and trying to get a line on her.

Felicity held Olga in front of her as a human shield, and he couldn't get a clear shot. But he sprinted in to body tackle her, calculating he could catch Olga as she fell.

From under Olga's head Felicity fired her 321. The recoil of the second depleted uranium cartridge sent Felicity flying backwards and threw Olga three feet up in the air.

Gravity did its worst and Olga plummeted nine feet, landing on her head with a snap: her neck and spinal cord breaking.

The .45 ACP D.U. round hit Crusoe with a kinetic energy of 2,000 foot-pounds – the pyrophoric effect of the uranium burning right through his ℧Armor and his ribs – exploding his chest cavity. His body was thrown back across the roof where it hit the air conditioning plant, throwing his neck back so violently that it snapped off his head, which rolled across the rooftop.

The depleted uranium bullet crossed the roof, terminating in a pallet of cladding on the roof of the Norman Shaw Building, where its intense heat ignited the building materials.

Emma, in complete hysteria, ran to the nearby edge of the rooftop. Construction scaffolding on the Norman Shaw Building almost touched River Heights, but a fire was now spreading from pallet to pallet with frightening speed.

A three foot jump seemed like a leap into the fires of hell for the three year-old, and she retreated back to the air conditioning unit. Seeing

Crusoe's head, she screamed, and ran to the far side of the plant, where she knelt and curled up into a ball like a hedgehog.

★

Smoke now poured into the sky from the fire on the Norman Shaw Building and everything rushed through Felicity's head at once. Fires from this life all rolled up with fires from her past life filled her with a sense of a job well done.

'Oh, I do love fire,' she shouted at Emma, moving closer.

But Operation Penthouse itself had suddenly gone clusterfuck. She couldn't go home to Balham now.

Plan B.

'We'll say it's *another gas explosion*,' she confided to Emma.

She'd go by ferry to her safe house in Dublin. Cool Hand Luke was at Pimlico underground station with a backup disguise and documents.

'Don't you *just love* Democracy?' she said, prodding the little curled up hedgehog with her boot.

1.4

*W*ith their Scanners working again, the OhZones moved quickly. 'There's another way in at the back,' shouted Farringdon. Running the OhZone AI software on the computer Felicity's husband of three months, Jude Robinson, and Farringdon had discovered an emergency staircase not used since the Second World War.

Nearby (a dead ringer for Felicity) sprinted around the side of the building to join them and heard Bob Dylan's *It's All Over Now Baby Blue* playing at full volume from one of the apartments above.

At the rear of River Heights Jude detonated an OhZone explosive called a 'China' (ten times more powerful per gram than C4) across a welded-up steel plate, ripping a large hole in it. *It's All Over Now Baby Blue* continued to play.

Jude and Paddington – armed with flashlights and Sig 320s – burst through the China hole and ran up the disused stairs. Nearby followed carrying, for the very first time in anger, her Sig pistol in her hand.

Pointing over Nearby's shoulder, Farringdon yelled, 'The Russians.'

Nearby looked around and saw Lara and her Sergeant approaching, Gyurzas drawn.

On her Scanner Nearby could see helicopter footage of a child on the roof. She couldn't see the face of the figure near her.

'Put those away and leave,' Nearby said in Russian. 'There's nothing you can do.'

'Grinin?' Lara asked.

'Almost certainly dead.'

'The children?'

'One on the roof.

Lara refused to take her eyes off Nearby.

'We don't know about the other girl.' Nearby said and was gone.

*T*he H175 helicopter swooped low through the smoke over Emma and the two bodies on the roof. The pilot-doctor called the major incident information into the radio:

'OhZone-Kilo-6-0-7 to MI6 Control. "Methane" repeat "methane," roof of River Heights, Victoria Embankment, Sierra Whiskey-1. Armed attack on children...'

As Blanka forced open the elevator shaft maintenance door, Felicity, having readied herself for Blanka's arrival and bracing herself for the recoil, fired three depleted uranium rounds at Blanka one after another.

The force of the blasts demolished the machinery and the lift shaft and sent Blanka and the elevator crashing a hundred feet to the ground: killing Officer Gabor and burying the River Heights lobby a foot deep in rubble.

From the helicopter's winch door Sokol Comarova – agent OhZone 5 – in fatigues immediately recognized Felicity through the sight of her sniper rifle, and pulled the trigger.

With lightning-quick reactions Felicity dodged the bullet. Meanwhile Prosthetics John opened fire from the Old Cabinet Office Building. Several rounds from his semi-automatic ricocheted off the helicopter legs and into Sokol's ℧Armor.

As Prosthetics John ducked out of the way of rifle fire from Lara's sergeant on the ground, Sokol jumped on a harness and cage in a desperate attempt to lift Emma off the roof. But Felicity, picking Sokol up on her AI vision, fired at the cage, sending it raining down in pieces as Sokol fell the thirty feet onto the roof.

Part of the cage hit Felicity's arm, causing her to drop her 321. The fall also knocked Sokol's P238 micro-compact from its holster and sent it flying across the roof to Felicity's feet.

The smoke from the burning building engulfed the helicopter. The pilot backed away, winching in the remains of the cage. Emma was now out in the open. With her AI microsecond reactions and OhZone resilience, Sokol had landed on all fours and was already on her feet.
'SUKA Robinson!' she yelled as she charged towards Felicity, a ten inch army knife in her hand.

Felicity picked up Sokol's pistol and emptied the clip of .38 rounds into Sokol. One round hit Sokol in the arm, another her hand, sending the knife flying. As Sokol continued to stumble on, Felicity used OhZone unarmed combat maneuvers to send her sprawling to the deck.

Felicity dropped Sokol's P238 in her bag. 'Plan B means new life, new priorities, she said to herself.
She trotted the six feet to get back her P321 and then, quite deliberately, aimed it at Grinin's remaining daughter, who was ten feet away curled up again in a ball.
She was a hedgehog clinging to a toy tiger, thought Felicity, and laughed.
'Let me see your eyes," she commanded, but all Emma could do was tremble.
'What a shame. But if I can't have you, no one will,' she added. '*Auf Wiedersehen Haustier.*'

When Felicity fired the sixth depleted uranium round, once again bracing herself against the recoil, it decimated Emma and splattered the roof and Sokol with pieces of bloody toddler.

Numb with shock, Sokol couldn't even look up from the ground.

'Bitch,' Felicity shouted in her face. 'See what you've made me do.' And she kicked Sokol in the stomach, making her groan. 'She'd have been safe with me...' she raged, chopping down on Sokol's neck with her Sig 321 and knocking her out.

Crouching over the unconscious OhZone's body, Felicity started stripping her of her fatigues and talking as if Sokol could hear her. 'Operation Penthouse sure turned into a clusterfuck, didn't it? And whose fault is that? You and Blanka and C and all the petty bureaucrats who don't give me resources and can't see past their asses.'
Felicity extracted Sokol's ℧Scanner and waved it in front of her face. 'For my new life. Compensation for the twins I never got to know properly.'

Unzipping Sokol's ℧Armor and pulling it off her, she stuffed it into her bag, and then screamed, 'Now I'm going to have to bale out of dear old William Blake's Jerusalem, and set up house elsewhere.' And with that she grabbed a piece of the cage to brace herself with.
'But I'll leave you with something to remember me by.' Then she raised her Jimmy Choo Myren boot and kicked the unconscious woman in the face, breaking her nose and cracking her eye socket.

She was readying herself for a second kick when her AI hearing picked up Blanka climbing toward the top of the ruined elevator shaft. All out of ammo, thought Felicity-fast-track. Then she did an extraordinary thing.

Leaving the fire and bodies behind her, she skipped across the rooftop merrily whistling Mozart's *Eine Kleine Nachtmusik*.
At the far edge of the roof, she clipped herself to a zip line (which Prosthetics John had erected earlier), easily slid the ten yards on to the roof of the Old Cabinet Office Building and made good her escape.

1.5

*W*hen Sokol came round, she got up and limped towards Olga's body. When she reached her, Sokol opened Olga's blue lips and gave her the kiss of life. At that moment Emma's charred blue shirt, which had been ripped from her body by the blast of the .45 D.U. round, was gusted by the wind to land at Sokol's feet.

Climbing up out of the ruins of the elevator shaft – covered in rubble and her own blood – Blanka, the leader of OhZone and agent Ʊ4, ran over to Sokol who was pounding Olga's heart.
Sokol looked up at Blanka grimly. 'She's gone.'
'No!' Blanka shouted. She ripped the top of Olga's dress open, pulled an Adrenalin syringe from a medical pack at her side and injected it into Olga's heart.
'Gone. Dead,' Sokol said firmly and lifted the girl's body gently into Blanka's arms. 'Look at her! Can't you see?'
But all that Blanka knew was that she felt Olga's heart trying to pump. She cradled the little girl.
'There's a pulse,' she cried.
Incredulous, Sokol carefully explored the back of Olga's neck with her fingers.
The helicopter had landed, and the pilot-doctor ran over with a portable defibrillator.
'Get it on,' Blanka told him. The pilot attached the pads to Olga's bare chest and hit the green button.
'Stand clear,' came the recorded voice from the machine. There was the sound of a shock being delivered followed by 'Analyzing now.'
'Blanka, her neck's broken,' Sokol said. 'Her spine's severed.'
'But she's alive,' Blanka answered. 'There's still hope.'
Blanka shot another adrenalin injection into Olga's heart. The cardiac monitor beeped feebly a few times.
'It's over,' the pilot said, about to get up.
'Shock her,' ordered Blanka.
Sokol gripped Blanka's arm to keep her from reaching the machine.
'I don't think –' started the pilot.
'You're not a fucking doctor,' screamed Blanka.
'He *is* a doctor,' said Sokol. 'Blanka, stop! We can't save her.'

The emergency stair hatch at the far end, blocked up with concrete, exploded open, showering the roof with chunks. Jude emerged followed by Nearby and Paddington.
Nearby surveyed the carnage, took a couple of steps to Emma's Rugby shirt and picked it up from where it had fallen next to Sokol.
Blanka and the pilot turned to Nearby as if somehow she could bring

them salvation. Sokol shook her head and gently closed Olga's eyes.
Nearby's CIA-Blue crackled, 'We believe the killer has entered Westminster underground station, we're in pursuit. Do we have an I.D.?'
Nearby turned to Sokol.
'SUKA Robinson,' Sokol said.
Nearby spoke into the radio, 'This is Nearby, MI6. The killer is female, five feet ten. ID OhZone 7, Felicity Robinson, formerly Furness. Armed and possibly disguised, extremely dangerous.'

Sokol stood up and faced Felicity's husband, Jude.
'The children?!' cried Jude. Then he saw Crusoe's head and body by the air conditioning plant and rushed over to his brother. Nearby signalled Paddington to follow. Seeing Olga's tiger, now soaked in blood, also lying by the plant, Sokol started the gruesome task of gathering up the body parts that had once been Emma.

★

Out of some macabre sense of what needed to be done, Paddington placed Crusoe's head next to his body.

Is she going to try to fit the head back on to the body? thought Nearby.

But Paddington sat down next to the sobbing Jude and cradled him in her arms. There were tears in her eyes too.

Nearby blinked. She wished she'd never come down from that tree and met Blanka. She wished she'd stayed in Ireland and never got closer to MI6 than Dublin Castle. She found herself looking at Blanka with an emotion she didn't think she possessed, something approaching disgust.

In an attempt to hide from those dark emotions, Nearby looked down and stared at the fragment of blue shirt that had for such a brief time been Emma's, turning it over and over in her hands.
The Dylan song still rang in her ears

It's all over now, Baby Blue   ↻

Through the Looking-Glass

Antony:
Blood and destruction shall be so in use
And dreadful objects so familiar
That mothers shall but smile when they behold
Their infants quarter'd with the hands of war;

All pity choked with custom of fell deeds:
And Caesar's spirit, ranging for revenge,
With Ate by his side come hot from hell,
Shall in these confines with a monarch's voice

Cry 'Havoc,' and let slip the dogs of war;
That this foul deed shall smell above the earth
With carrion men, groaning for burial.

WILLIAM SHAKESPEARE – JULIUS CAESAR

2.0

*T*he first three fire tenders wailed to a stop eight floors below the River Heights roof.
Black smoke from the Norman Shaw Building wrapped Blanka and Nearby in their own world, disconnecting them from the rest of the universe. In the black haze, Nearby knelt down beside Blanka and prayed part of the Rosary with her: the simple Fatima prayer.
Nearby started and Blanka joined in

O my Jesus, pardon us, and save us from the fire of hell;
draw all little souls to heaven, especially those most in need.
Amen.

Nearby felt Blanka sink her head into her shoulder and she listened to Blanka's erratic breathing. What would Blanka do now? Would she hide in some fantasy where she stumbles back in time and Grinin makes it to Ireland? Or does she imagine him returning to Russia where his children would still be alive?

Nearby looked across the roof at tear-soaked Jude who now sat stunned, immobile. Paddington gently placed Crusoe's head at the top of the bloody torso, then Sokol used a tarp to cover him.

Blanka repeated her Rosary, Paddington cradled Jude. And Sokol resolutely gathered up little Emma scattered, o, too far and wide. There was too much horror and grief to take in. Nearby let her mind drift, let anything distract her – thoughts of King Richard the Third and Leicester car parks and mitochondrial DNA and Ulysses. The Greeks had it right. We must live on surfaces, we can't survive the depths for long. Penelope.
No one had mentioned the bereaved mother – Grinin's now childless widow – no one had mentioned *Diana*.
How could she possibly bear this?

Nearby looked at the once-strong OhZone woman sobbing uncontrollably on her shoulder and whispered a childhood comfort (from one convent schoolgirl to another). The Beatitudes from Christ's Sermon on the Mount wouldn't have comforted most people.
But Blanka wasn't most people.

> *Blessed are the pure of heart,*
> *for they shall see God.*
>
> *Blessed are the meek,*
> *for they shall inherit the earth.*

Nearby realized she must leave Blanka and go to Diana now: she could get to London Zoo in three minutes by bird [helicopter PUT EARLIER] As Met police sirens screamed down below, Farringdon repeated the major incident alarm on the CIA-Blue and the ℧Scanner.

> *Blessed are they who mourn,*
> *for they shall be comforted.*

2.1

MI6 Headquarters, Vauxhall S.E.1

*W*hen the fire on the roof of the Norman Shaw Building took hold, Devices [director, Technical Division] had been looking out of the window of her corner office on Floor 10.

Within sixty seconds, she was storming into Miss Banks' office on Floor 13. 'Where's C? The Norman Shaw Building next to River Heights is on fire,' she said. 'There's a report in that Grinin's been killed.'

'Good heavens,' Miss Banks said, pointing out of the window.

'You just missed C.'

Devices looked out the window. The MI6 helicopter normally stationed in a hanger on the roof was just taking off and crossing the Thames.

'Pass me your radio,' said Devices, taking a red radio handset from Miss Banks.

'Office to C, come in. Office to C, come in.'

No answer.

Miss Banks jumped to her feet. Out of the window she could see flames leaping up from Victoria Embankment.

Devices grabbed an internal phone and dialed.

'Yes,' Probe answered.

'Penthouse is Charlie Foxtrot, C's gone. I'm on '13, get up here.'

Probe answered without emotion: 'Wilco.'

In C's absence the chain of command dictated that the head of the biggest and most important desk would be in command of MI6. That was the Russia Desk. But Russia was at a NATO meeting in Brussels. In his absence it fell to the most senior director.

Devices and Probe had joined on the same day, but Devices was the older.

Probe marched two of C's lieutenants, a man and a woman from the so-called anti-OhZone desk, into Miss Banks' office.

'I think you take precedence by age, Octavia,' he said. 'As far as I know no one's officially authorized a hit on Grinin. The directors voted for him to make the Metapox vaccine.' He turned to C's lieutenants. 'Did C authorize a hit?' he demanded.

'It's classified,' said the young man.

'Classified?! I have level nine clearance, young man.'

'With respect, Sir, it's over your level.'

'My level!' Probe chased the man around Miss Banks' desk, trying to cuff him.

Devices held out her arm, stopping Probe, and addressed the two agents. 'Slocombe and Worth, I'm acting Commander. I order you to answer'

'With respect, Ma'am, you are not acting Commander. C is still in transit; he's not on leave yet.'

'Yet!?' yelled Probe.

'He's not officially on leave until tomorrow,' said the woman.

'That means from midnight tonight,' put in Miss Banks. 'It's five o'clock now.'

2.2

RAF Northolt, West End Road, South Ruislip

*T*he British Foreign Secretary, L.B.J. [Lucien Barker Johnson], heard the news as he stepped off a flight from a stormy meeting with his Russian counterpart in Geneva.

A senior Foreign and Commonwealth Office aide ran up to him followed by two Special Branch officers, 'I have to speak to you, Sir.'

'What is it?'

'One of our agents has gone rogue and killed another agent and two children.'

'Children?'

'Girls.'

'How old?'

'Three years-old, sir. The Grinin twins.'

'My God. What, both of them?!'

'Yes and the MI6 agent, OhZone 3.'

'Fucking Jesus wept,' exclaimed L.B.J.

'It gets worse. Downing Street wants to know did you authorize a close-the-file action on Major Grinin?'

'What, a hit? Of course, I fucking didn't – he defected to us, didn't he?'

L.B.J. stood paralyzed in anger, incredulous. The senior aide and the

Special Branch officers stood awkwardly in those silent moments until…
L.B.J. seemed to see.

'Holy Mother of Christ. Get me to number ten, fast.'

L.B.J. got into the back seat of the official limo behind the tinted windows. Without another word the driver waited for two Met police cars to immediately pull out ahead and put on their blue lights, before all three vehicles sped into the night.

2.3

River Heights, S.W.1

*N*earby climbed into the H175 with the pilot-doctor, who fired up the engine. The pilot called London control on the radio. 'This is OhZone Kilo 6-7 Critical Emergency Flight Plan to Regents Park heli-pad. Notify all traffic.'

Rotor engaged, the bird rose five hundred feet from the rooftop and headed north down the river to Regent's Park Zoo. The radio crackled, 'Copy that OhZone Kilo 6-7.' came the reply.

Nearby looked behind her at the burning Norman Shaw Building, Big Ben behind it, and down at a sea of blue lights. Three blocks in every direction from River Heights were already sealed off by scores of MI6 officers. Fire tenders were playing their hoses on the burning building, and Westminster Bridge and Parliament Square were being closed off by the Met police.

Nearby surveyed the fiery chaos below, and remembered the old Catholic saying, 'If you can't go to the Father, go to the son. If you can't go to the son, go to the Mother.'

She would go to the Mother.

The gray of River Thames faded behind, in the approach to Regent's Park. Its green expanse resolved into the neat walkways and enclosures of the London Zoo, home of the animals Diana specifically worked with; the elephants, monkeys, lions, and tigers.

When the helicopter landed, Diana was waiting for her outside the main office building. She had heard the sound of the explosions and seen the fire and the lights.

Her anxiety, as she looked up into the smoke-darkened sky, had been for humanity in general. Seeing Nearby's face, the grim set of her mouth, Diana felt panic seize her. She closed her eyes.

Even when Nearby embraced her, held her for the longest time, Diana kept her eyes tightly closed. Finally she spoke:
'Tell me what happened. But please be kind. Dear God, please be kind.'

2.4

Five Minutes to Midnight (Wednesday)
C's Private Dining Room, Floor 13, MI6 Headquarters

When Bio [MI6's youngest director, Science Division: Marcia Miles] walked the mile from her apartment in Battersea Power Station, she knew she was being tailed. MI5? she thought, now *I'm* a suspect. The tails changed at the Waitrose on Nine Elms lane.

Now as she walked up from Floor 12 to C's Private Dining Room, the eyes of every agent on the night shift at the Russia Desk followed her.

Nearby was at Sokol's house trying to console the hysterical Diana (where it was thought best that she should stay for the next few days), Russia waited on Floor 13 for the other directors, and Jude Robinson's location was unknown. As a result, a nervous Paddington [young Black German woman; living with aunt in W.2] was temporarily in charge of the Russia Desk.

The directors had decided to wait until midnight when C was officially on leave before they met. Earlier, Devices and Probe had asked Dr Fox whether C could be declared mentally ill.

'He's unfit for duty alright,' Dr Fox had answered, 'But I'm afraid I can't classify him as mentally ill.'

'This is a pretty mess,' said Devices.

'I'm meeting L.B.J. at 10 a.m.' said Russia.

'The original gas explosion has been upgraded to a terror attack,' said Probe. His eyes fell on Bio who eyeballed him back.

'I've done nothing wrong,' said Bio, defiantly.

'I'll be the judge of – ,' said Probe.

'Hang on, old man,' interrupted the youngest man, *Bantu*, the Africa Desk director, an Afrikaner.

'Shall I take the chair as planned?' asked Asia sheepishly.

'Yes, please,' said Devices.

Asia looked at the clock. In the distance he heard Big Ben starting its sixteen note prelude to the hour.

'It's midnight,' said Asia. 'C is on leave. In his absence, Russia is in acting command of MI6. I ask him to make a statement to us in his new capacity.'

Russia stood. He looked each of the other seven directors in the eyes, finishing with Bio, who sat opposite him.

'C's lieutenants have been kind enough to debrief me. They are all temporarily suspended, and are being closely monitored. Major Grinin's murder...' Russia stopped for a moment to let his words sink in, once again surveyed the directors and settled his eyes on Bio.

'Major Grinin's murder,' he continued, 'designated Operation Penthouse, was a *close-the-file action* sanctioned by C after the Metapox conference one week ago at Castle Monkus. It was hatched against the majority vote by the directors in favor of a vaccine to Metapox. It was done in utmost secrecy and in breach of our agreement with the Americans. The Op was given directly to OhZone agent 7, Felicity Robinson who – after closing-the-file on Grinin – went rogue and murdered Grinin's children and agent Crusoe Robinson.'

Again he paused, but this time he only looked at Bio.

'These hits were not, I repeat, *not* sanctioned. In the usual way they, along with the second degree murder of police officer Gabor, will be placed under the heading of collateral damage.'

Russia sat down and Asia nodded and asked the room, 'Can I check which directors other than C had knowledge of Operation Penthouse before the fire on Victoria Embankment?'

Bio raised her hand.

Asia looked around the room. No one else moved.

After a moment's silence, Bantu pointed at Bio.

'She was having an affair with Felicity-fast-track.'

'As the only director who had prior knowledge of the operation, do you also acknowledge having an affair with OhZone 7?' asked Asia.

'It was a light affair,' Bio answered.

Devices pinned Bio with her eyes.

'A *light affair*? She killed two toddlers, Marcia. Couldn't you have *lighted* elsewhere?'

Probe coughed his official cough.

'I have video of Mrs Robinson leaving your apartment this morning, only eight hours before the killings,' he said.

'Can I clarify this for the classified record?' Asia interrupted and turned to Russia. 'In reference to 'not sanctioned', we are discussing the killing of the two Grinin children, Olga and Emma, Special Branch officer Gabor, and OhZone 3, one of our most trusted agents gunned down on the rooftop?'

'Yes,' said Russia. 'The Blue or Black Slip hit covered only Grinin himself. His daughters, the police officer and Crusoe were murdered.'

'Is this the first killing, *ever*, of an OhZone?' asked Asia.

'Yes, it is,' said Devices.

Asia turned to Bio. 'What kind of hit was it?'

'Black,' stated Bio.

'Can you prove it?' said Probe.

'I can. I have the Black Slip on security camera.'

'You better had,' said Probe.

'Chairman?' said Russia.

'Please,' said Asia.

Russia stood again and looked straight at Bio.

'This is not a time for recriminations,' he said. 'With the General Election just six weeks away, we cannot afford another scandal.'

A buzz of agreement went around the room.

'Since Bio was the one director with knowledge of this Op,' Russia continued. 'I would like the directors' consent to have Bio assist me in the full investigation of it.'

Asia turned to the room. 'I propose that Russia, assisted by Bio, launch an A.C.L.I. [All Classified Levels Investigation] into Operation Penthouse, its consequences, Grinin's killing, the children's murders and the loss of our esteemed colleagues, OhZone 3 and Officer Gabor.'

'Seconded,' said Devices.

All eight directors raised their hands in favour.

*D*evices wasn't yet finished with Bio. She reached forward and placed a forensic bag containing an empty tranquilizer syringe on the table.

'Two tranquilizer syringes were recovered from the scene. The dimethohexital from this was used to kill Olga Grinin, who died of a massive overdose. The same tranquilizer was found at a lower dose in the blood of Mick Mayall, 5's live-in placement. We did not recover that syringe, so we assume Robinson must have left with it.'

Devices placed another forensic bag containing a second syringe on the table. This one was still full.

'We don't know if this injection was intended for Emma,' she said. 'But it may well have been.'

She addressed Bio. 'Did you supply these syringes of dimethohexital to Mrs Robinson?'

'Yes,' said Bio, and a gasp of surprise went around the table. She panicked, 'For a Black Hit they're authorized! But dimethohexital is intended to knock out adults who –'

Bio stopped and lowered her eyes.

'The child's death might have been an accident,' she said.

The other seven directors stared at her. In the silence, Bio saw prison bars – again. As a young matelot [Royal Navy rating] she'd killed a chief who'd attempted to rape her. Although eventually cleared of all charges at Court Martial, she'd spent three months in the notorious Anchor Gate R.N. Detention Quarters at Portsmouth.

Devices broke the silence, completing Bio's previous sentence:

'Dimethohexital is intended to knock out adults who walk in on a hit.' She glanced quickly at everyone in the room, then addressed Bio again: 'You're not defending Felicity killing two small children, are you?'

Bio took a deep breath. 'No, 'she said. 'I'm not in any way defending her. She knew what dimethohexital syringes are intended for. She had medical training.'

'Wasn't there another officer involved in the Op?' asked Asia, coming to Bio's rescue.

'A Grade 2 technical officer,' said Bio. 'John Hunter, Prosthetics John. He reports to Devices.'

Devices blushed slightly. 'He's deserted,' she said. 'After using a sniper semi-automatic from the Old Cabinet Office building.'

'We have A.P.B.s out for him and Felicity-fast-track,' said Bantu.

'For obvious reasons,' Russia said, 'Felicity Robinson should be our primary concern. Her OhZone security and privileges are already rescinded, and I am asking Professor Hart to eradicate her OhZone and AI mods when she's caught.'

'Arms supplied the uranium rounds and gave her special training. Isn't that what you call it?' said Bantu, sneering at Probe.

'Did C authorize the use of those rounds?' said Asia. 'Can you find out, Devices?'

Devices looked up from her tablet. 'Arms is on a few days leave.'

'I'm seeing him tomorrow, today,' said Probe. 'The Pimlico Players are performing *Orpheus* Saturday, I'm in his orchestra. I'll find out from him.'

'When did Felicity's special training take place?' asked Russia.

'Sunday night,' said Bantu. 'In the firing range after she closed up the Cloud Nine bar.'

'What?!' yelled Probe.

'Maybe C wanted the training hidden from everyone else,' said Russia.

'This is most irregular,' said Asia.

'An understatement,' said Russia. 'Let's just say she didn't follow required procedures. But she has a history of that.'

'I have *additional security footage*,' said Bantu, looking pleased with himself, 'of Arms and Felicity having sex in the firing range –'

'Oh my God,' said Bio under her breath.

'– both before, and after, training with the D.U. rounds.'

'She's fucking Arms too?!' spluttered Probe, his reading glasses falling off his nose. He turned from Bantu to Russia.

'Sex before violence, violence before sex,' said Russia. 'The corruption is systemic.'

'Octavia,' said Probe sternly to Devices. 'Arms also reports to you!'

'Well, Felicity-fast-track's not fucking me,' snapped Devices. 'If that's what you're asking.'

Probe slammed his fist on the table, making the water glasses and pens jump. 'Devices and I are in our seventies! Is there anyone else in Wonderland, who isn't fucking Felicity Robinson?'

2.5

Thursday. 6:37 a.m.

A few cockney pigeons preened themselves as the long-awaited sun rose on the vast clean up team spread out across the rooftop of River Heights.

Under the watchful eyes of Blanka's Russian second-in-command, Sokol – her hand, arm and face bandaged – every hair, every shred of skin, every spot of Emma's blood was being gathered.
Since her futile attempts to save Olga, and Nearby's departure, Blanka had moved just a few yards to sit on the parapet.
She stared listlessly out across the London skyline and the Thames river, and upstream to MI6 Headquarters.
She was flanked by two other Americans, one white and one black. The CIA Director, Admiral Keith De Leon, and the OhZone chief scientist, Drox (Dr Ray Oxberry).
'It feels like it's happening all over again,' said Blanka.
After a pause De Leon spoke, 'It's not your fault.'
'And what happened in Rome was not your fault either,' added Drox.

⭐

Vauxhall Tower (aka St George Wharf Tower)

An hour later, and a mile away as the cockney pigeon flies, Russia and Bio approached the MI6 officers outside the entrance to the opulent apartment building which almost met C's materialistic sense of himself.
'An African-American gentleman, a Dr. Oxberry, will be along,' said Russia. 'No one else is to enter.'
The officers nodded in almost perfect unison.

At the door of C's ground floor apartment, Russia knocked three times. An eye came to the spyhole, dull gray in color.
'Little pigs, little pigs, let me come in,' Russia said through the apartment door. Several locks were undone, and Anthea Holland, a senior forensics officer, let them in.

'We need some privacy,' Russia said to Bio.

Bio nodded and spoke to Holland. 'Wait in the corridor please.'

'Yes, Miss-Chief,' said Holland. Holland nodded to two other officers, and the three of them filed out.

'You shouldn't let your subordinates take joking so far,' said Russia.

Bio bit her lip and turned to look around the hall and the luxurious front room of C's apartment. That curtain pattern, she thought. Like in my bedroom. A sour taste filled her mouth. Felicity had been fucking her, in front of that very same pattern eight hours before she killed the twins. Sex and violence. She hadn't come into the service for this.

Russia interrupted her thoughts. 'You will let me know if you see anything significant, won't you?'

Bio hastily whispered her assurances and then strolled into the bedroom. She walked around the bed and looked to see where the spy cameras were. One was carefully hidden in a gap inside the wood of C's bedside table, hair-thin to avoid detection.

The one inside his lampshade had fallen out when the lamp had been knocked over and lay conspicuously on the maple wood. Someone would get in trouble for that mistake.

She turned to Russia. 'I wanted to thank you.'

Russia looked at her across C's bed and raised his eyebrows.

'For not throwing me to the sharks,' she said.

'Think of it as a temporary reprieve,' he said. 'I've closed the anti-OhZone desk and the thirty most corrupt officers are on their way to safe houses for debriefing. Hopefully that will bring new information to light. In the mean time we have to figure out C's motives – and Felicity's. And what's hiding here, and in her house in Balham.'

'It *was* a Black Slip hit, Phil.'

'A Black Slip hit with four unauthorized bodies: two *children* and two *officers*. I'm the new broom, Marcia. Don't think for a second I'm giving you a permanent shield. If you hold anything back, Miss-Chief, anything at all, I'll see you're assigned a ten year posting to Science on Penguin Island.'

Bio didn't bat an eyelid. 'You were first secretary at the embassy in Moscow, weren't you?'

'Yes,' he said as he pressed down on the mattress and let it spring back. 'I heard about the *irregularities* in Wonderland.'

'Blow jobs on the fire stairs,' she said. 'And *The Cadre*...'

'It wasn't just sex in the building and pay-for-kill,' replied Russia, sitting on the bed and running his hand over the sheet. 'Power is a huge aphrodisiac and I found the weave of Wonderland's fabric steeped in corruption. But when I returned from Brussels last night, I saw things at River Heights that I never dreamed I'd see in Westminster. In peace time. Collateral damage, done in the name of *democracy*.'

Bio looked down at the bed. Then she looked at him. 'To be able to help you, you've got to trust me.'

'I agree.'

She crossed around the foot of the bed and stood in front of him. 'Having sex with your boss isn't against the rules. My affair with C was fifteen years ago. I was a hungry Grade 3.'

'Yes, we all know C preyed on hungry girls within Wonderland. That's old news. There are many others like him in the civil service. And some are female.'

Bio looked Russia in the eyes.

'I suppose we should be grateful he didn't prey on the hungry boys too,' he continued. 'Tell me about your hunger, Marcia. Felicity was a junior rank. Is the hunger a constant craving? Or has it been satisfied?'

Bio bit her lip again. Then she rallied. 'I'm nothing like C,' she exclaimed. 'I'm not going down with him. I had no idea Felicity was after children. And I can't honestly imagine that C was. In all my time with him he never showed any unnatural interest in children.'

'He was at an orphans' fair with Felicity on Saturday.'

'It's her *hobby*. "Blanka has her animals and I have my orphans," she used to say.'

'Could C have wanted to wipe out Grinin's line?' Russia asked.

'No,' said Bio. 'It doesn't make any sense. I believe C knew nothing about the children.'

But the word *orphans* ricocheted around inside her head like a pinball. 'We have to find Felicity for the answer,' she managed to say. 'Any chance of catching her?'

Russia laughed. 'For a Grade 3 with little field training, she is a master of disguise, as you know.'

'A mistress of disguise,' echoed Bio.

'We were all over her house yesterday, before someone reduced it to rubble during the early hours. She didn't go there.'

'She's gone,' Bio said to herself.

'Nothing from the A.P.B.,' continued Russia. 'Half an hour ago a tall Irish woman in Jimmy Choo boots flew out of Dublin. But it's nothing solid.'

'Where to?'

'Spain. Reus. Our man in Barcelona is heading there.'

And what if Felicity hadn't meant to kill the twins, thought Bio.

Then what exactly did she want them for?

'I'll be gone like the mist in the morning,' shivered Bio, remembering Felicity's warning the previous day.

Tasting stomach acid coming up into her mouth, Bio took a bottle of Evian from her bag and drank.

'Are you alright?' asked Russia. 'We have a lot to get through.'

'I'm fine,' lied Bio.

A voice over the radio informed them, 'Dr Oxberry's here.'

'Thank you,' Russia replied. He turned to C's wardrobe and told Bio, 'I want to show you something that I think will surprise you.'

She smiled. 'I already know what's in there. C was always into BDSM.'

When Drox was admitted into the apartment, he joined them in the bedroom. He had an earpiece in his ear and his gold Scanner in hand. It immediately beeped. To give him a Virtual Retinal Display, he put on goggles. 'There's a hidden passage,' he said.

'Have you been listening?' asked Russia, opening the wardrobe.

'Of course,' smiled Drox.

Russia pushed an array of bondage wear along the rail and pressed a screw on the giant wall-size mirror at the back.

The mirror sprung open a few inches. Behind it, Russia keyed in a ten digit code into the alpha-numeric pad. 'It took our top code breakers four hours to crack this.'

The mirror slid sideways on an electric drive until it revealed an opening five feet high and three feet wide.

Bio looked at it open-eyed, 'I've never seen this.'

Russia, being much taller than C, had to bend low to enter the passage, as did Drox. They descended a spiral staircase then stepped into a secure Comms room – called in Intelligence a *Skiff* [Sensitive Compartmented Information Facility] – concealed underneath C's apartment.

'His own private *Skiff*,' said Russia, 'hidden within the core of the tower.'
Drox examined the area with his gold Scanner. 'A perfect Archimedes
cage,' he said. 'Hidden from you, hidden from us.'
Russia and Bio looked at each other and then around the empty Skiff –
which had been completely stripped bare.
'C caught the 7 p.m. flight to Havana,' Drox added. 'He didn't strip this
bare. So, who's been doing the hiding?'
Just then his scanner beeped. 'There's residual signals from hologram
transmissions in the last twenty-four hours.'

Russia turned to Bio. 'Any other private ordnance C was hiding away?'
asked Russia.
'He had places in Tuscany and Rome. You know he's close to the former
Pope?'
'Professor Hart blew up the OhZone Machine in Rome,' said Drox,
'rather than let C get his hands on it.'
'Fifteen years ago,' said Bio. 'I went to his villa in Tuscany only once with
him. He was selling it.'
Drox removed his goggles and fixed Bio with his eyes, his finger pressing
down a polygraph setting on the Scanner.
'What do you know about the Fatima Secret?' he asked her.

'Operation Fatima, another black Op. You have the files. You should be
asking Blanka.'
Russia took a step closer to Bio. 'I'd like you to tell us what *you* know.'
Bio took her time to answer. 'I overheard C say one thing that's not in the
official file. The Fatima Secret involved Grinin somehow.'
The polygraph on the Scanner showed green. Drox looked at her search-
ingly, 'What about Felicity's house in Balham?'
'Never been there,' Bio replied coolly. 'Felicity lived there with Jude.'
Russia watched the polygraph screen stay green, then turned to Drox.
'She's a polygraph evader. As are all our spies; Grade 3 standard training.
So she could be lying through her teeth.'
'Good point, well made,' said Drox.
'Boys, sorry to interrupt you. I *could be* lying, but *I'm not*,' she asserted.
Russia's radio went again, 'The Prime Minister's here.'
Russia picked up his radio, 'Say again.'
'Mr Corduroy's here. He's canvassing.'
'What-the-hell! He's doing what?' Russia exclaimed.

'Mr Corduroy's canvassing, Sir.'

'Canvassing?'

'With the MP for Vauxhall.'

Drox shook his head, 'I've just decided life is a screenplay written by an idiot. Politicians are here to provide the sound and the fury.'

The radio crackled, 'Paddington's intercepted him, Sir. They're talking about opera. Do we let him in, if he insists?'

'Of course you let him in, he's the bloody Prime Minister,' said Russia. He then had second thoughts and added, 'But tell Paddington to keep him talking about opera as long as possible.'

'May I?' asked Bio. Russia handed her the radio and she pressed the call button, 'Holland?'

'Miss-Chief.'

'Cut the crap. The Prime Minister 's here canvassing for the Election. Put crime scene tape across the door and look like you're on duty.'

'We are on duty.'

'Badges?'

Mumbling came over the radio followed by Holland, 'Cumming's not got his.'

'Let Cumming inside then. The rest of you look alert.'

Cumming slipped in through the door and looked down at the floor.

'Cumming!' said Bio.

'Sorry Ma'am.'

'The same name as MI6's famous founder,' said Russia, shaking his head.

'And no badge. Any relation?'

Drox gestured to the stripped-bare Skiff room with his hand, 'Clean broom, you said? You'll need a Second Coming to get this cleared up'

2.6

11:25 a.m.
Jermyn Grove, London S.W.12

*B*lanka's Mini Cooper, with Russia and Drox also inside, pulled to a halt at the Met police barrier five hundred yards from the ruins of Felicity's house. Jermyn Grove was sealed off by Met police, and the gas board signs read

Keep Back! Burst Gas Main!

Two hundred householders had been evacuated to Balham Community Centre, and a few curious on-lookers talked in a huddle outside the barrier. They looked up as snow started to make its final and unwelcome entry into the March sky. One householder argued with the police about getting her possessions from number 409.

'It's ten houses away,' she said. 'I need it for my elderly mother.'

'No one's coming in until the all-clear,' said the Met policeman.

'Was it a gas explosion?' 'A Second World War bomb?' others asked.

Russia showed his MI6 badge; Blanka and Drox showed their OhZone badges.

As the Mini approached the vicinity of what had been numbers 424 to 426, they were met by Paddington and another agent, Debbie, dressed as army bomb disposal experts. Blanka pulled her car up next to a Met police Range Rover, and Russia got out and walked with Paddington and Debbie towards number 424. Blanka and Drox stayed in the car.

Blanka's eyes closed for a moment and a dream fragment flashed before her ...

A dream or a vision? Her band, Point Blanka's version of *Roads To Moscow* filled her ears. She heard Sokol singing, as she saw herself riding Caesar, chasing the steam train. The smell of pines, the fog again.

Two broken Tigers on fire in the night flicker
their souls to the wind

In the last car, two goats in the straw. From the locomotive a White Rabbit, wearing engineer's cap, looked back at her and sounded the whistle. Beside the Rabbit was Grinin at the controls! He hollered at her, 'Come on, Magdalena, snow covers the traces!'

Catching the front car, Blanka saw the black teenage girl from Bosnia – cross-playing *The Night They Drove Old Dixie Down* on a *Marine Band* harp [harmonica]. The girl waved at her ...

Could only have been a few seconds. From the seat behind, Drox tapped gently on Blanka's shoulder. 'You haven't slept. You sure you want to do this?' Drox leaned forward, cradling her, 'I'm so, so very sorry,' he said.

'It's my worst nightmare repeating. It feels like it's going to keep happening forever…'

'You couldn't have stopped it,' said Drox. 'The blame lies at C and Felicity's door. And whoever else they are working for or with.'

'Just because I can't make it okay, doesn't mean I won't try. Understand?'

'Yes,' nodded Drox. There were tears in the corners of his eyes.

'I won't rest,' said Blanka as she forced herself out of the car. 'Until the wrongs I'm guilty of have been righted.'

★

*T*he area surrounding Felicity's apartment was literally a bomb site. Numbers 424 to 426 had been levelled to the ground by a massive explosion that killed the residents of 426, a black British couple who'd been asleep.

Felicity's wrought iron bathtub, broken into two pieces, lay in the street where it had been thrown by the force of the blast. Blanka approached the tub and ran her hand along the enameled metal.

'We've searched everything,' said Debbie, 'there's nothing out of the ordinary. Felicity-fast-track's bath tub, her and Jude's possessions.'

'Where's Russia?' Blanka asked.

Debbie pointed towards a house with blown out windows, number 428. When Blanka reported to Russia, he said, 'I think you should know that when we got to C's apartment at 9 p.m., there was a full-scale Skiff hidden in the downstairs. It took us four hours to get into it but it had already been *cleaned*, stripped bare in fact.'

'What time did *this* explosion happen?' Blanka asked.

'About 2 a.m. We had the house staked out by agents front and rear all evening. No sign of Felicity.'

'Were they hurt?'

Russia nodded toward a car with a column of brick on its hood. 'They were inside but had a lucky escape. I arrived an hour later and we've been searching since first light.'

In a statement of defiance the snow-cloud filled sky opened, and heavy snow fell.

'It's been snowing on-and-off all morning,' lamented Russia.

'Can we get a hot drink around here?' asked Blanka.

'Hot chocolate, guv,' replied Paddington, cracking a half smile. Blanka and Russia followed Paddington into the Army Bomb Disposal tarp where Paddington made the hot chocolates.

Blanka looked out at the snow. She remembered Grinin's words from her dreams

Snow hides everything, covers all the traces.

Blanka took her hot chocolate and walked absent-mindedly into the ruins of Felicity's house, her AI eyes scanning for hints but seeing only disaster.

She picked around in the rubble and lifted a huge block of masonry out of the way. Drox climbed out of the Mini and joined her, putting on his digital headset and holding his gold Scanner.

Connected in this way, he was also connected to Blanka's mind unless she switched off the connection.

'You are keeping the connection on, aren't you?' he asked.

'Yes. Not sure what good it will do,' she said.

'Let me be the judge of that.'

Blanka intermittently sipped her hot chocolate and deployed her OhZone vision to see through the layer of snow. If she saw something unusual, she wiped the snow and had a closer look. When she saw something under the snow that rang an alarm bell in her AI-enhanced-mind, Drox also saw it in his headset.

'A very new carpet,' he said, seeing what Blanka saw.

Blanka cleared away snow from on top of it. Her hands revealed the remains of a new rug. Not out of the ordinary in itself – but something didn't add up – Felicity-fast-track hated carpet. She'd boasted how the house was woodblock floor throughout. Olga's 'secret carpet' from the twin's birthday party flashed into Blanka's head, and from there into Drox's. She took out her silver Scanner and set it on a little stand in the snow. Her eyes glowed and she connected to it, feeling it scan down through the ground and receiving its signals.

Then she lay face down on the remains of the carpet and used her OhZone vision to see through the bricks under the rug. She couldn't really 'see' but – half with her AI eyes and half with her intuition – she felt there was heavy metal down there.

And not the heavy metal she loved.

She turned to Drox.

'I see it,' he confirmed. 'Metal object in a recently bricked-in cellar. Most likely of interest.'

Blanka returned to Russia. 'There's a cellar,' she said.

'What?' replied Russia.

'I'll explain in a moment.' Blanka turned to Debbie. 'Blue light it to Wandsworth Town Hall, use emergency powers and requisition the master plans for the street. Let's find out what this thing is.'

Debbie nodded, ran out of the tarp, and jumped into the Range Rover. The driver started its engine and drove off. As it passed the barrier and small crowd at the end of the street, it put on its blue light and siren.

Russia was lighting a cigarette. 'You were going to explain?' he said.

'I thought you'd given up,' she said.

'On cleaning up MI6?'

'Yes. But I meant cigarettes.'

'I did,' said Russia. 'I give up smoking at least once a week.'

'We're going to need heavy lifting equipment. Not to clear the site. But to excavate the cellar.'

'A cellar? In this neighborhood? Are you sure?' asked Russia.

'Yes,' she said. 'Can we order in the Caterpillars first? Then go over the details?'

He called on his radio.

'Russia Desk,' a voice answered.

'Who's looking after Diana?' he asked

'Sokol. At Sokol's house. They're going to Heathrow to meet Diana's father.'

'Nearby?'

'Just arrived on the Desk.

'Put me through.'

'Nearby,' said Nearby's voice.

'We need emergency excavation equipment from the government depot at Clapham. Close the A24 to get it here.'

'Yes, Sir.'

Russia turned to Blanka. 'Now, what's this all about? Give me the short version, my head hurts.'

Blanka pointed at the ruined house. 'We have to get to the bottom of this.'

'I agree. There's something going on with C. But I don't know what it is and I bloody well don't know how to explain it to L.B.J. or Corduroy.'

'I meant the bottom of the house. The cellar,' said Blanka.

They walked out of the tarp and into the ruins.

Drox turned to them and said, 'Someone is covering C and Felicity's tracks very carefully. Someone who's constantly one step ahead of us.'

Russia turned to Blanka. 'Something nasty in the cellar you say? Are you sure? Not just a hunch?'

'It's down there all right,' she said.

Blanka showed Russia the fragments of carpet covering bricks. Then she wiped the new snow from the line of bricks in the ground.

'These are different bricks. Maybe the same team who cleaned out C's secure room and apartment also wanted to bury this cellar so completely we wouldn't know it existed.'

Russia examined the line of bricks. Blanka took a brush from her handbag and swept away more snow to reveal the outline of a stairway. It was completely filled with new bricks.

'They filled the cellar with bricks, and then blew up the house?'

'My guess is they filled it in during the afternoon,' said Blanka. 'This whole thing has been in action for a while now. All the time we were watching Operation Penthouse, they were watching us, ready to seal up Felicity's house at any time.'

'So when we arrived to stake out the house, the cellar was already sealed?'

'Exactly,' she said. 'Just waiting for the dead of night to set off the explosion. We need agents to take statements from the residents, find out if they saw building work going on.'

'Right. What do you think we'll find down there?'

'A large fire and theft-proof safe,' said Blanka.

'A mighty big one,' Drox added. 'Probably concreted into the floor.'

'Can you tell me what's in it?' asked Russia.

'You think C and Felicity were working for someone else?' asked Blanka in reply.

'Yes,' said Russia.

Blanka looked at the ruins of number 424. 'It's not going to be good.'

'Are we talking Metapox?' asked Russia. 'Do we need to cordon off Balham? Or what?'

'I don't think it's Metapox,' said Blanka, 'No one in MI6 has been able to make it.'

Drox looked worried. 'MI6 hasn't made it, but there are eight Metapox weapons in the world. Four are – or were – in the hands of the Kazak Mafia. They want to sell, but no one will pay the hundred billion dollars they're asking.'

'As far as we know,' said Blanka

'As far as we know,' repeated Drox. He looked at Russia. 'You're right, it's "Or what." If it's Metapox, cordoning off Balham won't be enough. You'd need to cordon off London and close the UK's airports.'

'Paddington,' yelled Russia. 'Get Bio here at the double.'

'Yes, Sir.'

Russia called on the radio again.

'Control. It's Russia. I want a hundred more agents deployed to Balham immediately. Cancel all leave.'

'Wilco, Sir.'

Blanka had not fully registered the last conversation and she continued, 'The Met can help with asking questions. Let's send a dozen of them over to the Community centre with the agents.'

'Absolutely, 'said Russia. 'And I'll talk to Army Bomb Disposal. It seems we're going to need them after all.'

⭐

*T*he Council master plans had arrived, and Drox and Debbie stood poring over them.

In front, a massive JCB JS330 tracked excavator dug carefully while Blanka and Paddington crouched in the ruins. A small fleet of tipper trucks quietly waited.

The official story was changed to: 'following a terrorist attack at River Heights, next to the Palace of Westminster, a gas explosion in Jermyn Grove Balham had detonated an unexploded German bomb from the Second World War.'

The cordon had been expanded to eight blocks and three thousand people had been evacuated; at the edge of it more Army Bomb Disposal vehicles arrived. Three hundred yards from number 424, a twelve-foot high screen had been erected on every side, preventing anybody outside getting a view of the site.

Bio, with Jude, and her two most senior Science Division captains, arrived in a convoy. A Met police car preceded their green Range Rover which was followed by two unmarked vans and then two more marked, 'C.S.I. Forensic Dog Unit'. One of the captains directed the vans to unload and set up their biological and chemical 'sniffing' rigs, while the other directed the three dogs officers to deploy the first of the sniffer dogs.

In the car, Jude turned to Bio.

'Cigarette please,' he said.

'But you don't smoke,' said Bio, handing him a cigarette. 'You're getting as bad as Russia.'

Bio looked at her face in the vanity mirror and quickly touched up her makeup, getting her thoughts in order. I'm not going to go down for this. But ex-lover of C and current lover of OhZone 7 doesn't look good. She glanced across at Jude:

The husband. The poor dumb-bastard-husband. How could he have been *so stupid*? With all the upscale training he's had in subterfuge and surveillance, his radar didn't pick up Felicity coming? Now he's wrapped up in death and destruction.

Bio looked out the window. And there's Blanka, like a refugee from a war zone. Looks like she hasn't been home at all. Here goes.

She put her hand on Jude's knee. 'You okay?'

'I'll finish this and come over,' said Jude, exhaling smoke.

A young sniffer dog picked over the ruins of the bombed-out house watched by Blanka and the dogs officer. Bio took a Samsonite from the back of the car and walked towards them. The dog scented something and moved into the yard followed by its handler.

It had stopped snowing and wreathes of mist wrapped around Blanka's legs as she stood alone contemplating the Balham skyline. Gone like the mist, Bio thought. Where *had* she read that before? She climbed across the rubble and set down the case next to Blanka. Being considerably shorter, Bio looked up at her. But Blanka didn't stir. 'OhZone 4?' said Bio. Blanka turned. After a second's delay she said, 'So I'm just a number now am I? What happened to Blanka? Or Queen Boudica even?'

'The Iceni aren't looking too good today,' said Bio. 'But then neither is Science Division.'

Blanka nodded. 'I was thinking of all the people living in London. In Great Britain. Sixty five million of them. Living their lives in total ignorance of a weapon that stalks them – from a perfume bottle.'

'There's no Metapox in the UK, I can tell you that,' said Bio.

'Yet,' Blanka answered.

'Okay, yet. My people would have sniffed out any trace of it.'

'You better tell Russia. He's shitting bricks.'

Gesturing to the Samsonite, Bio said, 'Nearby sent a change of clothes.' She got out a hip flask from inside her coat and offered it.

Blanka hesitated a moment and then took a drink. 'It's not like I have a reputation to uphold.'

From the car, Jude watched Russia heading over to Blanka and Bio. Two women dogs officers followed him, each holding a shovel and an older, experienced dog on the lead.

Wanting to appear somewhat functional Jude stubbed out the cigarette, jumped out of the car and stumbled over the rubble.

'Mmmm, caraway,' said Blanka.

Bio smiled, 'Venus aquavit, I brought it back from California.'

Blanka nodded and took a mighty swig.

Just as Jude reached them, he tripped and fell in the rubble. Blanka pulled him to his feet with her other hand, and the two women brushed him down. Russia put his arm around Jude's shoulder. 'We've all been pretty clumsy over the last 48 hours.'

Bio turned to Russia. 'Whatever you find today, I'm sure it won't be Metapox.'

'A hundred percent?' asked Russia.

'I'll sign off on it. Neither Felicity or C are good enough liars to conceal that from me.'

'It's definitely not nuclear,' said Blanka. 'Or a dirty bomb. Drox and I both ran the most sensitive Geiger protocols on our Scanners. They would have picked it up from half a mile.'

Russia turned to Norma, the lead dogs officer. 'Ready?'

'They work in a pair. They're ready, Sir,' replied Norma as she and the other handler squatted and readied to release the two dogs.

Russia turned back to Bio. 'Can you guarantee that Felicity didn't have access to other chemical or germ warfare W.M.D.?'

'No, I can't,' said Bio.

'Then "Cry *Havoc*, and let slip the Dogs of War," ' said Russia. 'Let them continue their good work. And pray they don't sniff out anything that will utterly destroy us'   ʊ

The Frankenstein Sector

3.0

Watership Down, The Hampshire/Berkshire Border

*T*he risk that Felicity's safe could contain a W.M.D. was taken very seriously. Sealed inside an OhZone impermeable shield, it was transported by Army bomb disposal truck, with heavy military escort, out of London and down the West Country (M4) motorway.

On deserted moorland south of Newbury, the safe was transferred into the secure biological weapons vehicle from Facility N (for Newbury). From above, Facility N had the appearance of a giant concrete bunker: it was a Cold War relic, a deserted regional seat of command (a chain of bunkers the length and breadth of the land, built to withstand a nuclear winter). But unlike the better known Facility P (Porton Down, further west in Wiltshire), Facility N was a secret biological and chemicals weapons development site, entirely underground.

In Facility N, staff undertook 'two week on-two week off' shifts and entered disguised as contractors at one of the industrial units at Greenham Park, the former Greenham Common Airbase: the site of the first US Air Force Gryphon Ground Launch nuclear missiles in Europe.

Each Cruise Missile carried a W84 Hydrogen Bomb warhead – just 34 inches long by 13 inches wide – but with thirteen times the destructive power of 'Little Boy,' the Hiroshima bomb built in the Manhattan Project by the USA, UK and Canada, and one of the two nuclear weapons used by the human race in anger – at the end of the Second World War.

The British Ministry of Defence and MI6 were quite right when they thought that nobody would suspect that Facility N had been sited underneath the old site of the Greenham Common Women's Peace Camp.

1982: Embrace The Base. Thirty thousand women encircled

In 1980, nine years before the Berlin wall came down, the British population awoke to find that their new political masters had printed fifty million copies of 'How to survive a nuclear war.' It was to be issued to every household and contained instructions on: what to do while holed up for two weeks under a table covered in sand, packing toys for the kids, and how to dispose of bodies. Britons were particularly alarmed by orders to remove their net curtains!

"Paint the inside of your windows to reflect away the nuclear heat flash."
"DO NOT GO OUTSIDE until the radio tells you it is safe to do so."

In 1981, terrified at the prospect of nuclear war, a group of Welsh women (Women for Life on Earth) walked 110 miles from Cardiff to RAF Greenham Common and chained themselves to the fence (see picture). On New Year's Eve 1982, forty-four unarmed women, mothers and grandmothers, quite easily breached the wire and climbed up the live nuclear missile silos where they sang protest songs for hours. All were arrested and given hefty prison sentences. Another time, the women occupied the USAF control tower.
The camp was occupied 24/7 for nineteen years. The women braving British weather and appalling conditions of mud and no toilets or running water, together with an increasingly violent response by the police to their peaceful

Greenham Common Women's Peace Camp

the five mile perimeter, linked together in a human chain

protests. They lived in makeshift tarps and were reviled by the British media for leaving their children and kitchens behind to protest.

Over the years the Greenham Women attracted great attention, and human chains of 50,000 and 70,000 took place. But like other anti-nuclear protesters, they were targeted by a British secret intelligence unit (the SDS) who established complete fake identities (at great taxpayers' expense) and spied on the women, forming intimate relationships and fathering children with some of them (which the Intelligence officers abandoned when the operation ended).

The Greenham Women had a profound effect on the anti-nuclear movement and the wider Women's Movement at large. It inspired women's protests across Europe and eventually the world, including the year-long artists' protest 'Window Peace' in New York City. Soviet President Gorbachev explicitly mentioned the Greenham Women when he said that the European peace movement enabled his decision in 1986 to meet US President Ronald Reagan and sign the Intermediate-Range Nuclear Weapon Treaty.

The hundred W84 hydrogen bombs left Greenham for the USA, where today they form part of the American nuclear stockpile of 5,000 hydrogen bombs – **itself less than a third of the world's total nuclear arsenal...**

Two visitors to lend their support to the human chains at the Greenham Camp were the young Working Party politician, Jermaine Corduroy, and the American filmmaker, Kitty Maguire. Unknown to her bosses at the oil company BP, Kitty made a moving documentary film
of the Greenham Women which she called
Plutonium Blonde.

Inside the biological weapons vehicle from Facility N, Felicity's safe was driven inside what appeared to be a farmer's barn. As the electrical barn doors closed, the vehicle stopped on a giant ramp, and Bio and a team of scientists surrounded it.

The ramp lowered the vehicle two hundred feet deep inside Facility N, and the safe was secured in a triple-airlocked Level Five Chemical-and-Biohazard quarantine laboratory. Blanka, clothed in canary yellow full body and helmet biological-weapon-protection-suit (with self contained oxygen supply) waited with Bio, similarly suited, for the final airlock door to open and admit them to the quarantine lab. They joined scientists and MI6 safe breakers, all suited up in the same gear. Blanka held her breath as the door of Felicity's gunmetal gray Chubb fire and theft-proof safe swung open.

*T*he inside of the safe was largely empty. But size didn't matter with W.M.D.s – after all Metapox fitted inside an eau de parfum bottle. Two suited scientists removed the contents of the safe: a black attaché case and a Toshiba laptop.

In the corner of the lab, the two items were X-rayed and scanned for booby traps, devices and hidden compartments. Once cleared, they were opened. There was no yellow vial of Metapox or any other W.M.D.

The attaché case contained fifty thousand dollars cash, and several passports in different names with photographs of Felicity in a variety of wigs and disguises. The laptop appeared to be, well, a regular office laptop. Blanka and Bio removed their protection helmets. Blanka took a deep breath and turned to Bio. 'Curiouser and curiouser,' she said.
Bio bit her lip, and nodded.

3.1

Slowly I learnt the ways of humans:
how to ruin, how to hate, how to debase, how to humiliate.
And at the feet of my master
I learnt the highest of human skills,
the skill no other creature owns:
I finally learnt how to lie.

THE MONSTER – FRANKENSTEIN
BASED ON THE NOVEL BY MARY SHELLEY – BY NICK DEAR

Friday. 2 a.m.
Basement 2 Level, MI6 Headquarters, Vauxhall S.E.1

*F*elicity's laptop lay strapped to a Science Division test bench, dissected into pieces and connected to arrays of equipment. Bio and Farringdon watched two other techies display the regular Windows files from the Toshiba 1.6Terabyte SSD [Solid State Drive]. C, D and E drives: operating system, documents, pictures and history, totaling about 1,400 Gigabytes.

But a further hidden sector of the SSD was 'invisible' from the laptop itself. Formatted in Linux, the 'X' drive was marked as 'disabled' for the Windows operating system, this 100Gb sector of the SSD wouldn't show up on any search of the machine – a device regularly used by Intelligence agencies to spy on the owners of the computers themselves. The techies ran continuous routines to extract and decrypt the files from the 'disabled' X drive. It contained confidential MI6 and OhZone files Felicity would have been privy to, and clandestine video recordings she had made of her husband, Jude, trying to scrutinize her laptop.

As Blanka arrived, Farringdon and a techie were examining the SSD with miniature tools, under a microscope.
'It sure looks like a Toshiba, and says PX05SHB series,' said the techie.
'Hi,' said Farringdon, absent-mindedly acknowledging Blanka as he took the SSD out of the microscope. 'Excuse me a minute.'

He took the SSD into another lab where, through a glass partition, Blanka watched Farringdon X-ray it.

He came back, shaking his head. 'Could I borrow your eyes? he asked Blanka.

Blanka blinked her blue eyes and nodded. She set her silver ℧Scanner on the bench, sat down and concentrated her AI vision on the Toshiba. The image from her eyes appeared on the Scanner.

'Can you calibrate the image? suggested Farringdon.

Blanka displayed calibrations on the X-ray on the Scanner.

'This is just not right,' said Farringdon to Bio.

'Nothing about this whole fucking thing is right –' said Bio and immediately regretted it. Drawing attention to herself only reminded everyone in the lab that she'd had sex with Felicity-fast-track the morning of the killings.

'Go on,' said Blanka.

'This one point six terabyte SSD should be 1,400 gigabytes. Manufacturers like to express the size of their hard drives in base-10 numbers, then call it giga and tera. It's factually incorrect, but the drives look bigger.'

'Your point is?' asked Blanka.

'This drive *really is bigger*. There's extra capacity on it that isn't included on the label.'

You mean the 'X' drive *we* put on?' said Bio.

'No,' said Farringdon. 'In addition to that. It's not Windows or Linux or anything we can read. It's some kind of Frankenstein sector Felicity's created.'

Bio closed her eyes, thinking, Can this get any worse?

'No fucking way,' said Blanka.

The two techies put their heads together and conferred with Farringdon.

'Never seen such a thing,' said one. 'Could Billy the Kid over at The Company crack into it?'

Farringdon shrugged his shoulders and turned to Blanka.

'Can we take this to Billy your Baker Street buddy? Do you have clearance to get me in?'

(When Blanka first joined the CIA she'd nicknamed her technical trainer Billy Da Costa – already in his fifties – Billy the Kid, because of his baby face. Now eighteen years on he had the same baby face.)

'Hell yeah,' said Blanka giving the Brits something to laugh at, albeit only for a few seconds. She looked at the two techies.

'All of us here should go see Billy. You okay for overtime?'

They nodded.

In her AI, Blanka checked the arrival time of Hart's jet from New York and worked out his ETA. 'My stepfather's arriving in two hours,' she said. 'We have time to call Billy, get coffee and drag our sorry asses over there.'

At 169 Baker Street – the London bureau of the CIA – there was no Ma Baker, but Professor Hart and Dr Fox watched Billy the Kid and the other CIA techies, together with Drox and his gold ℧Scanner, probe the freak sector of the SSD (wired into a bank of de-encryption equipment with black SATA-3 cables).

'It's technically ultra-invisible,' Drox explained to the MI6 techies. 'Beyond the invisible sector. Not even Toshiba would detect it.'

'Where do they make their SSDs?' asked Blanka.

'The Far East, Burma and thereabouts,' said Drox.

'What are you doing now?' Bio asked Billy the Kid.

'We're trying to look into it from the X drive,' he said. 'Like climbing to the top of the old Berlin Wall to see into the Soviet sector.'

Drox laughed at the analogy.

'It can't be more than 50 gig,' said a young CIA techie.

'If Toshiba didn't make the drive, then who did? asked Hart.

'We've found it,' both the CIA techies said at the same time.

At that moment, the fatal system error every geek dreads seeing displayed. On the large screen a 'properties' window opened for the Frankenstein sector, followed by a Blue Screen Of Death.

The Blue Screen Of Death screens rapidly spread around the room from one system to another, and into the operations room next door, setting off several alarms. Billy the Kid and Blanka both bolted up. Lightning quick Blanka tugged the SATA plugs apart from the Baker Street system.

'Holy fuck,' she said.

No one else spoke. Blanka looked around the room from the blank blue screens to the stunned faces of her colleagues.

Then Professor Hart turned to Blanka, rubbed his stubbled chin and said, 'Ow! This one bites.'

'Yes, I guess that's it for tonight,' Blanka said.

Dr Fox looked at his Omega watch. 'Or this morning,' he said.

Billy clapped his hands and his young assistants jumped into action and busied themselves with rebooting the several CIA systems.

Billy turned to Blanka and the others. 'I think we can safely say, that this drive is not a genuine Toshiba part.' It was a good joke, but nobody laughed.

'It's like something from another world,' Farringdon said, in awe.

'I did a detailed profile of Felicity,' said Fox. 'She is nowhere near capable of arranging this level of encryption.'

'Which means C did this,' said Hart. 'Science Division?'

'MI6 doesn't have this level of technology,' said Bio.

Hart turned to the room, 'Then C is a mole.'

'For the Russians?' asked Bio.

'This ain't Russian technology,' said Drox, looking at Hart.

'Then C is working for *someone else*,' Hart said.

'Yes,' said Fox. 'This is what I've suspected all along.'

'But who?' said Drox, wearing his worried face.

Unable to help herself, Blanka suddenly tuned out everything and sank her head into her hands. She hurt all over. Every part of her hurt. The human parts and the android parts hurt. Her AI eyes ached, her head ached: the AI part, the human part, the emotional part. And she smelt trouble big time. Trouble with a big fucking 'F' sign on it.

The 'F' word pounded in her brain. *Fatima.*

This smelt like the very same quicksand her mother, Kitty, had sunk in. All the way to her death.

'Who's supposed to be signing off on this Frankenstein drive?' someone said, breaking into Blanka's thoughts. It was Billy. Blanka looked up, and the various OhZone and MI6 people looked at each other.

'Me,' said Bio quietly. She had an unpleasant premonition that her words would come back to haunt her.

'Well, *good luck*,' said Billy the Kid. 'Can I go back to bed now?'

3.2

Wednesday, March 25

1 ***WEEK AFTER*** ***THE KILLINGS*** Dr Fox, avec black arm band, walked out the front of MI6 headquarters and heard a cry he'd not heard since the last newspaper vendors were banished by C under The Official Secrets Act. '*Socialist Worker*,' the bearded vendor cried, 'get your *Socialist Worker*.' Curious as to their version of events, Fox bought one of their weekly papers.

Five days had passed and the pain only got worse. Fox saw Diana each day at Sokol's, and now he'd signed Blanka off on sick leave too. She'd disconnected her Scanner and wasn't answering the phone. Her stepfather was holed up with her, and his way of dealing with grief, with vodka and Kahlua, was starting to appeal to Blanka. It was the day before she normally DJ'd at *Wilion*. No one had heard from her or Hart for 36 hours and there was considerable consternation.

Fox was a sprightly man with a martial bearing, quite tall, aging (but like Billy the Kid blessed with an ageless face) and with a full head of hair. Distinguished as much by his sagacious wit as by his thick gray beard, he was an old hand at many things, but driving was not one of them – so he arrived by train at Kensington Olympia station for his appointment with Diana. Twenty-five minutes early, he unlocked the gate to the community gardens behind 32 Russell Road and sought out a garden bench. Producing bird seed from his pocket, he fed the birds by hand, gathering dozens of sparrows, finches and black birds as well as the ubiquitous London pigeons. He even fed a pair of jays and a green parrot, not native to W.14. When he ran out of bird seed he watched the birds, and the birds sat and watched him. Unfolding the *Socialist Worker*, he nodded at the photograph of the Grinin family and the headline: 'Security Services Murder Father and Children.' Well that's not a conspiracy theory, he thought. He shook his head at another headline: 'Government hides Grinin W.M.D. in Balham.'

As the church bell chimed eleven, he rang the bell for the top flat at number 32. The door cracked open, and he squatted down and tickled Puppy around the face as the snow-white terrier ran out to greet him.

'Good morning Master Puppy,' he said, in his clipped cockney accent. The dog leapt up and gently pawed him, and Fox gave him a rub. Standing, he gave a broad smile to Sokol as she opened the door fully. 'Miss Comarova,' he said bowing. 'How are the injuries?'

'Improving thank you, Colonel Doctor Fox,' replied Sokol, her hand and face still bandaged. 'Won't you please come in?'

'Diana?' he asked, as he slipped his military-style overcoat off.

'She's waiting.'

Fox starting all his counselling sessions by offering his client a Fox's Glacier Mint. There was nothing quite like a mint – with Peppy the polar bear on it – to break the ice. It was uphill work attempting to channel Diana's terrible, all consuming grief away from what seemed her sole aim in life now – to track down and kill Felicity. In this endeavor, predictably, she was encouraged in word if not in action by Sokol. It was not the best way forward to work through her grief. Fox had often seen this toxic mix of anger, grief and pain. Being of military background as a Lieutenant Colonel and the most senior padre in the Canadian army, he had counselled hundreds for PTSD and seen first hand how many of the 'strong' hid their pain behind rage. Rage was something they could act on clearly and forcefully; grief was another matter.

Toward the end of their session, Fox had gotten Diana to talk about Blanka. She confessed, tearfully, that she wanted to stop Blanka blaming herself for the killings. 'Can I visit her, Don?' she asked. 'Will you come with me?

'Let's see how tomorrow afternoon goes,' said Fox. Because of Diana's compassion for the other victim of the atrocity, Special Branch officer Gabor, Diana wanted to visit the policeman's widow and baby, and Fox had arranged it for the next afternoon.

After the session ended, Sokol made black Russian tea for the three of them.

'How are you getting on?' she asked cheerily.

'Very well,' said Diana, lying. 'We may visit Blanka tomorrow. If we do, will you come too?'

Sokol's face darkened, but she masked her bitterness with a poorly faked smile. 'Unfortunately I'm really busy at work tomorrow. OhZone must keep running. And Nearby seems to have been requisitioned as your chauffeur.'

'We'll make it fun,' Diana said. 'She can wear her ball gown.'

Fox was puzzled and glanced at Sokol, who shook her head: no idea. 'Her ball gown?' he said.

'Yes,' Diana replied. 'The twins loved Nearby's ball gown. So it stands to reason that the baby will. He's called Homer.'

Colonel Dr Fox laughed and nodded. There was nothing to say.

*A*fter an emotional visit to Officer Gabor's widow and baby Homer, they got back in the car. Nearby was driving, but she had not worn her ball gown.

'Can we please drop round on Blanka now?' Diana said. 'I'd like to see her.'

'Are you sure you're up for it?" Fox asked.

'She's a friend, Dr Fox. Not a mountain I have to climb.'

'Nearby, what do you say?'

Nearby looked at Diana and Fox in the driving mirror. 'Buckingham Mews?'

'Yes, please,' said Diana.

When they arrived, Hart answered the door. He was sporting a four day beard, in shorts and a T-shirt, and looked as if he hadn't slept for several days. When he ushered them into the parlour, Fox was immediately concerned. The house had taken on the look of an opium den with liquor bottles and cocktail shakers everywhere.

Blanka was in her jogging pants but she looked like a dead woman walking. She'd just come off dialysis and had massive black moons under her eyes. After hugging and weeping, Diana took Blanka off to her kitchen to make a pot of tea leaving Nearby and the Colonel to talk to the Professor.

'This isn't Rome, Max,' Fox insisted. 'This isn't Kitty. You have to be strong.'

'I'm strong, Don. Just having an off-morning.'

'It's 3 p.m.'

'An off day then.'

'I'll help with the tea,' said Nearby and left them.

Diana loved Blanka's bee hives and cottage garden. Together, the three women took their cups of tea outside and walked under the trees and down to her fruit and vegetable beds. Escaping the hideous aftermath of the killings for a time, the women discussed cocktails and laughed at Devices' plan to replace MI6's vodka jello shots – served on the dot at five o'clock every Friday to the thousand employees on duty then at headquarters – with authentic Martini cocktails. Nearby did her imitation of Devices, declaiming:

'Not the James Bond vodka martini *rubbish*, but a fine *gin* and vermouth and instead of the olive, a tiny slice of *durian*. Now that's iconic!'

Diana laughed, 'But they smell so awful.'

'Devices is a very determined woman,' Blanka replied lightly, 'Being in command at MI6 for even a few hours gave her the taste for command. Unfortunately, its ruined her taste for cocktails.' But Blanka's mood suddenly turned. 'Command has a bitter taste. You can't avoid it. She'll learn, if she's not too old to learn.'

Back in the kitchen, Nearby made herself useful doing the washing up in the cute Butler's sink. When Diana caught her eye, she stopped, dried her hands and together they faced Blanka.

'We're coming to your gig tonight,' said Nearby.

'I'm cancelling it,' said Blanka, grimacing. 'I'm not – I don't – I can't –'

'I want to come,' said Diana. 'And I want you to DJ. Grigori loved Wilion. He loved dancing. He loved music. Do it for him, will you please? And for me.'

Blanka looked at herself in the mirror and said, 'I look like death warmed over.'

'We'll send the boys off and spend the afternoon getting ourselves dolled up,' said Diana.

Nearby giggled, and Blanka seemed to relax for the first time in ten days. 'Music might help. But it has to be very loud.'

'As loud as you want,' Diana said, and Nearby nodded in agreement.

'Good, that's settled. Now, may I use the restroom?' asked Diana.

'Of course,' said Blanka, 'you know where it is.'

While Diana was gone, Nearby took Blanka's hand, 'The funeral is the day after tomorrow. Diana needs to keep busy…'

Blanka's antique bell-pull sounded. 'Now who's that?' she sighed.

'I think it might be the heavy guns,' said Nearby. Blanka went into the hall and looked on the security cameras. Drox stood there wearing a locomotive engineers cap. He removed the cap and waved it at Blanka. 'My knight in shining armour,' she whispered.

3.3

But who shall dwell in these worlds if they be inhabited? . . .
Are we or they Lords of the World? . . .
And how are all things made for man?—

KEPLER - QUOTED IN THE WAR OF THE WORLDS BY H.G. WELLS

Club Wilion was quiet that night. It looked like only a couple of dozen hard-core Blanka music followers had braved the rain and turned out but it was enough to make the atmosphere cheerful. Blanka was up on the stage preparing for her set, looking a lot better, wearing a Russian-red dress and sporting a black arm band.

Nearby wore her ball gown, pristine in waves of blue. And Diana wore a ball gown – also Russian, 19th century. A sombre Steve Wright (the BBC Radio 2 DJ) walked in wearing a black arm band. He greeted Diana and Nearby in Russian-style and admired the gowns.

'It's what Grigori would have wanted,' Diana explained. 'He loved this dress.' She smiled at Nearby as Blanka put on the song *The Fox (What does the fox say?)* by Ylvis, during which a big crowd from MI6 arrived, to show their support for Blanka.

A surprise visitor – Foreign Secretary L.B.J., together with a political aide and full security escort, all wearing black arm bands, arrived on his Election campaign double-decker nicknamed the Barker Bus, with music blaring from inside. He stepped out and said in his loud voice to anyone who cared to listen 'Well I'd like to see for myself what Blanka's DJ-ing is all about.'

When the bouncer opened the doors wide for L.B.J. and his escorts, Ma Baker slipped in together with Billy the Kid. L.B.J. honed straight in on Blanka, who was talking with Steve Wright.

'Jolly good to see you,' said L.B.J. 'Very much looking forward to your show tonight! Is this your partner?'

'Not a partner. A friend.' said Blanka.

Animal noises were coming from *What does the fox say?* but L.B.J. used his formidable political skills and ignored them.

'I'm Steve Wright,' said Wright, holding out his hand which L.B.J. vigorously shook.

'Nice to meet you Mr Wright. If you're in the same '*Office*' as Blanka here, then you report to me,' he said laughing.

'I work for the BBC.'

'Excellent cover, well done,' said L.B.J., winking, and setting the two CIA men in stitches of laughter. 'Didn't know you two were together,' he said as he was led away by his aide.

Soon the two doctors, Oxberry and Fox, arrived, impeccably dressed to the nines, each with black arm bands. Blanka's phone buzzed in her pocket and she pulled it out to read a message from Nearby

Diana would like Rasputin by Boney M played x

'Excuse me, Steve,' said Blanka and then whispered to Drox on the way to the stage, 'Diana wants Rasputin.'

'That's sure to get L.B.J. excited,' said Drox. 'He missed out the first time. But if he tries to dance on the table, I'm afraid his aides will have to help him off.'

They glanced across to where L.B.J. was sitting at the bar, looking out of place with the aide and bodyguards carefully watching over him, his half-finished G&T in one hand, gesturing wildly and sounding off to a bored-looking man next to him.

★

*B*lanka stepped up on stage and took the microphone, drawing applause from the crowd.

Just before she stepped up, Drox told her, 'Remember your CIA training. "Lie like a rug, but make it sound like a magic carpet". '

'Just watch me,' she said.

'Good evening everyone, tonight my set is dedicated to the victims of the recent terrorist attack, in which five people were killed. Two of the dead were young, innocent children, Emma and Olga Grinin, taken from the world far too soon. The third was their father, Major Grigori Grinin, a well-renowned man very close to my heart. The other dead consist of my dear colleague and friend, Crusoe Robinson, and police officer Gabor. They died in the line of duty protecting the citizens of this country.'

Blanka could see that Diana was beginning to tear up, so she rushed her speech to its conclusion. 'I'm here to say the terrorists will be punished ten-fold, and justice will be served. But tonight we're gonna make a great noise and fill the world with rock and roll!'

She quickly put on the record. 'And we're going to begin by celebrating Grigori Grinin. Let's hear it for his Radio 2 theme song, *Rasputin*, by Boney M.

Cheers erupted as the 1978 song blasted from the speakers and the crowd began to dance

> *There lived a certain man in Russia long ago*
> *He was big and strong, in his eyes a flaming glow*

L.B.J. danced with everyone and everything, falling into the rhythm, and by the end verse he was dancing on the tables and singing along with great vigour. As Drox predicted, his aides had to help him off the table.

Paddington and Debbie danced together and then with Farringdon, and Bio danced with Russia. Diana, her face flushed with memory and grief, watched and swayed a bit then walked up to Blanka on the stage. 'Thank you,' she said. 'It's what Grigori would have wanted.'

'I know,' said Blanka, 'and he'd want you to dance *with somebody*.'

Wright stepped up to the mark and Diana danced with him for the rest of the evening. He was her late husband's height – slightly taller than her – and Wright knew that Diana was dancing for all she was worth, because she didn't know what else to do.'

*B*lanka continued to bring out tunes. Everyone was loving it, but eventually it came time to play the last song. Some people had drifted away, Nearby had left to take Diana home to Sokol's, L.B.J. and his entourage were gone. Drox asked Blanka if she was going to play her favourite, *Night They Drove Old Dixie.*

'No,' said Blanka. 'It's wonderful everyone's come, especially through the rain. But I don't want "favourite," I want to crawl up inside a little hole.'

'I understand, said Drox. I'm heading back to Paris. I'll see you at the Wash-up, but I'm only an hour away. Call!'

Okay, said Blanka, kissing him goodbye.

Colonel Doctor Fox lingered, as if to say he'd always be around.

To end her set, Blanka played a new mix composition comprising her signature *Robinson Crusoe* t.v. series theme, sampled with a new sound from a radio play broadcast in the USA on Halloween 1938, on the eve of the Second World War. The record sleeve read:

The original 1938 broadcast that panicked a nation

The radio play, in the days before television, had an audience of thirty two million and was so realistic that many Americans, thinking the end of the world was coming, took to their cars to flee the cities.

The piece began with the crackling old-radio sound of the CBS announcer

The Columbia Broadcasting System
and its affiliated stations present
Orson Welles and the Mercury Theatre on the Air
in 'The War of the Worlds'
by H. G. Wells.

At that point the *Robinson Crusoe* theme came in, and the words from the broadcast became fragments drifting in and out of the music with, 'we know now,' as a constant refrain.

We know now that in the early years of the twentieth century
intellects vast, cool and unsympathetic regarded this Earth.

We know now as human beings busied themselves about
their various concerns, they were scrutinized and studied,
as a man with a microscope might scrutinize the transient
creatures in a drop of water.

We know now that with infinite complacence people
went to and fro over the earth about their little affairs,
serene in the assurance of their dominion over this
small spinning fragment of solar driftwood,
which by chance or design
man has inherited
out of the dark mystery of Time and Space.

We know now ...
With infinite complacence ...
We know now...

3.4

Friday 2 p.m.
Russian Orthodox Cathedral, Kensington

*A*ll morning, the sun projected a foul yellow caste upon the clouds gathering over central London. Even for March it was unusual, and the people looked to the heavens and whispered to each other, 'It's like the end of the world.' Now, black storm clouds and thunder rent apart the skies, as if the wrath of the gods was to be vented on the populous.

Grigori Grinin's death may have been similar to Grigori Rasputin's – but his funeral was not. Following the three black troikas bearing the three coffins, in a state limousine, were Diana, her parents and brother, Nearby and the Prime Minister Jermaine Corduroy.

Despite the rain, large crowds turned out at the cathedral and on the route to see Grinin off. Each troika, drawn by three black horses, approached the Cathedral down Park Lane. In the heavy rain, the crowds pointed at the horses, and counted with relief: there were nine, not the four of the Apocalypse.

It was something Nearby had never expected in her wildest flights of fancy: that in three years she would go from hiding up a pear tree from MI6, to being at the British Prime Minister's side at what amounted to a state funeral.

But the Prime Minister sitting next to her was too preoccupied with his own thoughts to pay much attention to Nearby. Grinin had been a popular figure, and Corduroy genuinely liked the man.

L.B.J. had only informed Corduroy of the true chain of events the day after the killings. That Balham had to be sealed off – supposedly 'in an exercise in preparedness against terrorism' – beggared belief.
Privately, Corduroy expressed his outrage. 'You brought Grinin to me the day before *we* killed him. What the hell was going on?'
'The action was done without my knowledge or authority,' L.B.J.

had replied.

'Is this a democracy or a police state run by MI6?'

'I am happy to offer my resignation,' said L.B.J.'

'No,' Corduroy remembered saying. 'You don't get off that easy. I want changes there.'

The two senior civil servants overseeing MI6 had been retired early, murder warrants were issued for Felicity Robinson and her helper Prosthetics John [though Cool-Hand-Luke lived to run the London Eye another day], and C, wherever he was, had been put on indefinite 'medical' leave.

That's a start, thought the P.M., as he watched the twins' tiny coffins unloaded from their troikas. But it's only a start. I need someone who'll go beyond that. Someone who still puts servicing the public over his own plans. Arms is my man.

*

*I*nside the cathedral, sitting with Diana and her parents and brother were Sokol, Nearby and the P.M. Behind the P.M. sat Dr Fox, and Arms – suddenly brought out of the shadows of the firing range – and the PM's three armed security officers.

In a corner, which Blanka termed ironically *the killers' corner*, sat Blanka, with Professor Hart, Drox, Russia and Bio on one side and L.B.J., Devices, Probe and Asia on the other. Everyone knew that as the woman entrusted to bring the Grinin family safely to the West and protect them, Blanka had done everything humanly possible to protect the Major. Nobody had considered the scenario that his three year-old twins would be Felicity-fast-track's targets too.

*

*E*ulogies to Olga and Emma were given by their grandfather, the eminent doctor, and Diana's brother. Sokol and Nearby read poems in Russian and English that were the children's favourites. Tributes followed by the Nanny, the Russian Ambassador, by the Prime Minister, and finally by the Russian Orthodox Bishop of England who led the service. Diana could not bring herself to speak, but sobbed as quietly as she could under her veil, holding tight to her own mother's hands.

RAECHEL SANDS ≥ *75*

When it came to the Major, the eulogies were equally heart-felt and even more numerous. The P.M. talked about the forces that threaten freedom snuffing out this brilliant modern-day Leonardo Da Vinci.

Then it was Blanka's turn to give a reading. Blanka felt the walk down the transept towards the altar was the longest of her life. As she passed Diana, Blanka turned to her, and Diana tried to smile from under her black veil.

Blanka's reading was a poem that Grinin had read to her on two occasions. It had a curious effect on her: a Russian reading a Spanish poem that had been translated into English. After introducing herself in a voice so low few people could hear, Blanka went on in a louder voice. 'Major Grinin,' she said, 'shared with me this beautiful poem by the Spanish poet Juan Ramon Jimenez. It's called *El Viaje Definitivo* (The Definitive Journey). And I recite it now in memory of Grigori and Olga and Emma.'

> And I will leave. But the birds will stay, singing:
> and my garden will stay, with its green tree,
> with its water well.
>
> Many afternoons the skies will be blue and placid,
> and the bells in the belfry will chime,
> as they are chiming this very afternoon.
>
> The people who have loved me will pass away,
> and the town will burst anew every year.
> But my spirit will always wander nostalgic
> in the same recondite corner of my flowery garden.

Blanka wiped the tears from her eyes and started the long walk to her seat at the back.

As she approached Diana, Diana pulled up her veil and stood up. She embraced Blanka and they kissed each other Russian-style. As they had done that sunny afternoon at Zoo Zürich four years before, they looked into each other's blue eyes. Neither of them could have imagined what was to happen over the next eight weeks   ひ

МЕТАРОХ #2

PART TWO

ORPHANS IN ARMS

*T*he other fork of the road —
the one less traveled by —
offers our last, our only chance to reach
a destination that assures the preservation of the earth.

1962, RACHEL CARSON - SILENT SPRING

The Tragedy of Fatima

*The wolf shall dwell with the lamb,
and the leopard shall lie down
with the young goat,
and the calf and the lion
and the fattened calf together;
and a child shall lead them.*

BIBLE - ISAIAH 11:6 - ENGLISH STANDARD VERSION

4.0

Five days later
Wednesday, April 1, 2015
Leila's mountain village
Bosnia and Herzegovina, Eastern Europe

2 WEEKS AFTER THE KILLINGS A third pair of blue eyes blinked – Leila's – and her dark-skinned hand reached up to wipe the dust from her eye. Leila was milking the family's dairy goat, something she had done all the mornings of her life, at least all the mornings she could remember. She wore a blue dress, her second best, and the sleeve was threadbare; her first best dress was yellow. Now that Grandmother had joined Leila's father in heaven, her only family left was her mother, Fatima, who was lying in the main room of their shack, dying of tuberculosis.

They had bought the young brown and white goat, with money given by the local mosque, when their previous goat died. Leila was thirteen at the time and took naming the new goat very seriously. Being bookish, she decided that Cassandra was sufficiently melodic and beautiful, something a skinny goat could respond to with pride. But Cassandra's name was quickly shortened to Cassie; it was easier to shout, and the goat responded to it.

That morning flies buzzed around them and Cassie shook her coat, sending more dust flying into the air. She turned her head and looked at Leila as if to say, I've had enough of this milking. In a gesture of affection Leila flicked her tongue out and in at Cassie as she wiped her teats clean with a cloth, then got up from the stool and let Cassie's kid, Naughty, in through a ramshackle door to suckle on her mother.

Leila, now nineteen, slight and distinctive with her ebony skin and pale eyes, set the milk pail down at the tin sink, as the morning light reached over the mountains and poured through the kitchen window highlighting her face. It could have been the face of Cleopatra: noble, beautiful, both delicate and strong.

Hearing sounds, Leila looked out the window. An Imam and two other men stood at the broken pieces of wood that passed for their gate. They were arguing. Almost certainly over her mother's burial arrangements. Could fate have been any unkinder – to any woman – than it had been to her mother? Now, couldn't the men just wait for her to die?

The men looked at their watches. The mosque was paying for the doctor, who had somehow kept her mother alive the last six months. But the doctor had warned Leila: 'The TB is resistant to the antibiotics. It's only a matter of time. I'm afraid she has only a week or two to live at the most.' The consumption would take her mother's physical breath as surely as her Serb neighbours had taken her spiritual breath when Leila had been in her womb [1].

But, with a stubbornness that Leila recognized in herself, her mother had made it to her fortieth birthday. It was a subdued affair; her mother had no relatives other than an elder brother in Berlin, and Leila, and not a

---

1 An account of Fatima's ordeal during the Bosnian War of 1992-95 can be found in *Prologue to the Hiding Game Saga,* in the first book: *Metapox 1*

single friend. Leila had baked a coffee and walnut birthday cake and a few of her school friends came around. And yes, her mother seemed to enjoy eating a piece of the cake after the girls had blown out the candles. After her friends had left, Leila had sung African folk songs until her mother fell asleep. Then, secretly, out of her mother's hearing, Leila cried for her. That had been a week ago.

*L*eila looked at her bed beside the kitchen stove. Pinned on the doorframe leading to Fatima's room was a postcard from her uncle in Berlin: the distinctive shape of the Alex Tower in Berlin (the *Berlin Fernsehturm*) Germany's tallest structure. Leila unpinned the card that had reached her with no address other than her name and the name of the village.

A refugee from Ethiopia, with no relatives in Bosnia, it had been her mother's original plan to make it to Berlin where her brother, Sheriar, lived. Uncle Sheriar had visited on Leila's seventh birthday and a Polaroid photograph from that occasion, showing Leila and her African mother was pinned next to the postcard. Leila took down the Polaroid, sat on her bed – and with the postcard and photo on her lap – thought about her life. A father murdered when she was in the womb, a war-traumatized mother who couldn't or wouldn't speak, one relative two thousand kilometers away; crops that failed and goats that wailed, and chickens that the fox sometimes got.

She pulled open a drawer which held other tokens of her life. There were old school books, science books, poetry books, Huxley's *Brave New World*, song lyrics and harmonica chords.
Leila loved drama and poetry and music, and science. She'd wanted to make something of her life. But how can hope rise when you were born in a concentration camp… a minor one that nobody's even heard of? And if you live on the edge of a dirty war between Slavs that everyone wants to forget. What was it politicians said about putting 'boots on the ground?' U.N. peacekeeping troops still had their boots on the ground just twenty kilometers away. The only reason her neighbours weren't murdering each other was that NATO had taken their heavy guns away. Thank you, God, she mocked. It doesn't really get much better than this,

does it? Like you care at all, or exist, or even know I'm here...

She brushed years of birthday cards aside and took out one of a dozen harmonicas in the drawer. It was a Marine Band harp in G. A Hohner, a German harmonica, the first she'd owned. Uncle Sheriar had given it to her on his only visit. He'd just turned up one day out of the blue. Fatima had managed half a smile, but not a single word. Sheriar never came back. Leila couldn't blame him. She wouldn't have either.

Should she head for Berlin when her mother died? Uncle Sheriar drove a tram. She read the card he had put in the box the Hohner came in. He had written 'Happy Birthday beautiful niece' in both English and Bosnian-Croatian-Serbian followed by part of a poem by a Sufi poet

> I am a hole in a flute that the Christ's breath moves through –
> listen to this music. —Hafiz.

Listen to the music. She looked at the Hohner and wondered, What music would the Christ's breath make with my harmonica? A harp is not the same as a flute, there's more than one hole to blow through. Then she set it down to check on her mother.

★

As soon as she opened the door to Fatima's bedroom she gasped in surprise. Fatima was sitting up in bed pointing out of the window at the Imam by the gate.
'Don't worry, Mama,' Leila said. 'Don't worry. They're waiting for the doctor.'
'Leila...' Fatima whispered. 'My time has come. I dreamed...'
Leila stared open mouthed and ran to her side; her mother had not spoken since Leila was born.
'When you were inside me...' her mother began, then broke down coughing.
Laying her mother's head back down on the pillow, Leila gently wiped her brow. Fatima grasped her hand and looked into her blue eyes. Leila was astonished by the intensity in her mother's brown ones. After all these years of emptiness they had become animated, pleading, insistent.
'When I was in the concentration camp,' Fatima said, 'and you were inside me... a spirit came to me. Not a dream, a vision. At first I thought

it was your dead father, but it was a girl. Then I thought it must be you – but she was white. A white girl in the snow. She was at the foot of my bed, telling me to listen, to follow her, to believe…'

Leila heard the sound of the doctor's car pulling up outside the homestead.

'*Allah Akbar*,' her mother gasped, and coughed up blood. 'God is great.'

'Yes, Mama.'

'You will be great too, my Leila.' And somewhere she found strength to squeeze her daughter's hand more tightly, and to pour more love into Leila's eyes than she had ever known.

It was the last thing Fatima did in this world.

'Oh no, Mama,' cried Leila. 'Don't go! Oh, Allah, please!'

The saying by Jesus, Son of Mary came into Leila's heart

The meek will inherit the earth

By some sword of grace, Fatima's final breaking of her silence rent open her tragic, humble, suffering life and redeemed it, as she passed away. Leila laid her head on her mother's chest and sobbed, and did not answer the door.

Le Lapin Blanc (The White Rabbit)

5.0

The same morning – April 1, 2015
Westminster Cathedral, London S.W.1, UK

2 WEEKS AFTER THE KILLINGS Westminster Cathedral was one of the best kept secrets of London, and Father Flanagan was one of its longest serving Catholic chaplains. He stood in front of the mirror in the priests' changing room, looked at his sparse hair, and teased it into place with a small tortoiseshell brush. As he arranged his surplice, he thought about last year's April the first. That day, when he'd gone at 11.30 a.m. to start Confession, he had discovered a boy and three girls hidden in the confessional. As he was giving the Sacrament of Reconciliation to the eldest girl, the others had jumped up and shouted, 'April Fool!'

Smiling to himself, he donned his surplice and was tying it as he walked into the Vestry. Sister Lucia, one of the youngest members of the staff, was arranging a tray of tea cups and a huge pot.
'Would you like tea now, Father?'
'I would, Lucia. But unfortunately the confessional calls.'
She looked at her watch,
'Oh, to be sure,' she said. 'Now, Father, remember it's April Fools Day, so check for the young scamps.
'Once bitten,' replied the chaplain.
Walking from the vestry down the transept towards the confessional, the chaplain thought of the Sacrament of Reconciliation, or Confession. Little understood and much criticized outside the Catholic faith, he knew how helpful it really was.

The confession booth was already occupied by its first supplicant. When he opened the priest's door he immediately knew who it was. The fragrance the woman wore was distinctive – lofty and foresty – and she had designed it herself. He had inhaled its subtle aroma every day for the last two weeks. He slid the wooden shutter open. 'Good morning to you, Magdalena.'

The woman's confirmation name was Magdalena and with over a hundred passports and identities, Blanka had names to spare. She wore a blue dress and adjusted a blue headscarf over her hair. Father Flanagan was well aware of the reason for the black armband around her left arm. She gripped her Rosary beads tightly, and smiled thinly before she spoke.

'Forgive me Father, for I have sinned.'

'How long is it since your last confession?'

'One day, Father.'

What could she have done in twenty-four hours? he thought, reluctantly starting the response, 'What –'

Blanka looked straight at him, 'I have committed murder.'

The chaplain remained silent, then finally said, 'Magdalena, would you please step this way for a moment?'

Ironically, thought Blanka. These are the very words that every spy in the world dreads to hear.

*F*ather Flanagan led her into the Vestry.

Seeing Sister Lucia pouring tea, he said, 'I'm just going into the prayer room with Magdalena. May I have that tea? And an extra one?'

Lucia turned to Blanka and said, 'Good morning Magdalena. No sugar, isn't it? You're sweet enough.'

Blanka couldn't help smiling, and shook her head.

Lucia poured their teas. 'Is the kidney any better?' she asked.

'Much better,' Blanka lied. 'I've been doing dialysis.'

'That's great. And keeping off the chocolate?' Lucia asked, as she poured the milk into the three teas.

'I'm trying,' Blanka lied again.

'Rich Tea biscuits then,' said Father Flanagan, tipping a dozen from the packet on to a plate.

In the prayer room Father Flanagan sipped his tea and Blanka followed, her Rosary beads dangling from her wrist.

'Magdalena,' he said, 'We've been over this countless times.' He stopped as Blanka stared at the Station of the Cross behind him. 'I know you. You didn't murder anyone. You couldn't.'

'But…' She struggled to get the next words out.

Father Flanagan gripped her hand. Blanka looked him in the eyes.

'I *have* killed, Father. It weighs on my heart and I can't get rid of it.'

'What are you talking about?'

But Blanka couldn't answer; she just shook her head from side to side.

'I think the time has come,' said Father Flanagan, 'for you to sit down with Dr Fox.'

'Don? What can I do with him that I'm not doing with you?'

Father Flanagan kept silent, waiting for her to work it out herself.

'You think I'm mentally ill,' she said. 'That this can be fixed with drugs? Better living through chemistry?'

'Magdalena, you misunderstand me.'

'I've seen what drugs do. They hide or mask things. They numb you. What I have is a spiritual illness.'

'Spiritual healing is not confined to the clergy, Magdalena. Dr Fox is a wise, compassionate and insightful man.'

'I need to do this myself,' Blanka pleaded. 'You know me so well. You've helped me so many times.'

'Sometimes self-examination and the confessional are not enough. As a diplomat you can call upon the resources of the Foreign and Commonwealth Office,' said Father Flanagan. 'Don't be afraid to ask others for help.'

'I'll be seeing Don at the wash-up for the Op tomorrow,' said Blanka, drinking the last of her tea and setting down the cup gently. 'It's in Paris.'

'In the laboratory where The Machine is?'

'Yes.'

'The one that made the mechanical parts of you?' asked Father Flanagan.

'Yes,' said Blanka.

'You told me you don't like that Machine.'

'I don't,' said Blanka. 'But I like very much the scientist who runs it. He was my Mom's best friend.'

As she left Westminster Cathedral Blanka looked at all the graves surrounding it and thought of Olga and Emma and Grigori and her mother and of all the people like them who had been put to death in the name of the state. Then, a shaft of sunlight slid down from between the clouds and illuminated a single syllable on a gravestone in front of her: 'Hope.'

5.1

Later that same day
Castle Moncus, Dorsetshire

2 WEEKS AFTER THE KILLINGS Standing at the head of the medieval conference room table, with Probe, ever loyal, at her side, Devices addressed the other board members. 'Handling politicians is something we've been doing for a long time,' she began, passing round black arm bands. 'Put these on your left arms.'

'And try to look like you're sorry for these murders,' snapped Probe, brandishing his old-fashioned-MI6-issue sword-stick and exposing the blade. 'Or you'll be for the chop.'

Devices continued the metaphor: 'Heads are rolling in the changes.'

'Other than Crusoe's, you mean,' Bio whispered under her breath.

Though not AI enhanced, the hearing of the two oldest directors could be almost preternatural. Bio was reminded of this when they both tut-tutted in her direction. But it wasn't just a silent admonition.

'Why am I not surprised at your appallingly bad taste,' scolded Probe, 'considering your choice of bedfellows.'

'Just trying to lighten things up,' said Bio. 'Talking about choice, who chose April Fool's Day for a board meeting?'

Probe pulled his sour face. 'They have always been on a Wednesday.'

'Since time immemorial,' stated Chairwoman Devices, sitting down.

'You need to keep up, Queen Marcia,' said Probe smugly, 'to have any chance of remaining a director.'

'Thank you, Probe,' said Devices. 'Got your glasses?'

'Yes I have,' replied Probe, sitting and carefully concealing his sword-stick under the table.

'It's two o'clock exactly,' said Devices. 'Russia and Miss Banks will have to catch up. Item 1 is a small agenda item before much weightier matters, but it's something that's been bothering me.'

'You want to axe C's vodka jello shots?' laughed Bantu.

'*Replace* them,' said Devices, smiling and pointing at the agenda, 'with an authentic Martini.'

'Ditching Mr Bond's vodka? I hope ours will be stirred,' said Asia.

'Yes, the shaken version is called a *Bradford*,' said Devices.

'As Noël Coward so beautifully put it,' said Bio. ' "A perfect Martini should be made by filling a glass with gin, then waving it in the general direction of Italy." ' General laughter followed.

'Very good, Marcia,' said Probe.

'Actually a *Perfect Martini* includes equal amounts of sweet and dry vermouth,' corrected Devices, 'which I propose we shall use, garnished with a twist of *durian*.'

'A beverage in keeping with our exalted Olympian status,' laughed Probe.

'Rather than common as shit Greek olives,' said Bantu.

'All those in favor?' said Devices. '

Amidst considerable chuckles and utterings of the word, 'Durian,' the other six directors raised their hands. 'Carried unanimously,' wrote Devices in the encrypted minutes.

★

Outside, L.B.J. walked along the corridor, his arm around Russia's shoulder. 'It's just what we need,' he said, 'and Jermaine is quite sure it'll do the trick.'

Miss Banks followed behind, carrying Russia's briefcase and files.

L.B.J. nodded a perfunctory greeting at Arms who sat on the stone window seat overlooking the courtyard.

'Make it work, Russia,' L.B.J. said as they reached the great oak door of the conference room. 'I don't need to remind you of the alternative.'

'Merging with "5" will not be necessary, Sir, I assure you.'

'Not just that. We'll both be out of a job.'

Russia opened the door for L.B.J., 'Lead on McDuff.'

As L.B.J. strode in, the directors sprang up to welcome their political master. Bantu pointed to his agenda

> *Promotion, Senior Firearms Officer* **Marians, C.J. Mr** *(Grade 8), to Director QC Desk (Grade 9).*

and whispered to Bio, 'Arms is flavour-of-the-month, you can curry favour there, I know what a sweet voice you have.'

'Not as sweet as yours,' whispered Bio.

'Go for Arms practice and you'll get the lead.'

'It will all change with the election,' said Bio. 'Haven't you seen that

Corduroy's falling? Verdi will be out the door.'

'Sit down, please,' L.B.J. announced after he'd let them stand uncomfortably for an entire minute, giving him the chance to, as he liked to say, 'take in' everyone in the room. He also unfolded his prepared speech.
Devices stepped aside from the Chairman's chair and sat next to Probe who had his whiteboard pens ready.

'No sword-stick today?' was L.B.J.'s side comment just before he faced the directors, who were as uncomfortable seated as they had been standing. 'This isn't the first time a Foreign Secretary has had to give you lot a dressing down. Need I remind you of the illusive Iraqi W.M.D.s? There has been a veritable litany of disasters in this service, culminating in the killings, two weeks ago, by former agent OhZone 7. Major Grinin, may I remind you, was not only a Nobel Laureate and Chess Grand Master, he was our guest. Olga, Emma and officer Gabor were British citizens, and Crusoe Robinson a Commonwealth citizen. Some very senior heads have been scalped at the F.C.O., and your very existence is now in question. Animal Farm, Biology Farm, Chemistry Farm,' chanted L.B.J.. 'What the devil were you boys,' he paused, '– and girls – thinking?' Spending British tax-payers' money on a germ warfare factory underneath Jersey?!'
He looked around at the rows of red faces.
'I protested about it from the get-go,' said Asia.
'Turncoat,' said Bio and Bantu together.

'I'm sure you all know the Prime Minister's new initiative will involve you singing a very different tune which mandates serving the community, instead of killing them. Some of you might find that a novel concept, but I suggest you get familiar with it.'
'That's below the belt,' Probe murmured to Devices.
'If you think that's below the belt, you'd better buckle up,' Devices whispered back. 'It's going to be a rough ride.'
'At this very delicate time –'
'Meaning the General Election,' whispered Devices, just loud enough for L.B.J. to hear.
L.B.J. ignored her, but muddled up his pages. 'The P.M. wants to turn your minds from the wrong kind of thing and get you –. As you know, Arms, Charlie Marians, is an ex MI5 man – '
'Killing him with faint praise,' whispered Bio to Bantu, receiving a sharp

rap on her leg under the table from Probe's sword-stick.

'At this very delicate time, Mr Corduroy has personally asked Arms to lend a hand, by filling the vacancy for an MI6 director. He is also a very talented opera conductor, and – '

L.B.J. wisely decided to abandon the rest of his speech, and nodded to Miss Banks who opened the door for Arms to enter.

L.B.J. held out his hands, and announced, 'Arms.'

The directors all stood to place ceremonial cone-shaped scarlet hats on their heads. Together with the black armbands they looked quite a sight. Russia pulled out an empty chair for Arms and the directors applauded as he took his place at the table. After the Latin swearing-in ceremony, Miss Banks opened the door again and the bulky Marines Sergeant pushed the tea trolley in. There was tea or coffee, a choice of cakes (chocolate, lemon drizzle or Victoria sponge) and a bowl of Fox's Glacier Mints. The sight of mints brought to mind the January board meeting, when C had sucked his favourite mints only to foam at the mouth because they'd been replaced with denture cleansers. Bantu had played the trick (although C blamed Dr Fox) and now he was creased up in laughter along with Devices, Asia and Probe, who quoted C aloud: 'I think we should X-ray the biscuits from now on.'

L.B.J. had no idea what the joke was, but laughed anyway. After two slices of lemon drizzle cake, he departed leaving them to their own Devices, who again took the chair. The directors had been warned about the changes the P.M. was making to Wonderland. Staging three operas a year for the public was bad enough, having to cooperate with MI5 was much worse. Arms summed it up in the catchphrases: 'Less Lying With Your Spying,' and 'Opera for Every Occasion.'

Devices announced that Probe would outline the P.M.'s most important changes. Probe jumped up, walked to the front, spun his whiteboard and in his droning voice began: 'We have three options before us.'

'*Changes*,' prompted Devices. 'Major changes.'

Probe looked around the room, strangely lost without C to chivvy him along. Then he produced his sword-stick and waved it in the air. 'Yes! We may have *lost* Major Grinin but we've *got major changes*.' Only Bantu laughed; Miss Banks looked horrified and Bio shook her head sadly. 'Change one: less sex!' shouted Probe. Then turning to Bio he added, 'And none on Wonderland premises.'

'It wasn't in Wonderland,' said Bio, coldly.

'Maybe not. But the junior ranks are shagging up and down the rabbit holes – like – like –' He ran out of steam.

'Like *rabbits*?' said Bantu, stifling his laughter.

'With everyone except me,' Probe said with a sad smile,

Many of the directors looked at the table.

'You need to get out more,' suggested Devices. 'Get involved with new activities.'

Probe nodded, 'Perhaps.'

'You could help me with the new Wonderland drink and the durians.'

'What new drink?' asked Russia.

'Item one,' said Devices, pointing at the agenda. 'You were late.'

'I might do,' continued Probe. 'Anyway, from now on shagging within Wonderland will be classed as Gross Professional Misconduct and will lose you your Crown Pension.'

A murmur of disbelief went around the table. This was surely going way too far!

'What about blow-jobs?' quipped Bantu. Then, looking at Bio, he added, 'And petting?'

Russia was about to lose his famous diplomatic cool when Asia saved the day by asking, 'What about C's private dining room?'

'His butler has been retired early,' Russia replied, calming down. 'And his private dining room is being reassigned for Opera rehearsals.'

'Which brings us,' said Probe, 'to change two: opera.'

'Is this Divine Comedy or divine retribution?' asked Asia, making yet another bad joke.

A rap on the door was answered by Miss Banks. The Marines Sergeant handed her a dozen librettos for Verdi's opera *Macbeth*, which she distributed around the table.

'Arms joins us as the new ninth director,' Probe said. 'A new desk to be named, "QC Desk," after the Latin dictum: *Quis custodiet ipsos custodes?*'

'Who guards the guardians,' said Bio, looking at Bantu. 'For the benefit of those without a classical education.' She turned to Russia and he nodded his approval.

'The P.M. wants this staged at the South Bank's Queen Elizabeth Hall on the eve of Election day,' Probe concluded, nodding to Arms. 'Just five weeks to rehearse, so you'd better get on with it.'

Arms took over, 'Bio has volunteered to take the part of the leading lady.

She has a ravishing alto voice.'

Bantu burst out laughing and Bio jabbed him in the ribs.

Arms continued, 'I don't want any officers holding back. MI5 have an equal number of major parts.'

Bantu creased up with laughter and Asia turned to him, 'I don't get it.'

'*Major parts,*' Bantu explained to him.

'Silence in the ranks,' shouted Probe waving his sword-stick.

Devices shook her head and signalled to Arms to hurry up.

'All officers not on duty will be in the chorus,' he concluded.

'And the orchestra?' Asia asked Arms.

'GCHQ's standing orchestra is already practicing.'

'You're to be Lady Macbeth eh?' Russia said to Bio.

'Is this a dagger that I see before me?' she quoted.

'Yes. Quite prophetic wasn't it?' he said.

'Now *third*, Russia,' said Probe. 'Russia is to continue as acting Commander pending C's official dismissal for Misconduct in Public Office.' Probe allowed the directors time to savor C's fall from grace. In that time Asia, never a fan of Felicity, stood dramatically and turned to Bio. 'And Mrs Felicity-fast-track?' he said. 'I would like to ask our leading lady: where is the *real Lady Macbeth*?'

'Why does everyone keep looking at me for answers?' said Bio.

'You're in the spotlight,' said Russia.

'Ha!' snapped Probe. 'You made your bed, now lie in it! Really, Octavia, these new girls!'

'Yes,' laughed Devices, 'they don't know what they're in for! But leaving grand opera and Bio's sex life aside, just for a moment, where is the child killer formerly known as OhZone 7?'

Bio looked at Probe. 'As most of you know, we lost her trail on the Underground. The southbound Victoria line to be precise. In Dublin she emptied a dead drop box for supplies. We thought we picked up her trail again flying out of Dublin to Spain, but it was not to be. Another trail led to the west coast of Ireland.'

'Maybe she went swimming,' said Asia. Another bad joke.

'The Atlantic can be pretty damn chilly,' added Bio, smiling at Asia.

Russia looked at Bantu. 'I think we have something in from the Africa Desk?'

Bantu, without expression, replied, 'She's on safari in Kenya. The authorities have been alerted.'

5.2

The next day – Thursday, April 2, 2015
The OhZone Laboratory
Beneath the 5th Arrondissement, Paris, France

*F*ifteen years earlier, Kitty Maguire had made the same death journey to the other world as Leila's mother and Major Grinin. As a memorial to Kitty, Drox had named the new laboratory after her and erected a plaque in the entrance lobby. It read

The Katherine Dorothy Maguire OhZone II Laboratory

Drox had paid for the solid gold memorial himself. He also had music piped through speakers into the complex. Kitty had loved music, lived for music, and it reminded Drox of the St Petersburg Astoria where he and Kitty and Grinin had stayed – like H.G.Wells before them – when they were hot on the trail of the Fatima Secret. Now, *both* Kitty and Grinin were dead.

In the two weeks since the killings the dust had settled slightly and the time had come for the official Intelligence post-mortem – the 'Wash-up.' Since Felicity was an OhZone, the responsibility fell to the agents involved in the Op and the 'OhZone Committee.' Russia and Dr Fox (the chief, and senior psychiatrist, of MI6) would be there; as would the Secretary General of NATO, and Director Keith De Leon of the CIA (OhZone's largest sponsor). Professor Max Hart, the inventor of the OhZone process and the three surviving OhZone agents were also committed to be 'Committee' members.

Drox sighed, 'It's happened all over. The innocents are slain and the guilty go free.' He stared once more at the plaque. By one of those strange coincidences that marked out life on planet Earth, and had fascinated Major Grinin so much, the woman singing from the speaker that moment had the same initials as Kitty: 'K.D.'
If Nearby or Lara Starikova had been there they would have known and informed Drox that K.D Lang was also a Scorpio, like Kitty, but two years her senior.

As the words and melody of *Constant Craving* filled the air, Drox gazed at the speaker. The album *Ingénue* along with the movie *Philadelphia* had been major milestones in the early '90s LGBT rights movement. Not only had Kitty been Drox's best friend, she was the friend who encouraged him to come out.

He swallowed hard. The last time he had seen K.D. (Kitty) Maguire was at her post-mortem in Rome, at which he assisted the city coroner. Like C, Drox remembered her blue dress distinctly. But for Drox, it was with great tenderness and affection. Kitty had died in her blue dress, dark with the river water of Rome's Old Man Tiber.

Drox remembered how relieved he and Grinin had been, in St Petersburg. How they'd congratulated each other on saving Kitty's life! Kitty's host, Valentina, and her niece Lara, had gone back to Moscow... and only Grinin and Drox had stood between Kitty and her becoming another death statistic in St Petersburg. She'd only lived a few days more – until her murder in Rome – but they were priceless days, priceless memories for Drox.

He'd been haunted by their conversation at the Rome laboratory, and the silence that followed his request to tell him what she'd learned about the Fatima Secret from the Patriarch of St Petersburg. And it always came down to this: I should have pressed her more. With a taxi waiting outside, and the rain tumbling from the bleak and cold Roman December sky, Drox gave Kitty a tour of the lab. When they consigned The Magdalen Icon into his vault of vaults, Kitty saw the hard drives from The Machine. She asked about the drive for her daughter. 'Why did you and Max nickname her Blanka?' She suspected there was something about The Machine that her husband Max didn't understand. 'What's your Machine's hidden secret?' she'd asked, holding the hard drive labelled|

> ᴜ4   *Maguire, B.V. Miss   dob Sept 28, 1978*

'It's like the hard drive of the soul,' he'd answered enigmatically.

When the lunch with Cardinal Kratky had been changed to 'supper,' they'd found themselves with the afternoon to kill.
'We've got all afternoon, and damn, we can't have sex to fill the time,' she

concluded, letting out with her full-bellied, lilting laugh. 'I'm married to your best friend, and you play for the other side.'

That was the last time he heard Kitty's laughter. She didn't laugh after she'd entered the empty Machine; and lain down on its operating table after he'd connected the cyber-helmet to her head. She never talked about what she'd then seen – and Drox locked Kitty's hard drive away with the others. Alongside The Magdalen.

5.3

*T*he visitors for the Wash-up started to arrive, finally. Pushing his memories of Kitty to the recesses of his mind, Drox set off to greet the first arrivals, taking the AI-driven twelve seater OhZone shuttle.

In year 2000, when Professor Hart destroyed the original Machine in Rome, Drox, who'd retained almost all of his third of the massive wealth of *The Goldheart* find, contributed half a billion of his own money on what he called the 'refit. This was in addition to the billions poured in by the six OhZone sponsors (the U.S. contributing the largest share). The new OhZone Machine in Paris was fit for a prince! Or princess! As Drox travelled deep under the River Seine and the Île de la Cité, he looked up in the direction of the famous Cathédrale Notre-Dame de Paris above, and thought about his own past life in Paris. What did Saint Augustine say? If it weren't for memory, I wouldn't have a soul? As the shuttle hummed through the darkness, Drox pondered what depths he had uncovered of his own soul since he'd been recording the images from The Machine?

*T*he main entrance to the OhZone lab was buried below Paris' busiest Metro station. Châtelet is a station on lines 1, 4, 7, 11 and 14 of the Métro, in the centre of medieval Paris and the 1st arrondissement. Unbeknown to the world at large, the station had a twelfth platform, on a sub-level two hundred feet below the others.

When the shuttle doors opened at that private platform, Drox spoke to the driver, AI Paul, one of two androids he had created to operate the facility. AI Paul had been constructed in the form of a friendly compact man of below-average height and was instantly recognizable by his silver-colored synthetic skin.

'There will be two riding back with me,' said Drox.

'Yes, Doctor. 4 and Admiral De Leon,' the android replied. 'The Admiral has not been here for two years and thirty-nine days. May I greet them?'

'You may, Paul.' Drox pronounced the name, 'Pol', in the French way. 'Use the standard OhZone protocol.'

'Will you dispense with the N-SASS for the Admiral?'

'No,' said Drox curtly, strolling into the elevator lobby. The lights of the train and OhZone station blacked out behind him. He stepped into the elevator and pressed the button marked 'RC.'

RC stood for rez-de-chaussée (ground floor), and it always made Drox smile: it was actually a hundred feet under the ground. He walked across a metal landing and briskly went through the ritual of voice, iris and hand recognition. The lutetium-tungsten carbide door sprung open and Drox walked in and up the stone steps inside. As he climbed, his gait lost some of its lightness. He was going to meet Kitty's daughter, Blanka and would be obliged to put on his public smile, a mask she would see through instantly. He sighed. She in turn will put on her mask, and we will have to play the game again.

When they'd created Blanka, the sun was shining, God was in his Heaven and all was well in the world. Now Blanka is the sole survivor of the four, lamented Drox. He had augmented her synthetic parts and the AI part of her mind. She also bore the only other ƱScanner which matched his – her silver for his gold.

He heard her voice and removed his gold-colored ƱScanner from his pocket, allowing him a view of the security door above.

'Meet you half way?' said Blanka.

Drox stopped near a stone sill on which an oil lamp flickered, and took a deep breath. He was tired and feeling his age. These were dark days for OhZone: Felicity, the second to go rogue, with the mysterious safe under her house and the SSD Frankenstein sector they couldn't penetrate. And C had also vanished, leaving the remains of a covert Skif with hologram Comms under his apartment, stripped bare by some unidentified force.

'Who goes there?' he asked. It was part of the protocol.

'One OhZone, 4; one human, De Leon.'

Drox pressed a control on his Scanner. The lutetium-tungsten carbide door in an extra-mural janitor's office below the maintenance level of Metro Line 7 opened. Drox looked at the stone sill. It was deeply blackened by the soot from centuries' old oil lamps lighting the steps. He looked up as he heard footsteps above. Shadows from the electric lights stretched long around the corners. Heavy on his feet, the energetic seventy year-old De Leon made his appearance first. They shook hands warmly. De Leon was followed silently by the smiling Blanka.

'My knight in shining armour,' she said.

'My Celtic queen,' Drox answered. As they got in the elevator, he pressed the button marked, 'Platform 12.'

Blanka was the first to step out. The platform lights switched on to reveal the waiting OhZone shuttle. AI Paul saluted, shook hands, and greeted her effusively. '4, my favourite OhZone, the brightest and most glorious, a star amongst my heavens. Your sixty one days' absence from us have been a pain to my heart.'

Blanka gave Drox a look that said, 'And I know who programmed those phrases into him.'

'Thank you, Paul. I've missed you too. Have access,' she said, her eyes glowing.

In a second, AI Paul had checked over the insides of Blanka, human and artificial. 'All present and correct, Ma'am, apart from your left kidney. May I hope for good tidings about an OhZone donor for it?'

De Leon coughed politely.

'Admiral De Leon, Sir, most venerable upholder of honour in the world of Intelligence –'

'Can we do the N-SASS?' he said, shaking hands with AI Paul.

The 'nasal, saliva and sweat samples' DNA analysis was the gold standard for security. The only other premises guarded by it were the CIA Director's suite at Langley. When people complained about nasal samples, Keith De Leon would reply, 'You can't make omelets without breaking eggs.' Drox was more diplomatic. AI Paul completed his analysis, the three boarded the shuttle, and AI Paul jumped in his cab and drove off happily backwards.

The OhZone shuttle ran back under the Seine, one of the prettiest rivers in the world, under *La Rive Gauche* of Paris, The Left Bank, dropping to five hundred feet below the streets of the fifth Arrondissement. Half way between the original publishing house of James Joyce's *Ulysses*, and *The Sorbonne University* lay the OhZone laboratory complex. Its creators, Hart and Oxberry, were pacifists – or at least they were anti-war – yet this complex was the envy of every military in the world!

At its heart was The Machine, rebuilt with love, time and an endless supply of money. A direct nuclear strike on the Paris streets above wouldn't even make it miss a beat…

*A*s De Leon prepared the 'conference room' for the meeting, Blanka sought out Drox in his private study. Like the other décor at the laboratory, it was white and tasteful, with modern art originals on the wall.

'I have a question.'

'Only one?' Drox said as he ushered Blanka into a chair. 'About The Machine?'

'Not really, although you never talk to me about it.'

'You're right, I don't. Do you remember my visits with you at the convent in Mexico?'

'You came every Christmas. One of the highlights of my year.'

'I've known you since you were been born. Before you were made into an OhZone. I know you don't like The Machine and feel uneasy about being an OhZone.'

'You can't unmake an OhZone.'

'No, we can't. By the way, I've never thanked you for introducing me to Dr Fox. He has been a great help in ironing out some of my theories.'

'I thought you had known Don forever,' said Blanka.

'No, you introduced me to him when Grinin defected.'

A momentary silver tint washed over Blanka's eyes as, behind their lenses, her eyes processed the new chain of thought.

'Okay, one question is about him. I dreamt about Don last night. It was bloody weird. He was flying through the clouds. I was alongside him. We had wings.'

Drox shook his head. 'I'm not sure I can help with that. Your stepfather is the one to ask. What else?'

'My name. Why did you and Max give me the name – Blanka? Is it to do with what you saw when I was in The Machine?'

'Likewise, a fascinating question. Two reasons, really. When we first started we thought that OhZones should have special names, like the present day AI Paul and AI Matilda. Second –'

At that moment, De Leon knocked on the door as he walked in.

'Sorry to break in,' he said, 'but I'm all done.' He turned to Blanka. 'Don't you have to do the English pub stuff?'

The silver tint washed over Blanka's eyes again (processing new information). 'Paul has picked up the other OhZones, on their way from the airport to Châtelet.'

De Leon stretched to his full height and cracked his knuckles. 'Showtime,' he said.

Drox smiled and led Blanka and De Leon out of his study, around a corner and down a white corridor. AI Paul's voice gently listed the arrivals over a tannoy. 'Two OhZones, 5 and 6, approaching Chatelet.'

As she walked beside Drox, Blanka wondered if he had intentionally avoided the question about her name, and if he would ever truthfully tell her.

AI Paul opened a pair of large doors and ushered them into a huge 3D white-cove. It was hard to judge its full extent because the human eye could make out no end to it.

A round oak table with nine sets of papers on it was conspicuous, next to a white board, as the only furniture. AI Paul addressed Drox: 'Doctor, the Admiral has been one hundred percent effective. Everything is ready twenty minutes ahead of schedule.'

De Leon smiled. 'Leave it to the Marines,' he said.

'*Tres bien,*' said Drox.

'*Je m'inquiète pour le professeur,*' said AI Paul. '*Il est encore à Bar Saint Georges.*' (Blanka and Drox both understood French: AI Paul was worried that the Professor was still at his favourite bar).

A momentary violet tint washed over Blanka's eyes. AI Paul turned to her, 'I'm sorry to upset you.'

'Don't worry,' she said. 'But I need to put my contacts in so people and androids can't see my color shifts.'

Drox turned to her, 'Max will be here.'

He took his gold-colored Scanner from his pocket and paused his finger over a window. 'Now...' He turned to Blanka.

'Do you want *The Ship* from Wardour Street? Or *The White Horse* from Neals Yard?'

'Hah, I love this bit,' laughed De Leon.

Blanka put her finger to her mouth pretending to be deep in thought.

'I guess it's a no brainer,' said De Leon. 'You've seen *The Ship* so many times before.'

Blanka nodded, '*The White Horse,* please.'

'Stand back,' said Drox, 'there's quite a crowd.'

He waited for the AI, the OhZone and the human to all step back a few paces, then he pressed a window on his gold ℧Scanner.

In two seconds a gigantic life-size hologram of a busy London Soho pub *The White Horse* materialized in the space around the table, followed by the walls windows and doors of the pub and a hundred customers standing outside in the evening sunshine talking in cockney.

The four of them were set on the street outside. Blanka looked up at the pub sign of The White Horse hanging above her, and beamed.

'Hah,' said De Leon.

Drox swung open the pub door and one by one they walked inside.

5.4

*A*t Drox's laboratory in Paris, every OhZone agent had their own sleeping quarters and 'den.'

In the Rome laboratory, the pioneer OhZones had dubbed their bedrooms, 'The Catacombs' and the name had carried over to the new Lab when it was built in Paris in 2001-2.

Drox had wanted to make it a 'home away from home' for them.

'It's bad enough,' he'd explained to De Leon,
'that we turn them into hemidemi-androids...

Without giving them
somewhere to come home to...
just to be themselves...
somewhere only they know.'

Blanka emerged from her secret bedroom with her contact lenses in place and her emotions intact. *It's my life, since I was twenty. I wonder if OhZone is really… the only thing I know.*

OhZone Agents — In Service				ʊ
4	COMMANDING OFFICER: BLANKA MAGUIRE	F	CIA	v 3.1
5	EXECUTIVE OFFICER: SOKOL COMAROVA	F	KGB / MI6	v 2.2
6	ON PATERNITY LEAVE: DAVID MU	M	CIA	v 3.0
8	30 DAYS TO COMPLETION: HANS ZIMMERMAN	M	BND	v 3.0

She looked at Crusoe's room, next to hers in the corridor, and a lump came to her throat. They'd followed each other into OhZone in '98; decided which of them went first – on a coin toss. People asked, 'How come you're number four?' Crusoe did his 'forty days and forty nights' first. I followed on. That was how. She looked beyond Crusoe's bedroom to OhZone 2's. Pascal was dead too. 'These rooms *are* fucking catacombs,' she shouted. 'I am dead-OhZone walking.'

OhZone Agents — Deceased				ʊ
2	PASCAL SOUM	(1964 - 2014)	M	DGSE	v 2.2
3	CRUSOE ROBINSON	(1970 - 2015)	M	ASIS / MI6	v 2.2

She'd never known OhZone 1. He'd deserted in '97, never seen the lab here, was presumed dead. But Drox kept a bedroom for him all the same. Drox reminded people, 'If we treat our OhZones better perhaps they won't go rogue. And who knows maybe we'll see OhZone 1 again one of these days.' Well, thought Blanka, her sadness turning to anger. Felicity pissed all over that fucking theory. She walked down the corridor passing the other doors. Room 5 was Sokol's, and room 6 belonged to David Mu, a Hong Kong born CIA agent, who was on paternity leave but coming to the Wash-up at Hart's request. Room 7 had been Felicity's, but the room number had been erased and every trace of her removed.

OhZone Agents — "Gone Rogue"					↻
1	JOHN DOE	(1997)	M	CIA	v 1.0
7	FELICITY ROBINSON	(2015)	F	MI6	v 1.1

Then David Mu appeared, followed by Sokol, who held back and made no eye contact. However, Puppy knew no such restraint and jumped high up at Blanka, licking her hand. Sokol ignored Puppy's actions, while Mu and Blanka hugged each other like old friends.

'Long time no see. I've missed you guys,' said Mu. 'Shall we go into the Tank and see Hans?'

'Sure,' huffed Sokol, struggling to remain civil.

They stopped at a secure air lock with an illuminated panel above it displaying 'Operating Theatre.' A humorous sign had been erected on a pole with a piece of string

☺ *Welcome to The Machine*

Blanka pressed the button to open the microphone and spoke clearly into the intercom, 'We're here, Matilda.'

'Good,' said AI Matilda's voice, loud and metallic over the speaker. 'You may enter the changing room.'

There was an audible click from the stark white airlock door followed by a moment of silence, then a sudden 'whoosh' as the door opened. With an unlimited budget and a lot of space science to call upon, even the airlock made them feel like they were in space. 'Here we go,' said Mu, as pressurized air and disinfectant sprays showered them. Soon they stood in what would have been fog to the normal eye, but their AI vision saw through it clearly. As rapidly as it had been introduced, the fog was removed as oxygen and nitrogen from an independent air supply filled the airlock.

Sokol was dying to make a caustic remark about the 'special' but sterile air of the Paris underground, but she didn't. She wanted to use silence to punish Blanka, but was beginning to wonder how long she could keep it up. When the inner airlock door opened they stepped out into a well-lit changing room with rows of lockers (Sokol's vision counted thirty-six instantly). Scrubs on hangers covered one wall. As the airlock closed behind them, another whooshed open. It was parallel to the first, though the door was narrower. Out of it stepped AI Matilda, with the same metallic skin and facial features as AI Paul. The android's name reminded Sokol of her late former-fiance, Crusoe. He had suggested her name to Drox, from the Australian folk song *Waltzing Matilda*.

AI Matilda was a later version than AI Paul – more shapely, taller and faster. She existed to work The Machine. Her longer limbs enabled her to perform certain mechanical procedures within the Tank. She wore an android version of a nurse's uniform to keep stains off her skin, but her shoes were white plastic, inside which wires and boards controlled her leg movement. The human staff of nurses and doctors called her, 'Mother Matilda.' AI Paul had never needed 'backup,' but in a security emergency the larger and stronger AI Matilda would come to his aid within seconds. Their AI minds were linked to each other and to Drox's gold Scanner 24/7. Through her silver Scanner, Blanka could link to them too, when she wanted; a privilege given only to her, as the OhZone leader.

Matilda sped over to the three OhZones and greeted them matter-of-factly. 'Hello 4, 5 and 6.' She turned to Sokol, 'I am sorry for your injuries 5. I hope you will allow me to examine them and contribute to the repairs.'
'Thank you,' said Sokol.
'My records indicate you have all visited the Theatre during the OhZone procedure before.'
Sokol and Blanka nodded.
'Just the once when - ' Felicity was in The Machine, Mu had started to say.
'Matilda, what is former-OhZone-7 now known as?'
'She's currently referred to as Felicity-fast-track. Her arrest warrant says

Felicity Furness aka Felicity Robinson,' said AI Matilda.

Sokol cleared her throat. 'Suka,' she spat out. Blanka thought she might spit on the floor.

'Her husband Mr Jude Robinson is divorcing her,' continued AI Matilda, unawares. 'If you like I can send you updates on her name.'

'No thanks, it's okay.' Mu said.

Via her silver Scanner, Blanka's mind changed the subject. 'I see Drox hasn't taken the sign down.'

AI Matilda turned to her and publicly said, 'Dr Drox likes me to experiment with humour. I have erected other signs. Would you like to see them?'

'Sure,' said Blanka. Sokol frowned and went to a locker marked ℧4 where she started undressing, while AI Matilda showed off another child-like sign hanging above the lockers. It had a serious face and read

😐 *Tank wear*

Blanka and Mu smiled and made their way to the lockers. As Blanka opened her locker, Sokol stepped past her towards the sterilizing showers. Blanka gagged at the naked OhZone. Sokol's broken nose and eye socket, together with numerous bruises, made her look quite black and blue, and were accentuated by her nakedness. Blanka felt terrible all over again and the sight of the communal showers inexplicably unnerved her. She thought of Felicity and the killings. No one had access to the The Machine's images except Drox. *What images had he seen of Felicity – when she was in The Machine?!* Could that be why he had inexplicably programmed her with a primitive version of the software? And acquiesced when she had quit half way through the training?

Blanka carefully removed her necklace of Rosary beads and then her silver bracelet adorned with a cross. Laying these on the silk lining she had decorated her locker with, she stripped. She entered the women's showers as Sokol left, wrapped in a sterile bath robe. Again, no eye contact. Sokol donned her scrubs, and turned to AI Matilda, who kept constant vigilance over the systems inside the Tank. 'All ready, Mother,' Sokol joked.

AI Matilda followed Sokol as she walked to a third airlock. The outer door whooshed open and Sokol stepped inside. The short corridor looked like part of the international space station, apart from a sanitation terminal and a screen showing the inside of Airlock 03b. Sokol's hands were scanned for micro-organisms – the screen showed blue patches indicating the areas of microbial build-up – and then sanitized using SL18. Sokol liked the inner airlock, black like cut granite, with two doors set three feet apart. When she appeared on screen 03b, AI Matilda and the computer took thirty seconds to re-identify and re-scan her for micro-organisms. Then, a series of green lights came on.

Sokol stepped into what everybody just called the 'Tank,' an underground cavern with cut granite walls, hewed from the bedrock five hundred feet under the city. It was a circular chamber a hundred feet in diameter, with a domed ceiling rising from ten feet at the edge to thirty feet in the centre. Arrays of electronic equipment coordinated in the black color scheme lined the wall and were grouped in five stations: four for controlling the process, and the fifth for recording the dreams and mental impressions that the subject experienced during their days and nights in The Machine.

Sokol was the very first OhZone to be made in Paris and no matter how many times she visited, it filled her with awe! In the centre was a gigantic glass cylinder – Drox's 'Lava Lamp,' as Blanka had dubbed it. A room-within-a-room, with two inch glass walls, it was twenty-five feet in diameter, with a lutetium-titanium operating table at the bottom. Hewed out of Second World War underground bunkers, Drox proudly called his Tank 'an Archimedes cage within an Archimedes cage' and declared it to be the most secure room in Europe. The real magic was the reason for its nickname: the Lava Lamp was filled with a viscous violet liquid. Suspended in it – hooked up to dozens of tubes and cable bundles, but floating freely, serenely, in the thick fluid – was Hans.

A faint sound suggested that the others had come through. Sokol tensed, remembering her feud with Blanka. Her AI hearing formed a sonar picture from behind her: Mu was alone. She turned and smiled.
'So this is where I spent my forty days and forty nights,' he said. 'Shame I wasn't awake, it's majestic in here.'
'It's Ubercool,' replied Sokol, her mood brightening slightly.
'Why didn't you get your version 2.2 upgraded?' he asked.

'Never felt the need,' she said. '2.2 serves me fine and has got me this far. There aren't that many differences.'

'Hans'll be 3.0 like me,' said Mu. 'Drox has been dogfooding 3.1 [working out the kinks] on his systems and live on Blanka, and he's come up with a leap forward for 4.0. Double the time in the Machine though. Imagine how advanced the next OhZone will be!'

'Tres bien,' said Sokol, trying not to yawn, and realising reluctantly how much she missed Blanka's company.

AI Matilda entered the Tank from the airlock and sped over to the chief nurse, Adriana, who was working at one of the control stations that circled the Lava Lamp.

Blanka, looking a little white, finally emerged from the airlock.

'Whoa, girl. You okay?' asked Mu with his Californian accent.

'I've got what the Brits call a "gippy" tummy,' Blanka said.

'One oyster too many, dear?' quipped Sokol.

Blanka looked down, not wanting to fight.

Sokol regretted her joke.

AI Matilda approached with the chief nurse.

'This is the new senior charge nurse, Adriana.'

'I was the nurse on the blood transfusion at nights', she said in French.

The OhZones' AI minds translated quickly and they shook hands with her. Mu gestured to Hans in the Lava Lamp and said, 'Germany, Spain, Russia, America and Hong Kong, all in one room underneath France!'

AI Matilda laughed. An eerie laugh, half human and half machine. Sensing the reactions of the OhZones, AI Matilda explained:

'Dr. Oxberry will be editing my laugh in the next update. He also promises to upgrade my wit.'

'Yes...' said Blanka, uncertainly.

'He'd do well to upgrade his own sense of humour first,' Sokol said.

Everybody laughed – human, OhZones and android.

'I will make a note of that and let him know,' Matilda said.

As Blanka watched them adjust the Phosphorus and Lutetium transfusion rates for Hans, she thought about the concentrated blood. It made OhZones susceptible to dehydration (they needed to drink ten pints of fluid a day) and had led to her kidney disease. Thirty more days till completion, poor Hans. A month ago he was sitting in her kitchen discussing crystals and comparing the taste of different herbal teas. She pictured herself in her cottage garden giving Hans a tour of her fruit and vegetable beds, as she explained to him the principles of planting by the moon. Then she thought of her beehives. The queens would be waking soon and thinking about the year to come. The worker bees would be born and would live to serve the hive. Is that what she did as an OhZone?

With a jolt, she suddenly realized that she was the last survivor. The only one of the four original OhZones to make it through. And she had health problems. Did it matter, that in sixteen years of being an OhZone, she had derived no personal benefit?

She thought of her wild animal sanctuaries and of the people who cared for the animals. Of course, others had benefited; people as well as the hundreds of animals. She gazed at Hans. Is he going to turn out like Felicity, or is he going to turn out like me?

Pulling herself together, she told herself there were indeed many advantages to being an OhZone. She laughed to herself and addressed her internal back up AI: Hera, describe the second brain implant.

In what Blanka had always considered a Greek accent, Hera answered: The second implant is inside the hypothalamus. Using this, OhZones can optimize and regulate their own hormone production. They can manually override the hypothalamus, choosing when to sleep or be awake, for example. In female OhZones it allows manual regulation and timing of your estrogen-progesterone balance to suit your mood. You can decide if, and when, you want ovulation and menstruation.

Blanka was still smiling as she looked across the Tank at Sokol, who stood near Mu at the Lava Lamp. Three women had been made OhZones: Blanka, Sokol and Felicity. Felicity didn't complete the training so didn't know this App. But Blanka and Sokol both agreed it was their favourite feature.

It means dear Hera, Blanka said, that we can control our periods, the curse of womankind since the dawn of time!

She pictured Sokol in happier times: the twenty-five-year-old Sokol.

'Ubercool,' was how Sokol summed up being able to stop her periods.

5.5

REFERRING TO THE NEXT MORNING—
PROFESSOR HART WROTE THIS
IN HIS MEMOIRS TWENTY YEARS LATER, IN 2035:

Drox relocated OhZone to Paris in the early part of the century.
His hobbies were botanicals and old school black-and-white
photography. But if there was ever a person who fulfilled the idiom,
"still waters run deep," it was he.

Blanka told me of one spring morning.
She emerged from the photo booth at Sèvres–Babylone
Metro to walk to meet him for breakfast.

"I'll never forget that morning. It was Holy Week, Good Friday:
five days before I met the Girl-who-fell-to-Earth."
Blanka laughed out loud at the recollection.
"The sunshine, the light, the fountains, the little shops,
even a honey-house!" she told me excitedly.
"The River Seine sparkling, Drox's houseboat, Papillon,
bobbing against the bank.

"After the Cone hit –
when we found out that Paris had been spared –
I realized that Drox must have known all along.
He had foreseen the future."

Good Friday
April 3, 2015

*T*he sun rose, painting the medieval heart of the 'City of Light'
for the French festival, *Pâques* – meaning, literally, 'Passover.' While the
Jewish Passover commemorates the Exodus from Egypt, the Christian
Easter celebrates the resurrection of Jesus which, according to the
Gospels, happened during Passover.

Needing a break from OhZone, Drox had slept on his houseboat the night before. He'd invited the three OhZones to breakfast – of course croissants and coffee – what else?

Sokol was walking there from the house of her father (a perfumer) on The Left Bank. Blanka and Mu were ahead, having emerged from the back entrance to the OhZone lab – the 'Fotoautomatic' old school analog photo booth on platform 2 of Sèvres–Babylone station, the deepest part of the Metro. Blanka window-shopped as they strolled north on Boulevard St Germaine. Mu laughed when Blanka's face lit up on sighting a new honey-house, Miellerie Sant Germaine. She slipped in quickly to choose little gifts of boutique honeys for Drox and her best friend Sokol.

Passing Musee D'Orsay, they reached the unique Eiffel-design four-way pedestrian bridge *Passerelle Solférino* that reigned across the Seine, to the Jardin des Tuileries, in one unbroken span. They paused to look at the lovers' padlocks now arrayed there [sadly, the Parisian authorities have stripped *Pont des Arts* of them].

Mu didn't say a word, he didn't have to. Blanka was thirty-six and popular with both women and men. Selfless, sweet and beautiful; quirky, intelligent, kind to animals. Not a day went by without someone saying, 'Why isn't Blanka in love…? Why isn't Blanka with so and so…?' *Was it the job?* 'It'll happen if it's meant to,' Blanka always replied.

At that point, Sokol appeared. In the morning light, the two week-old wounds to her face gave it the look of a resurrected cadaver, partly because of the effort she had made to hide them with makeup. With deadly timing, and without even looking at Blanka, she pointed out her and Crusoe's lovers padlock. It was four years old but still clearly marked in Sokol's handwriting

$$Sokol \quad ❤ \quad Crusoe$$

The knife of the killings twisted again. Sokol was reminding her that she had lost Crusoe not once, but twice. Blanka's eyes teared up, misting her AI vision. Blinking hard, she turned to Sokol and handed her the gift. '*Je suis desolee*. Please forgive me,' is what she said.

Sokol opened the paper bag, glanced at the lavender honey and replied sarcastically, 'Sweet.' With that she headed off to Drox's houseboat.

5.6

*T*wo hours later, most of the delegates to the Wash-up had arrived at Châtelet metro station, been tested, conveyed to the laboratory, and greeted by Blanka, Sokol and Mu. The NATO Secretary-General was still to arrive, but the other three heavyweights met with Drox in his study. The Iceni had quickly nicknamed these four, *the four wise men*.

Professor Hart was clean-shaven. Drox, De Leon and Fox all sported beards. Fox's gray beard was so long it suggested a cross between Santa Claus and the god Zeus.

The Professor opened the conclave.

'Well, this is a sorry mess,' he said to no one in particular.

'We need to refine the positive from this,' Drox immediately insisted.

'What positive?' said Hart.

'Hopefully, an A positive for Blanka,' joked De Leon.

Drox caught the twitch in Hart's eye and gestured towards the bar. Hart crossed to it, examined the contents and looked underneath it.

'Sometimes you get the bar,' he quoted.

'Yes,' said Drox. 'The connection between bears and White Russians is clear to me.'

'And me,' said De Leon. Fox nodded too.

'The fridge is disguised as a wall safe,' Drox said, pointing.

'Hah!' said De Leon, then turned to Dr Fox. 'Cat got your tongue, doc?'

'I'm thinking about the selection of Felicity as 7,' said Fox. 'Nearby would have made 7 if C hadn't tampered with the psych tests. *Corruption,* in its many forms, is a hydra-headed monster.'

'Corruption in Intelligence is a chronic problem,' agreed Hart, his first White Canadian in his hand.

'I've struggled at Langley,' said De Leon. 'It won't go away. The problem is: at Wonderland you had corruption at the very top.'

'The CCU tests were there to protect the program,' said Hart. 'And protect the world from a psychopathic OhZone.'

'A second one,' said De Leon, looking at Hart who drained his glass of White Canadian and set about mixing another. 'OhZone 1 wasn't psychopathic,' he said. 'He was perverted by Wonderland.'

'According to them Felicity's in Africa,' said Drox.

'Makes the case for surgical tagging of OhZones for me,' said De Leon. Drox thought of the three OhZones eating croissants at breakfast. 'They're human beings, Keith, not machines.'

'You know my solution,' Hart shouted. Then regretted being so loud.

'Same old, same old, Max,' said De Leon. 'But there's far, far too much invested in OhZone to close the program down.'

'And let me remind you there's no contingency plan to decommission an existing OhZone,' said Drox.

'You can't make omelets without breaking eggs,' said De Leon.

'And there's no honour about thieves and liars,' burst out Hart. 'For God's sake, don't make cracks about "breaking eggs" at the full meeting.'

'Now isn't the time to rehash the surgical tagging debate,' said Fox. 'Drox, can you prepare a report on the anatomical and ethical issues involved?'

'On surgical tagging? I already have. Just have to dust it off. '

'Jens will want to see a road map forward,' said De Leon. 'As do I. It's not just about Felicity. He's also alarmed, as am I, by reports of Sokol's stand-off with Blanka, and by Blanka's failing kidneys.'

'We can fix the stand-off,' said Fox.

'How?' asked Hart.

'I'll bring it up in the group.'

Hart and the others nodded.

'And the second?' persisted De Leon.

'I'm hopeful something will come along,' said Fox.

The MI6 officers involved in *Operation Penthouse* with sufficient security clearance to visit the OhZone lab – minus Crusoe Robinson – were being served drinks at the busy bar of *The White Horse* by the android. The group consisted of Bio, Nearby, Paddington, Krishna and the technical officer, Farringdon. With the recent death of one of their own, not to mention the slaughter of Grinin and his daughters, they were somewhat subdued. AI Paul was dressed, incongruously, as a Parisian barman. 'It's my own little touch,' he confided to Blanka.'

Finally the NATO Secretary General, Jens Stoltenberg, the former Prime Minister of Norway, was shown in by AI Matilda who then left. Jens shook hands with everyone, was served a glass of aquavit by AI Paul, and then sat down at the round table next to De Leon.

'Welcome to The White Horse ,' said Drox. 'And as always we have four types of humanoids here,' he laughed. 'From the OhZone gods to ordinary mortals. From AI Paul to the holograms who don't usually react.' On cue, the two hundred hologram people stopped chatting and drinking, turned towards the table and shouted, 'Welcome Secretary General!' They then disappeared, leaving only those at the round table.

'It was quite unnerving,' Fox later said to Blanka, 'like being surrounded by zombies waiting to come in for the kill.'

Although Drox chaired the Wash-up, it was left to Russia, as the new Chief of MI6, to brief everyone on the details of Operation Penthouse. These were largely known, but Sokol felt obligated to bring the gruesomeness of the children's murders to everyone's attention by producing Olga's tiger from a bag. She slammed it on the table eliciting the Secretary General and Nearby (who didn't swear) to jump and curse out loud in their native tongues (Norwegian and Irish). Like Banquo's Ghost, the toy tiger, stained with clotted blood and stinking, rose and spoke in the haunted tones of Major Grinin

Come on Olga, come on Emma
Let's play the hiding game.

Whether it was the sound or the stench, Paddington jumped up saying, 'I'm going to be sick,' and rushed from the room. She had been looking after Sokol's wire fox terrier which now loose, howled and ran around the table threatening the meeting with further chaos. To bring things under control, Fox pushed his pub chair back, stood and addressed Nearby, who, having captured the dog, was trying to calm him.

'With the chairman and Secretary General's leave I'm going to ask you and the other ordinary agents to go outside with Puppy for a moment.' Jens and Drox nodded to Fox. Nearby took Puppy's lead, and Krishna and Farringdon followed them out.

Fox looked at Blanka and Sokol in turn and then picked up the bloody toy tiger.

'Although Russia has spared us quotes from *Macbeth*,' he said, fixing Bio in his eye, 'some might say Lady Macbeth is with us now.'

Rigid and expressionless, Bio remained silent, wondering if she was in for another round of recrimination.

Turning back to Sokol, Fox held out his hand. 'I know you witnessed the suffering more directly than anyone else. And you want everyone, not just Macbeth, to see Banquo's ghost – to witness the horrible deaths not only of Crusoe, but of Grinin and Diana's children. But there is already enough guilt in this room.' Fox paused. At that moment, all eyes glanced at both Blanka and Bio. 'Our job forward is to lay the ghosts to rest,' he concluded. 'There will be consequences. The guilty will be punished, even though the horror can't be undone. But Banquo's ghost must be laid to rest.'

After a second's hesitation Sokol handed him the bag. AI Paul made a timely entrance with a plastic trash bag and disinfectant wipes. Fox nodded, 'Now after we wash up we'll get on with the Wash-up.'

When the meeting broke up, Don gestured to Sokol and Blanka to stay behind. They stood at the table, several empty chairs separating them.

'You two have got to talk. I don't want to rehash what happened between you on the roof, or last Christmas. There's no point. You, Sokol, have got to move past this, past your anger and pain and grief. I'm not going to pretend it will happen overnight, but you have to start. Blanka, you of all people, should know what to do. If you two don't work together, don't work this out, there will be *no Iceni and no OhZone.*'

Blanka had tears in her eyes, but her face was stone, 'I keep saying sorry, it's coming out like a scratched record.'

Sokol stubbornly looked down at the table.

Fox sounded funny in his cockney accent, as he said, 'Play it again, Sam.'

'She won't forgive me,' said Blanka, also looking down.

'I've been counselling Diana Grinin,' Don exclaimed, ''till I'm blue in the face. It's her wish that the two of you should be friends again. And not just a wish. She needs for you to be friends. She needs help – and she looks to you two most of all for that.'

Blanka took half a dozen steps around the table to stand in front of Sokol, and looked into her brown eyes.

'I'm sorry,' Blanka said. 'I would do anything to bring Olga and Emma back. Officer Gabor, Major Grinin.'

Sokol looked up into Blanka's blue eyes. It was the look of a soldier standing inspection. At five foot six each, Sokol and Blanka could see exactly eye to eye.

'And dear *Crusoe*,' added Blanka. She took a deep breath.

'And I'm sorry for your injuries. …I made a serious error of judgement last Christmas. *I should have listened to you.* I see now how wrong I was about Felicity. Please find it in your heart to forgive me.'

Sokol nodded, and in her Russian way said, simply, '*Da.*'

Fox turned and addressed Sokol in Russian. 'Is it enough?'

'Da,' Sokol said again, 'It is enough.' She held out her hand, and Blanka took it and shook it. Then Sokol reached forward and kissed Blanka, Russian-fashion, on both her cheeks.

5.7

Gladius Legis Custos.   *The sword guards the law.*

PRÉFECTURE DE POLICE DE PARIS

Good Friday evening, Blanka went to mass at Cathédrale Notre-Dame de Paris accompanied by Admiral De Leon, Nearby, Bio and Russia [all MI6 directors were Catholic]. The two Intelligence heads were shadowed by armed bodyguards, and special arrangements had been made for them to be at the cathedral. As she waited in line for the Eucharist, Blanka was surprised to see Dr Fox there as well, just behind her in the line.

It was when they left the cathedral and walked into Place Jean Paul II, that *le lapin blanc* ('the white rabbit') incident happened. Notre Dame is at the very centre of Paris, on a rather stark island in the River Seine called *Ile de la Cite*. Blanka and the group were watching the sun set on the river, across from the Préfecture de Police de Paris headquarters.

Bio had just translated the Latin motto, 'Gladius Legis Custos,' above the station doors for Blanka – 'It means, "the sword guards the law," ' she said – when a heavily armed police patrol rushed past them. Three-person police patrols and four-person army patrols were the norm in Paris after the Charlie Hebdo shootings, so it was no surprise to see the woman sergeant reprimand another woman who was sitting on a small mat surrounded by children. This elderly beggar was letting the children feed a little white rabbit from a bundle of lavender grass she had. What was a surprise was how harshly the sergeant spoke. The children were frightened and ran away. The rabbit, who was attached to the woman by a thin pink ribbon, frantically ran this way and that. The old woman, as shaken and confused as the animal, started to gather her mat, lavender grass and rabbit, when the sergeant snatched her polystyrene begging cup out of her hand.

Blanka bristled and took a step forward, but felt the hand of De Leon on her arm. The sergeant – unaware that she was being watched by the head of OhZone, the head of the CIA and the head of MI6 – tipped the coins from the cup on to the ground, and then ripped the cup into three pieces. As the beggar struggled to walk away, the sergeant held out the shredded pieces of cup and yelled, 'Don't leave litter.'

At this point, Blanka's AI sight picked up Fox emerging from the cathedral. She was momentarily disconcerted when she thought she saw the shape of wings around him, caught in the glow of the setting sun. As the sergeant grabbed hold of the old woman and thrust the shreds of the cup at her, the terrified rabbit jumped from the her arms and ran onto the road, straight into the path of a truck.

Blanka was too far away to help the rabbit, but she felt – as she in later years described it – a 'breath of light' coming from Fox's direction. Just as the rumbling truck neared the rabbit, a four-soldier army patrol marched around the corner and stepped into the road. The woman corporal in charge held up her hand, and the truck stopped. Blanka dashed forward intending to pick up the rabbit – miraculously the soldiers' boots hadn't trampled it. Then the last soldier picked the animal up, smiling at Blanka as he crossed her path, and handed the rabbit back to the old woman (the obvious owner). Dr Fox winked at the soldier and thanked him in French. The police sergeant was itching to intervene again, but the presence of Fox dissuaded her. Blanka watched as Fox tucked a twenty Euro note under the rabbit's collar and, with his arm around the beggar, told her, 'Go on home now, mother.'

Fox noticed that Blanka was staring at him, so walked up to her and whispered. 'You see, *help was just around the corner.* Sometimes things have a way of working out. For people and for rabbits. And this rabbit really is a very lucky Easter bunny!'

5.8

*B*lanka had a little time before she had to return to London, so she spent the Saturday just chilling with Sokol. It was almost like old times. Although Sokol could not forget the horror that Felicity had wrought, she had made her first steps toward forgiving Blanka.

★

*O*n Saturday evening Blanka was out by herself perusing postcards at the little kiosks by the River Seine, when she ran into Fox on the footpath. They agreed to have dinner before Blanka flew home to London in Drox's jet.

'I'm not going back to England just yet,' said Fox. 'I'm going to a reunion in Croatia.'

As they sat in a candlelit restaurant on a river boat, Fox filled Blanka in on some OhZone back-story.

'The Roman name for Paris, Lutetium Pariseii, gave its name to the unusual element which you OhZones contain.'

'Lutetium? Max tried to explain relativistic chemistry but I didn't get it. I only remember one thing. Gold is *not really gold in color*.'

'It appears gold because of the lanthanide contraction,' laughed Fox. 'Things are not what they seem. You, for example, look like a slim, shapely woman.'

'Thank you.'

'You're welcome. But actually you have relativistic lutetium, iron, hemo-globin and ATP coursing around your veins.'

'And my poor kidneys don't like it. It's okay, Drox will dream up something to make a transplant unnecessary.'

'I hope you get what you need.'

'Que sera, sera,' she said, and looked out at the lights of Paris. 'What's your favourite city, Don?'

'I'm partial to Athens, the mountains along the Greek coast. I love the islands. The light is so dry and clear. Strange, such a bright place, yet they invented tragedy.'

'Yes, I thought that was strange,' Blanka said. 'The idea they had. That you were supposed to feel better after watching a tragedy. My mother's life was a tragedy. I don't think anyone feels better.'

'No,' said Fox. 'It's plain to see what it's done to your stepfather. But the Professor's star will rise again…'

Blanka studied him, but Fox said no more and seemed to become lost in the sprinkling of lights that made up Paris.

The man-made lights blotted out the night sky, hid so many of the stars. He could remember a time when the earth was dark and the stars were easy to see. They sat in silence for a long while, then Fox spoke again. 'Socrates didn't like tragedy. His disciple Plato invented a new art form, platonic dialogue, which was the prototype of the novel. And Aristotle says tragedy mixes compassion and fear to purify the emotions. Your mother's actions were noble but it's not just about a *noble* action; its about a *complete* action. Your mother's noble action is not complete. You, and others, will complete it.'

Blanka looked at Fox, puzzled by what he was saying.

'Did you know my Mom?'

'I never had the pleasure, when she was alive.'

'What does that mean?'

'It means Kitty didn't die in vain. Things are *not* what they seem, Blanka.'

'Mom said that to me in Rome, before she died…'

'I know.'

'You know? How can you know?'

'That, my dear Blanka, we won't be able to settle tonight,' he said, turning to the waiter. 'L'addition s'il vous plait. You're leaving, and I'm leaving first thing in the morning.'

'Your reunion in Croatia?'

'Yes. Old UNHCR chums.'

'UNHCR?' said Blanka.

'United Nations High Commission for Refugees.'

'I know what it stands for,' said Blanka. 'But you weren't in the army.'

'I must have someone else's parade uniforms in my closet.'

Blanka looked at him completely vacantly. Then she remembered that Fox was occasionally referred to as 'Colonel'.

'I was a chaplain with the rank of Lieutenant Colonel in the Canadian Forces,' he explained.

'You're Canadian?!'

'Didn't you know?' he laughed. 'Fooled by my British accent? I leant it at the Oxford debating society. "Pass the parsley old chap," ' he jested.

'But you're introducing Macbeth with a cockney accent...'

'Yes, now, that *is a tragedy*.' Fox laughed so hard his bright eyes turned red in the corners.

The waiter brought the check and Fox paid in cash.

'I didn't even know you were Catholic,' said Blanka.

'You observe someone, hear things about them and piece together a picture. But do you really know that person at all?'

'Do you have some special way of making sense of the world then?' she asked.

'I see it happening all-at-once and not at all; all at the same time.'

'What?! Am I supposed to understand that?'

'Not yet. Have you heard of a poet named Sappho?'

'The woman who lived on Lesbos, in ancient times?'

'Yes. Let me paraphrase some lines from her *Ode to Aphrodite*

> But you, oh blessed one,
> smiled in your deathless face
> and asked what I want to happen most of all
> in my crazy heart.'

Blanka smiled, 'I like that.'

'I thought you would.' He handed her a chocolate Easter bunny and said, 'Happy Easter for tomorrow. It's a big day.'

⭐

*L*ater, as Blanka looked out the jet's window at the lights of the Thames Estuary east of London, and unwrapped the chocolate bunny, she pondered on the mystery that was Colonel doctor Fox. But she had no idea how big the events of the following day – Easter Sunday – would be [2]   ℧

---

2 An account of this can be found in *Prologue to the Hiding Game Saga,* in the first book: *Metapox 1*

The Girl-Who-Fell-to-Earth

Deathless Aphrodite of the spangled mind,
child of Zeus, who twists lures, I beg you
do not break with hard pains,
O lady, my heart

but come here if ever before
you caught my voice far off
and listening left your father's
golden house and came,

yoking your car. And fine birds brought you,
quick sparrows over the black earth
whipping their wings down the sky
through midair—

they arrived. But you, oh blessed one,
smiled in your deathless face
and asked what (now again) I have suffered and why
(now again) I am calling out

and what I want to happen most of all
in my crazy heart. Whom should I persuade (now again)
to lead you back into her love? Who, O
Sappho, is wronging you?

SAPPHO - HYMN TO APHRODITE - TRANSLATED BY ANNE CARSON

6.0

The day after Easter Sunday 2015
Monday, April 6
The Dinaric Alps, just into Croatia.

*E*arly evening on the second day of Leila's journey to her new life, the sun was a burnished bronze orb sinking into the forested mountains to the west. Leila sang as she pitched her four-season mountain duty tent under the indifferent eyes of Cassie and Naughty. The song It was a Bosnian folk song about leaving her troubles behind. She considered the all-seasons tent her new home and the journey she was making a sign of her new freedom. She had buried her mother and left her village. Her old life was over. She had told no one, had simply packed what she needed and closed the door without looking back. Now she was heading north, on foot, through the mountains. Her initial goal was to find her uncle in Berlin, but her ultimate destination was America.

She'd worked as a goatherd for her cousin three months each summer to save the money for the rugged, all-seasons tent, made by a company in Scotland. When she ordered it, using her better-off friend's phone and credit card, the Scotsman on the line said it was the first tent being delivered to Bosnia since the war. The peace-keeping troops had used them then, he told her. The carton arrived two weeks before her mother's death. Pleased that it was even easier than last night to set up, Leila looked to her goats for approval. They only bleated.
'You're hungry, I know.'

She fed them, tethered them down for the night, and left her own meal cooking on a tripod fire as the sun sank below the horizon and darkness settled into the mountains. Leila unrolled her prayer mat, kneeled facing the east, and commenced the salāt al-maġrib (the sunset prayer) by saying the first two rak'at aloud. 'Akšam-namaz,' she began in Bosnian-Serbian-Croatian.

As she bade goodnight to Cassie and Naughty, she looked into the depths of the night sky. A clear, cold spring night, thick with stars. She located

Orion the warrior, and she thought she might need to become a warrior too, to make it through these mountains.

Climbing into her father's twenty-year old sleeping bag, she tried not to think about how utterly miserable and homesick she had been last night. She knew she no longer had any real connection to the village. No one, nothing there would better her life. No family, friends. The doctor and Imam did what little they could for Fatima after her grandmother died but no one, apart from her teachers, paid attention to Leila. Home was made up of family and the people who cared. But she no longer had any there. Wherever she was to have her new home, she would have to find a new family. 'From this day on,' she said to herself, 'I only look forward. I will live for the future, not the past.'

⭐

*T*oward the late hours of the night, a burst of thunder close at hand woke Leila from a troubling dream. In the dream a white girl with cropped hair wearing the pyjamas of Auschwitz was running through snow. Leila also had the strangest feeling that someone had been inside the tent. Another lightning flash jolted her into the present. The tent crackled in the rough wind and her goats were bleating at the top of their voices.

She unzipped the tent to a swirl of crystal-like snowflakes and rushed to calm her friends and bring them inside the bell end. She sat down between them, one under each arm.

'Cassie, Naughty,' she reassured them. 'It's only a spring snow. Did you have bad dreams too? Or is there something out there?'

She looked out the tent door and scanned the surrounding landscape. There was a snow-muted shape not more than twenty yards from her, sitting and watching. At first she thought it was a wolf.

'Get away! You don't frighten us,' she shouted, throwing a canteen at the animal.

The animal kept very still and looked directly at her. Then the snow stopped and she saw it more clearly. 'It's not a wolf, darling dears,' she whispered to her goats. 'It's a fox. He's just seeing who we are.'

The fox continued to sit calmly, watching, its eyes interestingly translucent, and kind it seemed, almost human. So Leila talked to him.

'Have we disturbed your neighbourhood, Mr Fox? We won't be here long. My goats are not for eating. And I don't think I should let you play with them either.'

The fox seemed to consider what she was saying. Slowly, even casually, he turned and walked back into the night.

Leila wasn't taking any chances. She settled Cassie and Naughty down inside the bell end and zipped up the outer tent door.

★

*T*he next morning, through the sides of the tent, the daylight had a strange but not unpleasant orange hue, like a sustained palette of the setting sun. To her surprise, Leila had slept in late and was awakened by her goats nuzzling her. 'Good morning, my darling sisters,' she said, still sleepy, as she undid the tent and persuaded them to run out. 'They're wary after their fox-fright last night. Who says they're dumb animals?' thought Leila as she climbed out after them.

Only an hour after striking their camp, Leila and her goats found themselves on a wooded mountain slope being engulfed in thick fog. It hugged the pine trees and blanketed out the sky and the mountain tops. Leila clambered to the top of a grassy knoll on one side, and emerged into the clear. The goats followed her and together they looked down into the slow swirl of gray all around. She tried her Noa cellphone to check her location but there was no signal, even though the battery was full from her solar charger. She checked the map she had brought for back up. It made no sense relative to where she thought she was, so she lifted out her magnetic compass and sighted a bearing due northwest. She muffed the goats hair and walked down the other side of the knoll and back into the fog.

Toward midday, she found herself climbing up a steep slope and the trees thinned out. Without a path she hiked over the clots of thick grass and heather. At times a breeze picked up and tore the fog apart in places. In the distance, further up, she could see the first sun of the day shine through. As the three rambled along, Cassie found an oblong tin on the ground and pushed it over with her mouth, ready to chew it. Leila smiled from ear to ear to see the label of her favourite brand

Dolmades

and surprised herself by saying the word out loud, as she picked it up. She sat down, opened the tin, fed one to herself and one each to the goats, who munched happily while she popped a couple more in her mouth.

It started raining heavily that night and continued all the next day, accompanied by thunder and lightning, finally ending at dusk. Every so often between thunder rolls, Leila thought for certain she could hear the refrains of an accordion from far away.

*L*eila woke early the next day hoping that the fog would have cleared. The light glowed orange through the tent wall as she pulled herself, shivering, out of her sleeping bag, kissed Cassie and Naughty on their noses, ate hard cheese and bread with them, and broke camp. She tried to pick up a signal on her Noa, but still nothing. She looked at the maps again, but they still made no sense, so she trusted her compass and followed it northwest. 3km ahead, mostly shrouded in fog, was a saddle between two snow-capped mountains. You don't need a weather man to know which way the wind blows, thought Leila, recalling the Dylan song. I must be somewhere near the Hungarian border, unless I got totally turned around and lost. She climbed the saddle, the wind biting, through her damp hat and coat and blowing gusts of snow and hail down from the mountains above upon her. From the top of the pass she looked down into a valley.

They spent a long cold day following the valley, half in and half out of the persistent fog. For brief periods, the sun was bright enough to penetrate it here and there, warming her a bit. Leila was weary, getting blisters, feeling down. She was so grateful for the companionship of her goats that she stopped once in a while, just to hug them. At times she swore she could hear the accordion music again, sometimes distant sometimes closer.

'Someone is playing for us,' she said to her goats. 'Or else my hearing is playing tricks on me.'

Late in the afternoon, a gap in the fog cleared enough to reveal an army post on the other side of a small ravine. A white painted sign on the roof read

U.N.H.C.R.

Leila danced a little jig which started Naughty capering after her. 'Don't worry, Naughty, we're saved!' she shouted. Thank you, Allah. They will give us food and maybe I can have a shower. At the very least they'll tell me where we are.

Looking more closely she saw a bearded man in the doorway of the building. For a minute or two she stood looking at him, when suddenly she registered that he was playing an accordion: making the sound that she had been hearing in her head the last couple of days. She considered him to be a soldier because he was in army uniform and wearing a blue UN beret, otherwise, judging by his face, she would have called him a musician or a joker.

Leila scrambled up the ravine, the goats keeping pace. When she next got a glimpse of the army post, the bearded soldier was looking at her through binoculars. As Leila climbed closer, the soldier lowered the binoculars and walked to meet her. 'I say,' the soldier shouted. In a splinter of a moment, with some gift of inner sight, a vision of her past and future flashed before her. She stopped dead in her tracks and stared – she didn't know why or how – but she somehow *knew* this ancient-looking man.

'I say – over here,' he called, in a crisp Michael Caine accent. 'Up here, above the fog,' indicating she was to climb to the far end of a small stone wall. A bit dazed from the flash of recognition and now very curious, Leila made her way along the wall. Again, time both stopped and expanded, and a knowing rose from within. She saw towers – towers of gold. And heard a voice.
'But what happiness did they bring you?' the voice asked.

As she reached the soldier she noticed his eyes. Where have I recently seen those? A fleck of silver in them rippled like a mountain brook. She felt comforted and confused. He was wearing the crown and pip of a lieutenant colonel on his epaulettes. '*Kalispera*,' Leila said, in Greek, then wondered why she had said *that*.

'Kalispera. I've been waiting for you,' he said, holding out his hand. 'I'm Lieutenant Colonel Fox, Canadian UN forces.'
Leila took his hand. (huge, rough and solid like a statue's) and shook it.
'I'm Leila Muhic from Bosnia and I'm lost,' she said breathlessly.
'Well, Leila Muhic from Bosnia,' said Lieutenant Colonel Fox. 'Perhaps, all you need is a little change of direction. A re-branding we could call it.'
The goats scampered up to Fox and he produced a packet of Manna Pro apple flavour wafers from his pocket. Amidst copious bleating Cassie and Naughty gobbled up the wafers from his hand. Fox was much taller than Leila, and Leila just stared at him.

'You've got very blue eyes –,' he said, stopping short. Leila guessed he had been about to say, *Now.*
He took a packet from his other pocket and held it out. 'Like a mint?' he said.
Leila took out a Fox's Glacier Mint. It had a polar bear on the wrapper, she'd never seen anything so cute.
'I find they refresh the parts other mints don't reach,' he said.
'Thank you,' said Leila, popping one in her mouth.
Fox smiled and led her towards the building on the other side of the wall. Parked next to it was a truck with giant white letters painted on the door

    U.N.

A pair of olive skinned soldiers, a man and a woman sergeant also wearing blue berets, were playing cards on the tailgate.
Leila let go of her goats' tethers and let them graze.
'What are you playing?' Leila asked.
'*Koupes,*' the sergeant replied. 'Hearts.'
'I'm sure you could do with some coffee,' said Fox leading her inside the building, which among other basics contained a row of bunks, four beds neatly made with blankets on them. 'It should have come first.'
'Pardon?' said Leila, quite mesmerised at the thought of sleeping in a bed.
'The coffee – before the mints,' he said.
Leila just nodded.
'We can give you a bed for the night, a shower and food.'
He pulled out a chair and motioned for her to sit in front of a battered desk that had an old and well-worn accordion on it. 'I play the French

harp, blues harmonica,' said Leila, her head swooning from all that was happening.

'Perhaps we'll play together,' laughed Fox. 'But first, down to business. So the fog blocked signals to your Noa? Good you had an old-fashioned *map and compass.*'

Leila nodded again, wondering how he knew she had a Noa and a compass. 'A Canadian chaplain gave it to me.'

'May I see your papers?' he said pouring her a mug of coffee from a jug and handing it to her.

Leila reached into her knapsack and handed Fox her Bosnian birth certificate. In the background, she saw a fourth soldier peppering supper at a small stove.

'Pepper...' said Leila, hazily.

'For supper,' said Fox. 'Passport?'

'I don't have one.'

'Money?'

Leila shook her head and looked down at her yellow dress – the only thing she had had to wear without any holes in it.

'No passport, no money. Unfortunately, not unusual in these times. *Leila Muhic,*' said Fox, as he wrote her name in a book. '*From Bosnia.*'

Leila nodded.

'Can you write?' asked Fox.

Of course I can write, thought Leila, but stopped herself from saying so. 'I write, I'm no savage,' she said.

'I'm very glad of that.' Fox smiled and pushed the book across the desk to her. 'We try not to invite cannibals in. Write your village of origin and last known address, please.'

As Leila wrote, he continued. 'We have a standard procedure, we'll grant you refugee status. Do you know what that means?'

'Yes,' Leila said. 'My mother was a refugee.'

'Again, not unusual.' He slid the book back, picked up one of the stamps on the desk and pressed it in the space next to her name.

'Where am I?' Leila asked. The coffee was strong, even by Bosnian standards, and her question was followed by a rough cough. Fox took his time answering her, allowing her cough to subside.

'Croatia, forty miles south of the Hungarian border. You were hiking northwest. Your intended destination?'

'Berlin. Or America.'

'I'm afraid you're still a long way from either.'

Fox's pragmatic tone disconcerted Leila. She glanced around at the soldier in the kitchen. She felt suddenly foolish and exposed, and buried her face in her hands. I am Leila Muhic from Bosnia and *quite lost*. What on Earth was I thinking? She struggled to get words out. 'I'm not hiding anything. I haven't done anything wrong.'

'No, no,' Fox hastened to reassure her. 'You have nothing to worry about. In fact, you could say I'm familiar with your case.'

Leila broke down. ' I – I – just buried my mother,' she confessed. 'But I couldn't stay in my village anymore. There was nothing there for me. And – and – I always dreamed of going to America.'

'Everybody's dream is America,' Fox said, quietly. 'But it can be harsh. You'll need someone you can trust. And a strong sense of what you want to do.'

'I loved my mother very much, but I have no one else. I want – I need – a new life.' Leila looked up at this old man whom she felt she knew, and trembled in her determination and desperation.

'That might not be as hard as you think,' he said gently. 'But first, let's eat. Then we can talk. I have some things to show you.'

The fourth soldier approached with a tray holding appetizers, a bottle of red wine and two glasses. He looked slightly comic in his blue beret with a matching blue apron over his army uniform. 'The appetizer you asked for, Sir.'

Fox smiled at him, 'Thank you,' and set the appetizers down in front of Leila, as the soldier poured the wine.

'Wine!' said Leila. 'Ooh… *dolmades!*'

'We're having lamb stew shortly, the sergeant's own recipe. But I thought you might like these,' he said, smiling.

'I *love* dolmades,' said Leila. 'I found a tin –,' she stopped, as Fox nodded knowingly.

*After their meal, coffee was served and the other soldiers disappeared. Fox returned to his desk and gestured to Leila to sit opposite. He opened a burlap bag and spilled the contents on the desktop: two red passports, an airline ticket, and a chic designer handbag. Fox handed one of the passports to her.

'This is the start of your new life – your new name.'

Leila tipped her head quizzically, in a manner uniquely hers, looking at the passport from different angles before she opened it.

She saw her photograph. 'How did you get this, already?' And the name under it was Houston Jane Nightingale.

'Do you like the name Houston Nightingale?' asked Fox.

'What's not to like? But it's an Irish passport. And that's not my name. Am I supposed to be Irish?'

'Is that a problem?'

'I saw an old film about working class kids forming a band. One of them said that the Irish are the *niggers of Europe*.'

Fox smiled. 'The Commitments, a great film.'

'But I'm not Irish. And I don't want to be thought of as a *nigger*.'

'Of course not. But you speak English. You can pass for Irish. People generally don't pay much attention.'

'But they do at the borders.'

'No, not even at the borders. I guarantee it.'

He handed her the airline ticket. 'Your ticket from Budapest to New York. You'll change planes at Zurich.'

She looked at the ticket and the name on it.

'I know the English saying, "there's no such thing as a free lunch," Colonel. What's the catch?'

'Catch? I didn't say there was a catch. Another dolmades?' Leila wavered between comfort and mistrust.

'It's *first class!*' she exclaimed. 'Do you give all your refugees first class tickets?'

'No. But you're special, Leila Muhic from Bosnia.'

'You're scaring me,' Leila whispered.

'You want a new life, don't you?'

'You talk about *my* new life, but we seem to be talking more about *your* plans.'

'Yes.' Fox gave a short laugh. 'Always stubborn, always full of questions. In all your lives, that never changes.'

'Stop talking in riddles!' Leila said coldly. 'What exactly is the trade off? Is this about sex? Slave trafficking?'

Fox paused, looked at her calmly, and chose his words carefully. 'I want you to discover your real self.'

'My real self?'

'In time it will be revealed to you. Once that's done, you'll have to act on what you know.

'I do want to start over. That's why I left. When I buried my mother I didn't bury my love for her but I did want to get rid of that unbearable weight of being responsible. I want to be free.'

'Free?'

'I don't want anything more to do with suffering.'

'Being free doesn't do away with suffering. Not even the gods –'

'I don't care about the gods. I just want freedom to live my life, for myself. I don't know what that means, but I get the impression that *this* isn't it. And I haven't agreed to anything yet. What am I supposed to do in New York, according to your plan?'

'You won't just be in New York. You'll go to London, Paris, Moscow. Asia. *Antarctica* even.'

Leila's mouth dropped open.

Fox took out his bag of mints and handed her one, pointing to the polar bear with a glint in his eye. 'See polar bears.'

'That's the *Arctic*,' corrected Leila.

'Your quite right, I beg your pardon,' he said, frowning and spreading his hands in a gesture of contrition. 'I'm not as young as I used to be. *Penguins*.'

Leila laughed at his antics.

'But start with this address,' said Fox as he wrote it on a pink post-it slip

Metropolitan Museum of Art
Central Park East 10016
Room 451

'Go straight from JFK. You'll meet friends.'

'I don't have any friends there, I don't know anybody.'

'Trust me, an old friend is expecting you. And you'll love his sister.' He lifted up a hundred dollar bill. 'This will cover the cab.'

'The cab?' Leila didn't even bother to hide her confusion.

'From Jamaica to the Museum.'

'Jamaica?'

'Fox paused for a moment and gave her a wry smile. 'No, she wanted to,' he said, roaring with laughter.

Leila pulled a face, 'I don't think that's very funny.'

'If everybody laughed more, the world would go round a deal faster than it does,' quoted Fox.

'The Duchess, in *Alice*,' said Leila. 'But you've got it all wrong! Anyway, is your joke supposed to be Canadian or British humour?'

'I suppose it's in a league of its own,' he said. 'Well, have a second passport. Swiss. *Dual* nationality. You can't have *too many nationalities* these days.'

She opened the Swiss passport to see she looked strikingly pretty and professional – the same as in the Irish passport.

'How'd you get my photo and have these together already?' she asked, glancing at, then turning away from her reflection in the mirror opposite the desk – dusty face and clothes, tangled hair. 'I look a mess.' She looked troubled. 'My hair is black. And my skin ...'

'Don't you like it?'

'Of course I like it: it's my skin, my hair,' she said. 'But the name doesn't go with the colour of my skin,' she said showing him the inside of the passport. 'I don't look Irish, and I certainly don't look Swiss.'

'I thought it would be fun,' Fox said. 'You know –'

'Yeah, I know.'

'If you don't like it, I can get it changed. I'm afraid you're stuck with Nightingale on the ticket –'

'I can live with Nightingale.'

Fox leaned back in his chair, and Leila realized she was trusting him, in spite of having every reason not to. He rubbed his eyes. For a moment, when he looked back at her, they seemed translucent. 'Discovering your real self is not a harmless child's game of hide and seek,' he finally said, speaking to her as she imagined her father might have spoken. 'And you're no longer a child.'

'So I must give up childish things,' she said sarcastically.

'I'm afraid so,' Fox said. 'Not right away, but you'll be a woman sooner than you think.'

The woman sergeant entered and saluted the Colonel.

'It's time, Sir. You wanted me to let you know.'

'Thank you,' Fox responded. 'We'll be right out.'

'Before we get into a quarrel about childish things, let's go outside. There's something you need to see.'

After the cramped warmth of the building, the mountain night scape was overwhelming in its vastness and early spring chill. Fox led her around to the back of the building. Leila tucked the two passports and the airline ticket in her pocket, and followed. She could make out what seemed to be another low wall near a mountain creek that had been hidden from view when she first arrived. A moonless night, yet it was so clear and thick with stars that the narrow bank of flowing water sparkled silver. Next to the creek was a gnarled silhouette of a tree that had yet to unfold its leaves. Fox put his hand on the ragged line of broken stones.

'This is not what it seems,' he said. 'It's not a common farm wall, but a column, a column from a Greek temple. Scattered around, unrecognizable, are the pieces of other columns. Some of the stones have even made their way into scattered huts. Perhaps five hundred years ago, people would have seen the outline of the cornice and been able to decipher the images on the frieze. But nature has long since reclaimed what men have abandoned.'

'This is what you wanted me to see? It may have been a temple, but it's nothing but rocks now.'

'It was a temple to Zeus. Like you, Zeus had different names at different times and places.'

Leila looked into his eyes again, translucent in the darkness.

'He was called Indra, Jupiter, Perun, Odin. Different names, but the same king.'

'I'm not a king, queen or princess,' she laughed.

'I wouldn't be quite so sure.'

'I'm only Leila Muhic from Bosnia!'

'But you announced to the mountains you would change the world.'

She paused a beat to register silently, He couldn't have heard what I said after burying my mother. Then changed the subject. 'Well, this heap of stones isn't exactly inspiring.'

'Look up and see the rest,' he said spreading out his arms.

Leila looked up at the night sky with its thick never-ending cluster of stars. She was about to dismiss the sky too, when a wash of green and purple partially hid the stars. Like waves from a vast, gentle lake the Aurora Borealis ebbed, flowed, and twisted like a rippling translucent veil. The display lasted several minutes before the immense veil disappeared as silently and quickly as it had come.

'Oh! It's so beautiful! Yet so fragile,' Leila said.

'Nature on display,' Fox said. 'Occasionally it's so overwhelming, people actually stop and look. But there are some who will also see what else it is.'

'What?'

'A warning.'

'A warning?' she said.

'The Aurora should not display this far south at this time of year.'

They stood together in silence, contemplating the night and breathing in its cold. Then the girl looked down from the sky and her blue eyes settled on Fox's pale eyes. 'A warning of what exactly?'

Fox spoke without taking his eyes from the sky. 'That all is not as it should be in our solar system…' Then he turned his gaze away from it and changed the subject. 'By the way,' he said, handing her a small metal object. 'Here's a knife to go with the Swiss passport.'

'A Swiss Army Knife!' shouted Leila, 'I've always wanted one.'

'It's to help you in your task. After tonight your memory of your life up to now – that is your memory thus far *in this life* – will be extremely foggy.'

'You said *this* life. That means I've lived before?'

'Yes.'

'And my task involves that past life?'

'Precisely.'

'Am I going back there? To that past life?'

'No, but you will remember it when the time is right.'

'And my task?'

'I will tell you –'

Leila interrupted him before he could finish. 'When the time is right?'

'Yes, when the time is right.'

'So I'm going to see you again.'

'I'm afraid so. I can tell you that you personally will give the phrase 'between a rock and a hard place' a new meaning.'

Houston weighed the knife in her hands as her mind reeled. She took out the largest blade, felt its edge and ran her finger along it.

That she'd lived before was not a new idea to her. She had learned of re-incarnation several years before, and secretly embraced the principle of the transmigration of the soul. She wondered why Muslims, Christians and Jews all hated the idea of it so much. Now here was this aged soldier talking about it so matter-of-factly.

The blade cut her, and she pulled her finger away, licking the blood from it.

'I said the knife would be handy,' Fox said. 'But like most things, you have to learn how best to use it.'

'What if I decide not to follow your plans. What will happen if I don't go to the Museum?'

'You could live in America, Ireland or Switzerland.'

'Or Bosnia?'

'Of course. There'll always be Bosnia.'

'I can keep the knife?'

Fox laughed. 'Absolutely.'

'But what exactly is the job? Can you explain it again.'

'You'll be a sort of "diplomat" based at the Foreign and Commonwealth Office of the United Kingdom.'

Laughing mimicking the accent, 'Foreign and Commonwealth Office. Oh please pass the parsley, old chap.'

They both laughed.

'So I have choices.'

'Yes indeed.'

'What makes the pass the parsley job and the mysterious task a better option than my Plan B that I'm madly trying to formulate? It all rings of James Bond, New-Age and sci-fi you know?

'I know,' Fox said, looking directly at her. 'And your Plan B is?'

'To party till I drop. I *can* drop out of this, can't I?'

'You can fly to New York City – and instead of going to this address, you can party.'

'And the stuff will never happen.'

'It will happen. It just won't happen *to you*.'

Leila continued to ponder the two red passports. 'Don't you need someone older, more experienced?'

He laughed.

'Don't laugh at me!' Leila said, suddenly irritated.

'I wasn't. I was laughing at what you said. I don't think I could find anyone older or more experienced than you.'

'Oh,' she said. She opened the airline ticket and looked at the name on it 'Is that what they'll call me?'

'They'll call you lots of things, you'll be famous.'

'Ha, ha,' she said with a twinge of sarcasm. 'Houston? They'll call me Houston Nightingale?'

'Yes. Houston like Texas, Nightingale like the bird. See how you get on with it.'

'But I can back out of this, right?'

'You have two choices to make. One when you get to New York, one tonight.'

'Tonight?'

'You have to tell me whether you'll accept the new passports, the new identities?'

'I'd be stupid not to, wouldn't I,' said Leila.

'But must understand what you are losing. You are losing your life as Leila Muhic. You won't clearly remember her.'

She turned and looked southeast up the valley back from where she came. Where she'd buried her mother and her old life. Her heart ached like never before and she felt a glimmer of hope she'd never known. 'Hey, I'm like the song, *Like A Rolling Stone*,' she said. 'I ain't got nothing, I got nothing to lose.'

Fox looked into her eyes and studied them, and nodded.

'I need to be alone,' she said, turning away and walking quickly towards Cassie and Naughty.

6.2

Wednesday, April 8

3 WEEKS AFTER THE KILLINGS The next morning, the girl formerly known as Leila Muhic from Bosnia was finishing her breakfast while recounting a dream to Colonel Doctor Fox. 'I had this great sword in my hand, it was glowing golden and a crowd was looking at me.'

'It may have been the meal last night, I told Zoria to go easy with the curry powder.'

'Seriously.'

'Seriously, you can turn back if you want. You can forget you ever met me.'

'No, I don't want that. I've decided I like being *Houston Nightingale*. But everything is so new and changing so fast.'

'You'll be so famous they'll write songs about you.'

Houston gave Fox the quizzical look that had been Leila's.

'And more plays,' Fox added. 'I'll come to all your opening nights.'

The truck drew up at the front of the building, its brakes squealing. A few seconds later, the sergeant stuck her blue-bereted head in the door.

'Time, Sir, Houston. Time.'

It was the first time she had been called *Houston* and she let the sound of it sink in and echo around her mind for a bit. When she looked up, the Colonel and the sergeant were both studying her.

'Houston,' Fox said, 'this is Zoria, she'll be in charge of getting you to Budapest and helping you pack.'

Zoria smiled stiffly, and Fox put Houston's Bosnian knapsack on to the desk. He took out the Noa smart phone, 'I'm afraid this won't work where you're going.'

As Houston's face dropped, the Colonel produced a gold-color iPhone 6S from his desk. Her mouth dropped open.

'But it doesn't come out til September,' she said in amazement.

Fox turned to Zoria.

'*Próoro montélo*,' Zoria said.

He turned back to Houston, 'It's an advanced model.'

Without a word, Zoria transferred the remaining contents of the knapsack into the new leather bag: harmonicas, spare T-shirts, socks and panties. There were books, and Zoria showed an English edition of *Brave New World* to the Colonel.

'An excellent book,' he said, 'worth keeping.'

Then came a Koran. 'I'll need that,' said Houston.

'Of course,' said Fox.

Finally, a journal. Zoria gave Fox a look.

'I write my poetry and thoughts in it,' said Houston and held out her hand, but Zoria gave the journal to Fox. He leafed through it.

'You need to understand that you won't recognise the things you've written in it,' he explained. 'It will be like reading someone else's history.' Fox passed the journal to Houston. 'It will be a strange sensation.'

'My mother's dead isn't she? said Houston hesitantly, already fuzzy about details in the recent past.

'Yes. I'm afraid you're an orphan now.'

Fox and Zoria stood quietly as the realization of this hit Houston.

'I'm an orphan,' she repeated. Fox nodded, 'But you won't be alone, you'll soon meet friends.' He handed her four Hungarian 5,000 Forint bills. 'Travel clothes and suitcase in Hungary.'

The passports and Swiss Army Knife were the only items left on the desk. Houston opened up the knife, caught the sun's rays on the blade and shone it into Fox's eyes.

'I'm sure I'll dazzle them with my brilliance,' she laughed, playfully.

He laughed too, and then said, 'You have a truck, two busses and two planes to catch.'

'But I can turn back at any time, right?'

'Any time before the Museum. Once you walk up the steps and into The Met, your new life will take over. But,' he gestured to the UN truck at the front door, 'the truck can drive you back to your village right now if you prefer.'

'No, I don't want that. But everything's a little blurry.'

As they stepped outside to the truck, Cassie and Naughty came running up to Houston. She seemed just the same to them and they nuzzled her, bleating.

'Oh, my God,' Houston declared, tears suddenly in her eyes. 'Cassie and Naughty. What have I done? How will you get to New York?'

She looked at Fox then Zoria, and then back at Fox.

'You have my word,' Fox said, 'I will take very good care of them.'

'What can you know about caring for goats?' Houston scoffed.

As Houston looked on, he produced the packet of Manna apple wafers from his pocket and the goats ran to him to be fed. 'It's one of the things I've learnt along the way. Will you trust me, Miss Nightingale?'

Houston swallowed hard and blinked back the tears. 'When I'm in my mysterious new life "passing the parsley," I want to see them again, even if I can't remember them. Okay? Is that a deal?'

Fox thought for a moment. 'Alright, it's a deal,' he said. 'In the meantime let me give you this to remember them by.' He took a Fuji Polaroid camera from the front of the truck, arranged the goats next to the door of the army post (with a view of the mountains behind) and clicked the shutter. The Polaroid wound out from the camera and he peeled it off and handed it to her. She looked at the blank white photograph and then at Fox. He gestured to it and she looked back. Slowly the color image appeared and got clearer. She nodded, understanding.

'Houston! Ante figame!' Zoria pointed to her watch and opened the passenger door, as the driver restarted the engine with a roar. Before climbing up into the truck, Houston turned one last time to Fox.
'I'm so excited and scared, I'm not even sure whether to thank you. Should I?'
'You're thanking me already,' he said. Pulling the packet of Glacier Mints from his pocket, he tipped a dozen into her hand. 'Good luck and re-member when you're in a tight squeeze, help is just around the corner.'

*T*he driver, blue beret on his head, drove the UN truck down the track into the depths of the fog; he looked across at Houston and Zoria as the truck shook up and down, heading out of the mountains and into the West.

Houston quit staring at the iPhone 6S and stowed it in her new bag. She unwrapped a Glacier Mint and popped it into her mouth. Zoria held out a mint packet, full of the wrappers, for her to place hers in. They obviously all ate the mints.

As Houston sucked on it, she opened her Irish passport, stared at the photo and tried to get her bearings. She held out the Polaroid of Cassie and Naughty to show Zoria. Zoria nodded then looked intently into Houston's blue eyes for a moment. 'How does it feel,' Zoria asked in broken English, 'to be like a Rolling Stone?'
Houston smiled but didn't answer. Zoria took a fragrance bottle from the dash and sprayed her neck and wrists. The unusual fragrance filled the cab.
'Mm,' said the driver, as Zoria offered the bottle to Houston. Houston

sprayed her wrist and inhaled deeply. She tilted her head this way and that. *'Efaristo'* she said, spraying her other wrist and rubbing it onto her neck.

Zoria nodded with approval, *'Paragalo,'* and set the bottle on the dash.

Houston looked out of the truck window into the fog. It had a strange quality, as if it was alive and sentient.

The next moment the engine stalled, and the truck idled down the track, the three of them enveloped in an eerie silence. They watched curious ice crystals materialize in and out of the fog, then disappear. A few seconds later the ignition turned over and the engine thrummed as usual.

'What just happened?' Houston asked.

But neither the driver nor Zoria could give her an answer.

6.3

2 p.m. US eastern daylight time

*T*he American Airlines B767-300 shook up and down as it hit turbulence descending through a belt of cloud toward New York City. Houston woke violently in Business Class seat 4G and looked around in terror. Where was she?

She tried to get up, but her seat belt stopped her; she tried to unbuckle it but she couldn't. With a shock, she realised she was on a plane. The seat was like a throne, was her first thought. A massive armrest space recessed from the aisle on each side of her. Then Zoria's fragrance worked on her sense of smell and triggered her memory of the morning. She sniffed the scent from her wrist to be sure. Yes, it was the second airplane flight of Houston's life; the first had been the thirty minute hop from Budapest to Zurich.

Zoria's fragrance was lofty and foresty, unisex like cK1. As she breathed it in, Houston had a flashback, a fragment from another life. She saw herself sitting at her high school, searching perfumes online. The room had tall windows and she could see buildings, a small village in the mountains! She remembered: she'd been friends with her teacher's daughter until the family had migrated to America, to a place called Beaufort Falls, California. She had wanted to go to California. That was her first memory of wanting to go to America.

She grabbed at her new bag to check what was inside. Ticket – in the name of Nightingale, Houston Miss – passport, hundred dollar bill, Polaroid of two goats with mountains in the background. 'Oh! Cassie and Naughty.' Delighted, for a few moments she looked around the cabin for them. Then she remembered Fox's words: 'To help you remember.' And her heart dropped.

The steward approached her.
'Are you okay Ma'am?' He was quiet and well spoken — and African American — and she felt reassured. 'You've been asleep most of the flight.'
Houston nodded.
'I've saved you the dinner. I guessed fish. I hope you like fish.'
'I love fish.'
The steward disappeared and even though only a dozen hours had passed since she had left the UNHCR post in the mountains, Houston found herself desperately trying to reconstruct her old life and her old world that had slipped away.

The steward had come back with the fish. 'I'll check back with you in a few minutes, Miss Nightingale. You'll need to eat quickly. We're landing soon.'
The steward had called her Miss Nightingale, but the name still sounded strange to her.
She looked at the Polaroid again. She had hidden her other passport and the Swiss army knife inside a red and white striped T-shirt in a gold-colored suitcase she had bought from a street market in Budapest.
She looked down at the knife and fork in her hands and the largely uneaten meal on her tray.
'Ma'am,' she heard the steward say again. 'Are you finished?'
'Yes. I wasn't as hungry as I thought.'
'Would you like it to go?' he asked.
'To go?' she asked. 'What's that?'
'I'll pack it in a box for you to take with you if you like.'
Houston smiled vacantly, 'Thank you.' She was trying to remember what

else the colonel had said: 'An old friend is expecting you.'

'A drink? Coffee?' repeated the steward.

'Please…'

Her brow furrowed as she recalled Colonel Fox's voice. There was something else he said.

'You have choices.' A place you have to be. He had written an address down, and she had put it as a bookmark in her novel. She pulled out *Brave New World*, opened it to where a pink post-it slip had been inserted, and read the address on it

> *Metropolitan Museum of Art*
> *Central Park East 10016*
> *Room 451*

The steward set her coffee down with a white mint on the saucer. She remembered the Glacier Mints Fox had given her, and unwrapped one. She popped it into her mouth and set the wrapper on the saucer. That's where you should go, but you must choose, he had told her. He'd given her the knife to help her in her task. Or was it the job? In any event, she loved the knife. She'd bought the suitcase mainly so she could check it through. The woman selling bright coloured suitcases near the bus terminal in Budapest had also given her a sandwich.

As the American 767 made its approach west into J.F.K., she looked out of her window and down at upstate New York. This can't be a trick, there's America. She looked around at the businessmen and women in suits and designer clothes. Fox had given his word, and people traffickers don't ship their victims in First Class.

6.4

*H*ouston got out of the JFK shuttle train at Jamaica. She exited onto the street and stood dazed, the myriad sights sounds and smells of New York City flooding her senses. A lot of the men and women were black like her, and she found that reassuring. Immigration had been a doddle. She had enrolled in something called 'embark gold' and had cleared all the formalities and got her suitcase within twenty minutes.

'Taxi, Ma'am?' called a black voice. Houston looked at the man and his yellow cab. 'Where you'all going now?
She handed the taxi driver the pink slip from her bag.
'Okay uptown, The Met.'
He put her almost empty gold suitcase in the trunk, 'You're traveling light.' Then he quickly opened the passenger door in the back. Houston just looked at him in confusion.
'Ma'am,' he said and laughed again. 'If you don't mind my saying so, people could tell that you're new to this town from a mile away. Ever been to the big city?'
'I got a bus to Budapest this morning, and stopped at Zurich. But I didn't leave the airport.'
The driver looked at Houston in the rearview mirror as he exited the airport toward Manhattan, and let out a chuckle. 'You're what's called a country girl. They don't get more country than you. And you're mighty pretty. Meaning no disrespect. Black skin and blue eyes. Man doesn't see that often. Girl like you could have a great time in New York. But you could get into trouble real fast, if you know what I mean.'
He tried to catch her eye in his rear view mirror, shook his head and chuckled again.
'Nope, I guess you don't. Going to the Museum's well and fine, but there's lots of other things you can do in this city. And since you was lucky enough to get my cab, I'm willing to offer you my services in case you want to do more than just look at a bunch of paintings and old statues that are mostly broke.'
'The UN officer who gave me my passport said I could choose, but I think I should go to the Museum,' Houston said softly.
The cab driver smiled broadly, 'Well, if you can choose…' Getting no response he studied the girl in his rear view mirror, tried to figure her. After several minutes he asked, 'Are you some kind of refugee?'

But Houston was miles away. She was looking through the window glass at the pretty people.
'There are so many people,' she said. 'Where are they all going?'
The driver laughed. 'Well, this time of day they're generally leaving work,

heading home or out looking for some fun, looking to relax in a noisy bar with a cold drink after a hard day. And there's clubs, but nothing really happens until much later. Dancing, music. You name it.'

'What kind of dancing?' she asked.

'You name it and people in the Big Apple do it.'

'I like to dance,' she sighed, and her mind flashed back to a picture of her twirling in a buttercup field with two goats.

*

*T*he driver pulled his cab up to the curb. 'Metropolitan Museum of Art, Central Park East.'

No response.

'Miss Blue-Eyes,' he said.

Houston just stared into space.

'Ma'am, we're here. That's thirty eight fifty.' Then he shouted, 'Miss Blue-Eyes!'

Houston stirred and looked at him blankly.

She rubbed her eyes. Had she slept in the taxi?

'Do you want me to help you to the entrance?' he asked.

'I think so… please, I feel strange.'

'Ain't that the truth,' said the driver as he got out to collect the gold suitcase from the trunk. After he opened the door and helped her out, Houston looked at the fountains and the children skate boarding into Central Park. Her pale blue eyes darted around trying to take everything in, registered nothing. I'm losing my mind. I should have stayed at home. But where is home?

She turned to the cab driver, 'Where did we come from?'

He laughed. 'You mean where did we start the fare?'

'Yes.'

'Jamaica.'

'Jamaica,' repeated Houston. 'No, she wanted to…'

'What?' said the cab driver.

'It's some Canadian joke.'

'Canadian? I thought you said you'd come through Zurich?'

'Did I?'

'You flew into J.F.K.'

'The airport?'

'Well, *the president*, he been dead a long time,' he said, screaming in mirth as he took her arm gently and helped her up the steps to the main entrance of the Museum. At the doors, he set the suitcase down. 'I have to go, will you be okay?' he asked, for a moment genuinely touched by her innocence.

'Yes, I'm meeting someone. I think.'

'You think?'

She showed him the slip again. 'Room 451, that's one of the galleries isn't it? I've never been in here.'

'Me neither. Truth be told, long as I been in the city, I never set foot in that impressive structure. Now ask me about Central Park any day.'

'How much do I owe you?'

'Thirty-eight fifty.'

On the plane, Houston had read about tipping in America and how it was the main living for a lot of people working low paid jobs. She remembered the phrase, 'Keep the change'.

She handed him the hundred dollar bill.

'Keep the change,' she said.

'What?'

'Keep the change.'

'It's a hundred.'

'Yes,' she heard herself say, 'I don't need money. It has no meaning.'

'Has no meaning, how about you? Get that! Eleven fifty is a fine tip, I thank you for that. You take this fifty and put it in your purse.'

'I don't have a purse.'

'What do you call that fancy boutique number?'

'I call it a bag.'

The cab driver roared with laughter.

'You put the fifty in your bag and you look after yourself, Miss Blue Eyes.'

'One last thing,' he said, pulling a slightly crumpled business card out of his bulging wallet. 'If you decide you want to have some fun, call or message me first. I'll show you the *safe places*. Where you can have a good time and where they'll appreciate you.'

'Thank you,' she said, staring at the card and impulsively hugging him. The cab driver smiled sheepishly.

'Yep, you're definitely country. Must be a real nice place,' he said as headed back to his cab.

Houston entered the main doors and walked to a booth. 'What's that fabulous fragrance?' asked the young female student who was working the ticket counter.

'I don't know what it's called, the UN woman let me have a spray. Want a better sniff?' Houston raised her wrist and the girl inhaled the fragrance again.

'Wow, I love it,' she said. 'My name's Michelle. You said a UN woman let you have some?'

'I just got off the plane,' she explained. 'At the airport.' To make sure the girl understood, she added, 'The J.F.K. airport.'

The girl nodded.

'How much do you want to pay for your entrance?'

'I have fifty dollars,' said Houston.

'What do you mean you have fifty dollars? You mean you want to pay fifty dollars?'

Houston lifted up her gold case to show the girl, 'I got a near empty suitcase and fifty dollars in the world,' she laughed.

'OMG, where are you from?' the girl asked.

'Bosnia,' said Houston proudly. 'The UN flew me from Budapest and here I am!' she said, showing the girl the pink slip. 'I need to meet someone here.'

Michelle read the Met address on the slip. 'You're a refugee!' she exclaimed. 'Awesome! I love refugees. I'm doing a paper on them. They've suffered so much. Did you suffer?'

Houston wasn't sure how to answer. 'I don't remember.'

'Oh my God,' said Michelle, 'you've blocked it out. It must have been terrible.' The girl's eyes suddenly started to tear up. 'Look,' she said. 'I'll let you in free. And you can leave your suitcase with me.' Michelle went through her purse. There were half a dozen one dollar bills and a twenty; she took out the twenty. 'Here's twenty dollars to help you,' she said, 'it's all I can spare. I'm here until we close. I would really appreciate it if you would tell me about your experiences. But only if you want to.'

Houston looked at her and smiled. 'Thank you so much. Everyone's so kind here in America.'

The girl beamed. Houston took the last couple of Glacier Mints from her pocket and handed the girl one.

'Try this,' she said, unwrapping her own. 'They're a special British mint.'

'A polar bear, it's so cute,' Michelle said, following suit and tasting the mint. 'Tastes really cool.'

'Which way to Room 451?' Houston asked.

'Oh, that's European Art, second floor. Take the elevator or stairs and it's on the right.'

As Houston approached the main elevator, the lights and power suddenly went out all over the Museum, and the emergency lighting glowed dimly.

6.5

*I*n the darkened Goldheart wing of The Met, Professor Max Hart confronted two security men who were trying to call Met security on their radios.

'It's not working,' one of the men told Hart. 'We can't get through.'

'Then I'll go myself,' Hart shouted and stormed away from the main exhibit. He had barely gotten to the exhibit archway when he tripped on two skateboards.

'Shit!' he exploded as he pulled himself off the floor and pushed his way through a group of six armed guards rushing toward the exhibit. They had been assigned to guard the most valuable artefact in the Museum – in fact it was the most valuable artefact in the world – a seven foot high solid gold heart.

Surrounding the Goldheart in the semi-darkness, the guards, bristling with weapons, looked bewildered. Just an hour earlier the security screens for the Goldheart had been dismantled so that Drox, and Hart's son, Will, could do a 3D scan of it.

The security screens lay at the side of the gallery and Will had attached a pair of giant paddles connected by conduits of wires to a bank of complicated scanning equipment operated by Drox on his gold Scanner. Will's heavyset skateboard friend, Buddy, held the wiring conduits off the Goldheart. Blanka, who had come along to mediate between Will and their father, stood off to the side.

When the Museum lights suddenly went out and the alarms came on,

Will turned in panic, 'We didn't blow the power, did we?'

Blanka shook her head. 'It's affected the whole Museum, Will. I doubt your little machine set it off.' She turned to Drox, 'Shouldn't someone look after Max?' she asked.

'He's sick with worry about .w . everything! Just leave him be.' Drox checked his cellphone. 'There's no signal — is this city-wide? In fact the cellphone is dead. This, I believe, is what's being called a "U.P.S." protuberance. Didn't you witness one in London last month?'

Blanka looked at her dead cell phone and then at the tense security guards with tactical flashlights around her.

'Now where's Will gone?' she asked, not responding to Drox's question.

'He's round the other side, Miss Maguire,' said Buddy, smiling at her.

Blanka walked around the Goldheart. Will had his head pressed against it in the darkened gallery, his eyes closed.

'Are you off away with your fairies again?' she whispered.

An officer of the security squad approached Drox. 'Sir, we can't guarantee security, everything's gone down.'

'Do what you can. I'm not worried, we have an OhZone here.'

As Blanka watched Will, she could hear the hubbub in the Museum coming from every direction. It got louder and softer in her ears like a wave pattern. She rubbed her ears. For reasons she didn't understand, the Neil Young guitar instrumental from *Like A Hurricane* surged through her head. She took her silver-colored ᴕScanner from her bag and checked it. A failure log line displayed, 'Normal service will be resumed as soon as possible'.

Within seconds it returned to normal, and the lights, alarms, AC and services in the Museum came back on. Blanka could feel her cell phone vibrating back to life too. 'Well, Drox, that wasn't so bad. Guess you'll have to study your protuberances some other time.'

Drox kept one eye on his own gold Scanner, and one eye on Will with his head to the Goldheart. 'Unfortunately, that will be sooner than you think. Worldwide, they're getting more frequent.'

At that moment Will leapt out from underneath the Goldheart making both Blanka and Drox jump.

'Fuck,' said Blanka.

'She's here,' Will yelled.

'Nothing on my Scanner,' said Drox.

'What?' said Blanka.

'She's upstairs,' said Will. 'Room 451! Come on, Blanka, meet me there! I need the rest room, I'm bursting.'

Will ran out of the Goldheart display area and off to the men's room. Buddy dropped the wire harnesses and hurtled after him, picking up their skateboards on the fly. Blanka raised her eyes at Drox, who shook his head.

'Do as the boy genius says. Given the current panic, I'd take the stairs. I think these armed gentlemen and myself can guard the Goldheart now.'

Will disappeared into the Level 1 North male restroom followed by Buddy and the skateboards. Blanka headed for the stairs and Greek and Roman Fine Art gallery, with *Like A Hurricane* lyrics pounding in her head.

In Room 451 some visitors, having recovered from the power outage, returned to contemplating the oil paintings. The Museum alarms had switched off, but distant sirens continued to wail from the streets. When Blanka entered the room she immediately noticed, on the far side, a black girl with one of her Iceni handbags over her shoulder. She did a complete double-take: how did she get hold of that?

The girl was looking at the original of *The Judgement of Paris*, a 1528 oil-on-wood painting by Lucas Cranach the Elder.

The girl started to turn, not so much in slow motion, but in a bubble of slow-time engulfing the whole room.

Blanka stared at the girl's face – transcendent, as if enraptured. Her Slavic blue eyes even more luminous for her dark skin.

The visitors in the gallery felt the thick energy too and turned to look.

Slowly fluttering her eyes, the girl spoke in a curiously dazed chant

> *I would not have you be deathless*
> *among the deathless gods*
> *and live continually after such sort.*
> *Yet if you could live on such as now*
> *you are in look and in form,*
> *and be called my husband,*
> *sorrow would not then enfold my careful heart.*

'That's wonderful,' Blanka said, cautiously. Something told her this etheric young black vision was in a remarkable and delicate state.

'It's a poem, isn't it? Did you write it?'

'I don't know,' the girl said. 'I was looking at the women in the painting. And the young man on the ground. Is he hurt?'

Blanka smiled. 'No, that's Paris. He's in awe of the women. He has to make a difficult decision.'

'Decision? What does he have to decide?'

'Which of them is the most beautiful,' said Blanka. She could see tears coming to the girl's eyes.

'But all of them are white. None of them look like me,' said Houston.

Blanka gently held Houston's shoulders, passing her gaze over her.

'It's a very old painting. If you had been there, I'm sure Paris would have chosen you.'

'Thank you for saying that. My name is H-He-Houston. Who are you? I mean, what's your name?'

'My name's Boudica,' Blanka managed to say.

'No, no… That's not right. You shine like the god Apollo,' exclaimed Houston. 'Your name is Apollo!'

'Okay,' said Blanka. 'Then you're the girl-who-fell-to-Earth.'

No, Houston was just about to tell her, in a flash of recall, I'm *really* Leila Muhic from Bosnia. When at that moment, startling the visitors, Will ran in at full speed holding his skateboard, followed by Buddy.

Houston's gaze shifted from Blanka's face, over her shoulder on to Will. Her eyes opened wide, she turned to face him, and the pink post-it slip fluttered out of her hand to the floor.

'It's her,' Will screamed at the top of his voice, pointing at Houston.

His legs froze and he skidded, like Skooby-Doo, in slo-motion, to a halt, his eyes glued all the time on Houston.

Time paused. Neil Young played in Blanka's head

… like a hurricane

Will came to a halt by Blanka. 'It's her,' he whispered, as Buddy's two hundred pounds crashed into the back of him, sending them both crashing to the floor and the skateboards flying through the air.

Will ended up at Houston's feet, and she stared down at him in surprise. She tipped her head quizzically – in that way that Leila had always had, looking at Will from different angles – before she blinked her blue eyes and said, 'Oh…it's you.'

Then she fainted clean away and collapsed in a heap on top of him.

Blanka was close enough, and quick enough, to catch Will's flying skateboard before it hit the beautiful face of the girl-who-fell-to-Earth.

The Girl from Ipanema

The more we do to you,
the less you seem to believe we are doing it.

DR JOSEPH MENGELE — "UNCLE" — AT AUSCHWITZ.
THE WORLD'S WORST ESCAPED SERIAL CHILD KILLER.

7.0

Sunday, April 12
Havana, Cuba

Walking off a beach near Havana followed by a wiry body-guard, C, Sir Mark Rolland Loveless, approached a classic Cadillac. The driver opened the door and C climbed in followed by his body-guard. The driver looked in the rear view mirror, 'Your hotel, Sir?'
'No, plans have changed. Hotel Nacional.'

Once at the old time Cuban hotel, C walked through the lobby to an empty lounge at the back. Staying behind, the bodyguard, now holding a bunch of yellow roses, got in the elevator and pressed the 6 button.
C picked up a hotel telephone and dialed 8660. A man's voice answered, (highish like Graham Norton) 'Have you brought the flowers?'
'Hydrangea's are out of season,' said C.
'That doesn't make me very happy.'
'Well, roses are red, violets are blue.'
'Chrysanthemums then, lovely,' said the voice.

C hung up, returned to the lobby, and took the elevator to the sixth floor.

Stepping out of the lift and walking down the corridor to the left, C turned a corner and continued down another corridor. At the further corner, his bodyguard was waiting. The bodyguard walked to the last door, room 660, and knocked. A young white man opened it, checked that the corridor was empty and took the yellow roses. The bodyguard walked past C and stationed himself at the corner.

When C walked into room 660, he found himself in a large suite that seemed occupied by a rich American couple with a generic taste in decor. The young man told him (in the Graham Norton voice from the phone), 'This way with the flowers,' and ushered him into the main bedroom.

Inside the bedroom a hologram Comms link was set up. The young man shut the metal screened door and handed C a headset. 'London calling. Encrypted, *you're* on holocam, but you'll only get voice.'
C sat on a chair and the hologram Comms link lit up eerily. As he stared at the vacant space, an encrypted robot-like voice spoke:
'I'm sorry to interrupt your vacation. How are you enjoying Cuba?'
C decided to be diplomatic. 'It's – tropical.'
'Do you miss me?'
'Of course,' said C laughing.
'Your leave from Wonderland will be short I assure you,' said the voice.
C cringed at the use of the nickname 'Wonderland'. 'Does that mean you have a surprise for me?' he asked in a noncommittal way.
'Are you keeping up to date with the UK Election?'
'The Working Party has a big lead.'
'Had,' the voice corrected. 'And Wonderland's tired old soap opera has been replaced by a *real one*.'
C forced himself to smile. 'Yes, I know. Bio is singing Lady Macbeth.'
'Is she now? Isn't Macbeth a tragedy?'
'They expect it to be a success.'
'I've made some arrangements. It will indeed be a tragedy – for the Working Party. How do you get on with June Glendinning?'
C rubbed the folds of his leathery face, 'Arts and Farts out?' he said, 'Queen of Tarts in?'
'I will send her your regards.'
'Thank you.'

'Prepare to return to MI6 the day after the election. The new Prime Minister herself will invite you.'

'Of course, I'm grateful,' said C.

'You bloody well should be,' said the voice.

C took the plunge. 'There's one other piece of business.'

'Which is?' asked the voice.

'Former agent OhZone 7.'

'Oh bless – you sad old man – you miss her, do you?'

C locked his jaws. 'We've lost her on safari in Africa. I apologize. She's a great loss – for both of us.'

'I'm not so sure. I warned you it would be on *your head* if you couldn't control AI-Felicity-fast-track,' said the voice.

C looked down at his feet like the naughty British schoolboy he was.

'I hope all that expensive Uber-BDSM kit came out of the British taxpayer's purse,' the voice continued. 'And not out of mine.'

C remained silent.

'Anyway,' said the voice. 'Fortunately my worker bees are a lot more competent than the Queen's. Mine know just where Felicity-fast-track is.'

'Is she –'

'But there's a new show in town. Langley Town. Houston Nightingale is her name. I want her next into OhZone. Don't fuck things up – and don't fuck her. I don't want her Civil-Service soiled. Use her on the raid you're planning on the *Russian Metapox.*'

At this point, the young man walked forward, pulled a face at C and handed him a dossier labeled

Nobaroz Bio-Weapon Facility
Sokolniki Park, Moscow

There was laughter at the other end of the link as C sat in stunned surprise and spittle nervously ran from the corner of his mouth. C fumbled about for a handkerchief. The young man handed him a tissue and he wiped his mouth dry.

'Our guest seems slightly disoriented by his assignment,' the young man said, laughing.

'Do try and get control of yourself, old chap,' said the voice. 'And no cumming in your underpants when you meet her.'

C opened his mouth, but could not command his vocal chords to speak.

'I think under the cover of snow, perhaps,' the voice concluded, 'Christmas…'
The screen went dead and C sat in silence until the young man interrupted his thoughts. 'Well, Sir Mark, that's you told!'
C took the headset from his head, suddenly more concerned about his own fate than Felicity's.

7.1

Monday April 13, 2015.
St. Vincent's Hospital, New York, NY, USA

*A*fter Houston's collapse at the Met, she remained unconscious; and Blanka had her taken to ER at St Vincent's Hospital where she spent the weekend unresponsive in intensive care. But on Monday at lunchtime, Houston opened her eyes and struggled to break free of the IV lines and other wires attached to her. The nurse watching her calmed her as best she could and immediately called the duty doctor.
'The young lady is agitated and has asked for a "looking glass,"' the nurse explained.
'Get her one,' the doctor replied bluntly. 'It's not like she's disfigured.'
The nurse had found a mirror and held it for Houston as she felt her face and her hair. After looking around the room she turned to the nurse and said, 'Is this the house of the dead?'

Blanka, who had been in the waiting area going through the contents of Houston's Iceni handbag over and over, arrived in the room before the doctor and was greeted by Houston's beaming face and a single word, 'Apollo!'
The IC doctor rushed in prepared to sedate the girl-who-fell-to-earth but found her perfectly calm and showing no physical symptoms.

None of the tests they did showed any physical signs that could explain the girl's apparent amnesia, and she was moved to a private room on

Stabler ward. After several hours with her, Professor Hart, Dr Oxberry and the hospital psychiatrists all confirmed that she indeed had complete amnesia. The only person she seemed to recognize was Blanka, who she insisted on calling Apollo. She didn't recognize her own name and had no memory of any events before waking up in the hospital.

She did, however, show slight reactions to a Polaroid of two goats and to her Koran, but other than recognizing them, she could give no details.

Blanka's initial investigation provided only a few facts. The grid showed Nightingale H.J. Ms had appeared, apparently out of nowhere, when an American Airlines ticket was bought for cash in Zagreb, Croatia on April 7th in her name, originating in Budapest, Hungary. US Border and Immigration confirmed that she entered the USA on an Irish passport at J.F.K. on April 8th. Security camera footage showed her collecting a gold-colored suitcase from the belt and taking the J.F.K. AirTrain to the Long Island Rail Road station at Jamaica in Queens.

Houston continued in her devotion to Blanka.
'My shining Apollo,' she proclaimed cheerfully.
'Isn't Apollo supposed to be a god?' Blanka said. 'I'm not anywhere near a god. And I haven't been shining much lately.'
'My beautiful shining Apollo,' Houston insisted.
'Okay,' said Blanka, mothering her. 'I'll be your Apollo, and you'll be my Girl-who-fell-to-Earth. But I can't call you that, so I'm gonna use the name on your ticket: Houston.' Houston nodded enthusiastically. 'Then they go together. Not Apollo the god, but Apollo the space mission that nearly ended in disaster. Only to be saved by NASA's mission control, called *Houston*.'
'Then I'll save you,' Houston teased, 'And you can save me.'
'We'll see about that,' said Blanka. 'But I do have good news. The doctor says you're fine to leave the hospital tomorrow.'
Houston made the bed shake with her eagerness. 'Then we can party like anything,' and celebrate everything, and take turns saving each other.'
'But there's one more thing.'
'What's that?'
'You're going to have another visitor.'

⭐

*B*lanka had no intention of contacting Admiral De Leon and Hart would not have dreamt of doing it. Blanka felt it her duty to care for Houston and planned to take her back to London to be her guest. That was as far as her thinking went. Hart, on his side, felt Miss Nightingale still required weeks of psychological tests, medicines and brain scans – to which Blanka's reaction was, 'that's not going to happen.'

Will, however, Hart's son and Blanka's half-brother, was a fifteen year old boy with more than a small amount of his mother Kitty's stubbornness and tenacity. Letting people know that he was 'OhZone 4's brother' had gotten him put through to the senior OhZone liaison at the CIA, Adelle Wasson, and then to the Director, Admiral De Leon.
The news that a mysterious nineteen year old woman had landed in New York possessed in equal quantities with amnesia and devotion to Blanka, had peaked the Admiral's interest. During the call, he had Houston's Meds traced at St Vincent's.
'She is an *A positive*,' whispered Wasson.
De Leon asked Will two questions:
'Have you told your father or your sister you're calling me?' And, 'Can you get Miss Nightingale to come down to Langley?' When the answer to both was no, De Leon said, 'Well, if the mountain won't come to Mohammed, Mohammed must come to the mountain.'

At 14:00 hours Monday, De Leon, Wasson and De Leon's security brief climbed off the Amex at Penn Station to be greeted by Will and Blanka. Blanka immediately said, 'Sir, I want you to know at the outset that having your come was exclusively Will's idea. If he had told me about it, I would have stopped him bothering you.'
'At ease, OhZone 4,' said De Leon.
'It's out of the question,' blurted out Blanka. 'You can't recruit a girl to the CIA like this.'
'I recruited you easily enough.'
'I bet you recruited her in a snap,' chipped in Will.
Blanka pretend-cuffed him around the ears.
'I didn't have total amnesia,' she said.
'But you were younger than nineteen,' said Will.
'Let me run the CIA, okay?' De Leon interrupted.

'If you don't think she's suitable for OhZone or if Miss Nightingale doesn't want to join the CIA, knowing she'd be considered for OhZone, which means becoming part-AI, putting on a little weight and all that,' he teased Blanka, while winking at Will. 'We'll call the whole thing off.'

★

*F*rom Admiral De Leon's perspective, his visit to St. Vincent's hospital was a complete success. Houston quickly and freely decided that if joining OhZone would help her *be like Blanka*, she was only too eager to oblige. As she pointed out, she didn't have anything else to do.

The medical tests confirmed that Houston, aside from her amnesia, was exceptionally fit. But Blanka still had doubts. And she wanted to be sure that 'on her watch' there was not going to be *another Felicity*. Houston seemed genuine and Blanka's intuition told her to trust her. But was this too good to be true? How had she got hold of one of Blanka's Iceni handbags when there were only a hundred made? And what about the Koran in the bag, thought Blanka, reverting back to her upbringing as a Catholic convent girl.

While Houston spent her last day in St Vincent's Hospital, Blanka was doing one final check of the chain of events that had brought her to The Met. Sitting at her stepfather's loft, Blanka activated her mind interface to the silver ΩScanner. Every reference to and mention of 'Nightingale,' with and without 'Houston,' 'H.' and 'H.J.' since she went on the grid, were arrayed inside her AI enhanced mind.

It didn't entirely surprise her that both the Irish and Swiss passports came from a large inventory of standard alias passports held within Langley. So was De Leon behind all this? And how did they get to Bosnia? The grid held no information about the passport photographs. If they were forgeries, the mystery was: why were they *our* forgeries?

She called Langley on her Scanner. After voice, iris and codeword recognition, she got the central alias document store. 'This is OhZone 4. Can you check on two foreign passports for me in real time.'
'Sure' replied the voice. Blanka gave the details.

While she waited she went through the trail of events again. De Leon had sent officers to interview the Jamaica cab driver, who was obviously stoned when they talked to him. But he remembered the fare to The Met distinctly and said that Miss Blue Eyes was a 'real classy lady' and that she'd tried to tip him nearly seventy dollars. The US Border and Immigration supervisor on duty at J.F.K. said there was nothing out of the ordinary when Miss Nightingale passed through immigration. And the student working at The Met could only repeat that the girl was a refugee who'd come straight from J.F.K.

The voice came back on the line: 'They were loaned to the MI6 station in DC on January 4th.'
Blanka took a reference and picked up the electronic trail. on the grid. Michelle at the Met was working a shift today and she decided to re-interview her. She took the elevator to the ground floor and hailed a Yellow cab. In the back of the cab she followed the passports, while deciding to pose as a Social Worker caring for Houston. That would be a good way to get Michelle to open up. The electronic trail ended in a common pool at MI6 in London. As the cab approached Central Park East, Blanka messaged Nearby with the link: 'I need you to physically check if these passports are in the MI6 alias store.'

*B*lanka was known to The Met management and given a room to interview Michelle. 'I've told the police everything,' Michelle said, immediately defensive. 'Is the refugee in some kind of trouble?' she asked.
'Not at all,' said Blanka, quite sincerely. 'I'm just looking after her case and I want to go over your account of her arrival.'
'She made a real impression on me,' said Michelle.
'I can see that,' said Blanka, her blue AI eyes looking hypnotically into Michelle's. 'Like I said, I'm helping her.'
'I'd like to help her.'
'I know you would,' said Blanka.
'I gave her twenty dollars,' Michelle blurted out.
'That was very generous of you.'
'She's a refugee. Does she have parents?'
'Not as far as we know –'
'She's an orphan,' said Michelle. And a lump came into Blanka's throat. 'I looked after her luggage. For security, I searched it of course.'

'Naturally.'

'It had a blue dress with holes, underwear, a pirate T-shirt, a compass, *Brave New World* and her Koran.' Michelle started to tear up. 'Is she gonna be okay?'

'Yes, I promise you she is.'

'She had a Swiss Army Knife. It was in the case, not inside The Met.'

The story checked out.

'Anything else?' Blanka asked.

'No,' said Michelle.

Blanka handed Michelle a card as she left, 'If there's anything you can add that you might not have remembered before, call me.'

*A*s Blanka walked out The Met onto Central Park East, Michelle's words rang in her ears: 'She's an orphan.'

Although C endlessly bragged that 'orphans make the best spies,' it wasn't something Blanka liked to talk – or think –about. Kitty had died fifteen years ago and Blanka had never known who her father was. Of course she had run her own and her mother's DNA on the government computers both sides of the Atlantic. No match meant a man not in public office or law enforcement and with no criminal record. He might well be dead for all she knew.

In 1999, in floods of tears, Kitty had confessed to her, 'I was fourteen-and-a-half when I got pregnant with you. I didn't know what to do.'

Blanka heard her twenty-one-year-old voice asking her mother, 'Why didn't you keep in contact with the man? Did he rape you?'

'No,' Kitty said. 'No. But I was running any which way. I told him I was eighteen. I lied.'

Her cellphone rang and she answered it. It was Michelle.

*S*he met her outside The Met on the front steps. 'She was following hand written instructions,' Michelle told her.

This had not been picked up.

'I see' said Blanka.

'On a pink post-it note. I don't want to get her into trouble, but I was brought up to tell the truth.'

'Thank you for your honesty,' said Blanka. 'That's extremely helpful. Anything else?'

'I loved her fragrance,' Michelle continued. 'She let me smell it. It was like a foresty version of cK1.'

Sounds familiar, thought Blanka. She knew one person who wrote on pink post-it notes and had one of her designer handbags. Her intuition and AI both lit up the word *Fox* even before Michelle mentioned being given a mint with a polar bear on it.

'Peppy the polar bear,' said Blanka to herself.

'Is that his name?' asked Michelle. She took out her purse, removed the Glacier Mint wrapper and held it up for Blanka to see. 'Yeah, she was eating these. She gave me one.'

As Blanka climbed into the back of another yellow cab, a message from Nearby came in on her Scanner:

'The passports from the DC station are not there. They were requested on February 25th by Dr Fox.'

'Roger that,' messaged Blanka.

Our forgeries then, she thought. Fox's photographs. She removed Houston's two passports from her bag and examined the back of their photographs with her AI vision. Not much to go on, just faint traces, but it was enough – *they were Polaroids.*

She dialled Don's landline number at MI6.

'Blanka, how lovely to hear from you,' Don's voice crackled down the line. It was familiar and reassuring, but Blanka had reason to be more direct with him than usual.

'I have a little conundrum here, Don. And it's tied up in a Fox's Glacier Mint wrapper.'

'I say, conundrum. I do like puzzles.'

'Care to explain how two passports from the central store, one of my Iceni handbags and some Glacier Mints have ended up in the hands of a young mixed race woman from Bosnia,' Blanka said.

'Yes.'

'Okay?'

'I gave them to her.'

'Why didn't you tell me?'

'They're only *mints*,' Blanka.

'I don't mean the mints. Why didn't you tell me the passports came from
you.'

'You didn't ask.'

'What were you doing in Bosnia?'

'I wasn't in Bosnia, Blanka my dear. I told you I was looking up my old
UNHCR buddies in *Croatia*.'

Blanka smacked her head, remembering, 'Fuck!'

'Did you say, you're stuck?'

'You said it was a reunion.'

'Yes, it was. A lovely time was had by all!' laughed Fox.

Blanka pictured him in his psychiatrist's consulting room on Floor 7:
rocking back and forth in his leather chair as he roared with laughter. She
waited for him to stop.

'The young woman was not keen on the Swiss passport name, although
she liked the Swiss Army Knife.'

'This isn't a joke, Don,' Blanka snapped. 'De Leon's enrolling her in The
Company for Christsake.'

'And she'll make a quite splendid CIA field agent, Blanka. Lighten up a
bit, can't you?'

'You're talking about Houston Nightingale,' Blanka said, suppressing all
the questions she really wanted to ask. 'She was one of your "old
buddies"?'

'She *was* looking for a job.'

Blanka shook her head. How was it with Don that he always seemed
three steps ahead and taking a stroll on another planet? 'So you were
trying to get a job for an "old buddy"? Care to give me any details?'

'You know, Blanka, where I come from, "old buddies" don't kiss and tell,'
said Fox. 'Otherwise we'd be around all day listening to tales.'

'She's got total amnesia.'

Blanka caught the slight pause before Fox replied.

'I hope she's alright otherwise.'

'She's okay. De Leon wants her in OhZone.'

'Well, you are short staffed,' Fox reminded her.

'I guess this was your way of trying to help me out.'

'Something like that.'

'And you are aware we still have *Felicity out there somewhere*,' said Blanka.

'Yes,' said Don. 'Your bête noire, Felicity-fast-track. But that's another
problem, isn't it?'

7.2

Ilhabela, São Paulo state, Brazil

*F*elicity had not been idle, but she had also not been careful enough. She hadn't gone to Brazil straight away. Because she had been a Grade 4 field agent on the South American Desk, with many assignments in São Paulo State under her belt and good Portuguese, Brazil would be an obvious place to look for her. But unknown to MI6, she had a small room on the archipelago of Ilhabela (half way between São Paulo and Rio de Janeiro) where she kept her 'personal' supplies: cash, weapons, disguises and multiple fake identities and passports.

Francisco, the old Brazilian priest who owned the rambling house and who she'd run as a spy since her first visit to Brazil, was desperately in love with Felicity. And strangely, because she hated Christianity, he was the only human being on earth who Felicity felt any real love for.

Francisco Mateus was the same age as Major Grinin and was also a defector, but in his case he had defected from The Vatican, in Rome. He'd talked about being involved with something called The Fatima Secret, but Felicity hadn't really listened. He had been on the run for decades. Maybe if he'd been younger, she often told herself, she might have stayed with him and had a different life.

In the weeks since she had fled from Ireland to Spain, Portugal and then South Africa (using one of her superlative disguises) she had seriously started to plan such a life. The Black Slip hit had been a disaster. She had soon learned of C's disappearance and the arrest and trial of Prosthetics John, as well as the explosion that reduced her Balham home to rubble. Forces bigger than C, MI6, or the KGB were at work, and she determined to keep one step ahead of them.

But Felicity, ever impatient, was in a hurry. From the fifty thousand dollar stash she had hidden near Dublin airport, she now only had nine hundred dollars left, and she knew her bank accounts were being watched. In Cape Town she obtained extensive laser treatment to the wounds on her right leg from a plastic surgeon with whom she had friendly dealings. He also removed the large tattoo from her left arm: a fearsome portrait of Genghis Khan with a black swastika in it. With their special blood filled with relativistic-haemoglobin and their special cells filled with relativistic-ATP, OhZones had amazing self-healing properties but there were limits. The surgeon apologized when he could not repair the hole in the helix at the top of her ear; (it required an ear transplant and they had no suitable donor).

Felicity offered to pay (from an old savings account in a fake name, which she knew was still secret) but the surgeon declined payment. It was a lucky escape for Felicity; extradition on a murder charge was a fairly straightforward process in the British Commonwealth country.

Felicity had arranged a false trail suggesting she was on safari in eastern Africa. As a result, MI6 director Bantu, and the British and Kenyan authorities were still looking for her in Kenya, while she made her way to Brazil.

★

*F*elicity's journey to Ilhabela was uneventful. She got the money for her airfare to San Paolo via Cairo and Madrid by turning half a dozen tricks at the seven star business hotels in Cape Town, putting her five grand ahead.

Francisco's house was deserted and the fountain wasn't running, which didn't surprise her. She simply found the spare key where it always was: down the garden, past the fountain and under an old stone crucifix in a cavity concealed by moss. Francisco was often gone for days at a time – where he went, he never told her – so Felicity decided to turn the fountain back on and stay until he showed up. She opened up the house and locked away Sokol's ℧Armor, Scanner and P238 micro-compact pistol in the safe in her room. In the mornings, she swam naked in the pool. As she looked at her breasts (with their conning-tower nipples) she reflected on how the water rippling above and around them gave a strange life to the tattoo of the world-as-conquered-by-Genghis Khan which spanned them. A reminder of her earlier life.

When Francisco first saw the tattoo, he gently kissed her breasts, traveling through all the areas depicted, and said, "Such detail. I can only imagine the pain involved in having that delicate skin pierced so deeply."

Then, before lunch, Felicity cycled to the grocery store, navigating the narrow cluttered aisles. In the evenings she sat in the yard by the fountain, cooked moqueca (exotic fish and seafood stew) in the clay barbeque, looked out over the Atlantic Ocean and remembered just how much she loved Ilhabela. And Francisco. The man who never judged her. But what would he think now, now that she was a quarter-AI? Night after night she waited for him to show up. She dreamed about the life she could have had with him – told herself she could still have with him. She watched her Brazilian iPhone, which only he knew about, and checked for emails on his Mac. She slept in his bed (under the mosquito net he never used) and worried about him and about his unusually long silence. He knew she was on the run. Why hadn't he come or at least messaged her? She made a few days stretch to twelve nights. Waiting for him.

One part of her OhZone programming was to broaden her mind. So, during her stay, she watched a few movies in bed including the Coen Brothers story of a hitman with no remorse or compassion: Anton Chigurh in *No Country For Old Men*. Chigurh was certainly a CCU 8, she thought. 'I think I'll buy the book'

7.3

5 **WEEKS AFTER THE KILLINGS** One particular night at the end of April, in the early hours, Felicity awoke from a dream clutching at her nose and mouth and struggling to breathe. She found the bed quite soaked, and her body dripping with perspiration. (These 'nighttime sweats' had been a problem for her since childhood and her ritual of lengthy bathing came from a desire to cleanse them away.) This was different, and what made it different was the intensity of the nightmare she had been trapped in.

Vivid and distinct in Second-World-War-style-black-and-white-film, the nightmare had started at an exhibition. She recognized it as the one Jude had taken her to just after her return from Paris by Eurostar. The war time documentary being run at the exhibition, *Listen To Britain*, was mixed up with her arrival home on becoming agent OhZone 7. In the documentary, school children – girls in white dresses, boys in dark shorts – were skipping in pairs hand-in-hand around an English school playground. What seemed like a harmless victory celebration, slowly turned out to be lonely and surreal. It was midnight, and Felicity found herself the only passenger in the twenty-car Eurostar as, puffing steam, it slid into Kings Cross/St Pancras station. Disoriented by the pervasive stream, Felicity stumbled as she disembarked. Then she found herself riding the travellator and turning into a black-and-white-1940 documentary version of herself. The whole dream was now set in the Second World War. As she approached immigration, a severe announcement on the travellator warned, 'Attention, you are approaching the end.'

As she stepped up to passport control, the soldier there (with gas mask strapped to his side) looked up at her. It was Jude!
'Jude! What are you doing here?' she asked.
'Hello, Felicity,' Jude replied, gesturing for her to put her passport away, and handing her a gas mask. 'Put this on, they're expecting you.'

With the gas mask over her face, Felicity walked into the customs hall where three Jewish-looking men dressed in Nazi uniforms smugly watched her. She looked down at her body and found she was butt naked and carrying her Jimmy Choo boots in her hands.

In the final chamber before entering Britain, a tall pale woman turned and pointed at her. Felicity recognized a ghastly version of Diana Grinin. 'She's *the killer*,' Diana said to a petite girl, black or mixed race, dressed in the robes of an ancient queen. The girl tilted her head this way and that, studying Felicity, before pulling a lever which opened the door to the station concourse. Amidst the sound and shock waves of German bombs exploding all around her, Felicity wanted to tell the girl there'd been a mistake, wanted to say that it wasn't her. But she couldn't speak, couldn't breathe, couldn't get the gas mask off her face…

Through the door, steam trains whistled. Lit by gas lamps, a small group of Second World War musicians surrounded two figures she recognized as Flanagan and Allen, playing two old pianos and singing *Under the*

Arches. Old fashioned British bobbies, carrying gas masks, patrolled the concourse. When they saw Felicity, they blew their whistles and gave chase. Covering her nakedness with her Jimmy Choo boots and still with the gas mask stuck on her face, Felicity ran from them down an old railway track, into the foggy mix of drifting steam and escaped gasses from the London sewers, train whistles sounding all around her.

Suddenly she heard someone whistling Mozart's *Eine Kleine Nachtmusik.* Ahead in the fog, she saw a small man with a pockmarked face and a large nose. He looked like Dustin Hoffman's Rizzo out of *Midnight Cowboy.*

'*Gute Nacht, Herr Doctor,*' the Rizzo man snarled, tearing at her gas mask and grabbing her boots.

At that point she awoke, frantically trying to untangle herself from the blanket clutching her.

7.4

Friday, May 8, 2015
Copacabana Município, Rio de Janeiro, Brazil

*A*fter her nightmare, Felicity grew increasingly restless. She had to get away from São Paulo State or she would be found, so she decided to head the 220 miles to Rio where she had no history. On the final evening at Ilhabela she cried. Tears streamed down her face for having missed Francisco. But there was anger too. Why hadn't he contacted her? Had he stopped loving her? In the morning, she left a hidden note under the crucifix. Well armed, and re-supplied with cash, burners, prosthetics and disguises from her room, Felicity headed off for the ferry.

*B*razil had always been pleasantly familiar to Felicity and in no time she found her feet in Rio. She shaved her head, bound her chest with bandages and used forged documents to adopt a male identity – and obtain a local hospital post as Dr Andreas Casadevall (an identity replete with a bank account, thirty thousand Brazilian real and a social security number) – which she had set up on a visit two years before.

The job was in the pediatric department of the large Samaritano lying between the Sugar Loaf and Corcovado mountains. She rented a house below the Corcovado range. It came with a strong fire-and-theft safe where she kept her weapons, valuables and identities, as well as the ΩArmor and Scanner she'd stolen from Sokol. When she first arrived, she rode the train up to view the 125 foot statue of Christ the Redeemer and reflected that former illustrious visitors – two Popes, Albert Einstein and Princess Diana – were all dead now.

On her days off, Felicity would emerge from the alley at back of her house as a Latino-looking blonde, hail a taxi that took her a few blocks away to a small room she rented in Ipenema. There she would change into a black bikini, don a hi-tech ocean-proof black wig and walk to the ocean. But on the morning of May 8, after taking in Copacabana beach (someone had to do it), she walked along the wave-patterned Portuguese pavement on Avenida Atlântica and headed to her familiar Ipenema. According to urban myth, the original *garota de Ipanema* (girl from Ipenema) had been the very first girl to dare to offend the rigorous stand-ards of Catholic decency and wear a 2-piece bathing suit on the Ipenema strand! The song was Felicity's all-time favorite and she prided herself on having every movie that used the song from Steve McQueen's *The Thomas Crown Affair* to the two Angelina Jolie films *Girl, Interrupted* and *Mr. & Mrs. Smith*. The songwriter Vinicius de Moraes, the poet, was also, like Felicity, a diplomat and Intelligence agent. Things hadn't worked out so badly after all, Felicity reflected as she dived under the waves along the beach. Even without Francisco she would make her come back. Later, as she walked to her favorite beach bar with her Bra-zilian iPhone playing the bossa nova song in her ears, she put on a Samba swing, indulged herself in the hundred pairs of eyes eating her up and imagined herself as the original garota de Ipanema. It was only when she noticed a newspaper banner on a kiosk reading
Corduroy slips!
that she realized the General Election results back home in Britain had come in.

At the bar she sipped a Caipirinha and watched the Sky news coverage of the National Party's unexpected landslide. A loyal former lover on the South American Desk had messaged one of her burners the evening before with the buzz that the production of *Macbeth* at Queen Elizabeth Hall had been a big success, but that Russia was perceived as being too soft.

'C may return,' said the message.

'When?' Felicity had typed.

'Nobody knows,' relied her contact. 'Another buzz: Blanka's found a replacement for you!'

Behind her contacts, Felicity's AI eyes flashed deep purple in color.

'Where?' she messaged.

'CIA, New York,' came the reply.

7.5

Sunday May 10, 2015
Chevening House, Kent, UK

*T*he opera had indeed been received with great public acclaim. But when a terrorist attack claimed the life of three police officers at a children's hospital being opened by the Queen, it was an easy shot to say that MI6 officers should be diligently using Intelligence to protect the Royal family, the public and uniformed police officers from terrorism threats and not singing Macbeth. The media roundly condemned the government for not being tough enough, and Corduroy's Working Party lost in a landslide defeat. June Glendinning's National Party had returned to power.

When it comes to politics, the UK is very thrifty. Unlike America where an incoming President has two months before he takes over the reins of power, a new Prime Minister takes over the same day. One of Glendinning's first acts was to cancel the Opera Initiative and reinstate C to MI6.

The day after, L.B.J. moved out of the Foreign Secretary's residence, Chevening Park (the inspiration for Rosings Park in Jane Austen's *Pride and Prejudice*) and the new Foreign Secretary sat in his splendid study, waiting for Russia to arrive. As he half-listened to an aide telling him what a popular chief Russia had been at Wonderland (if only for a short time), he remembered his first meeting with the new Prime Minister. With the support of his Permanent Secretary and other senior aides in the Foreign and Commonwealth Office, he had decided to stand up to the new resident of 10 Downing Street. It was short-lived in her presence. 'They'll be considerable resistance,' he had begun, 'to Sir Mark returning as C, particularly as the directors of MI6 abolished that position.' 'Never mind the resistance,' she'd countered. 'Get him back as one of the directors and leave the rest to him.'

'I'm not completely comfortable with that decision,' he'd said.

'If that's the case, you needn't take the Foreign Office portfolio, or move into Chevening Park. Perhaps Culture Secretary would suit you better?' she'd countered.

'I believe I can better serve my country in the Foreign Office,' was his reply. He'd backed down of course.

The news of C's imminent return had been leaked and was generally unwelcome. Russia, when he was shown in, was blunt in his summary of the situation.

'There'll be open mutiny,' he predicted. 'He's got children's blood on his hands, and no Intelligence officer is likely to forget he was responsible for OhZone 3's death. Or forgive the fact his protégé blew the man's head across a London rooftop using banned depleted uranium ordnance.'

'Quite so,' the new Foreign Secretary replied. 'I'd like you to issue an order banning the use of that *vile ordnance* within the service. With immediate effect.'

'And C?'

'My hands are tied,' said the Foreign Secretary, squirming. 'You'll all be equals. He'll just be one of the nine. In charge of the…' he checked his square cut folder (color: yellow) 'the QC desk.'

'*Quis custodiet ipsos custodes?*' said Russia.

'Yes, guarding the guardians,' said the Foreign Secretary, quite missing the irony. Despite his own angst, he wasn't totally oblivious to Russia's despair. 'I'm sure old hands like you, Probe and Devices can keep him in check,' he offered.

'Like we did before, you mean?' Russia didn't bother to remove the edge from his voice.

'Far be it from me to tell you your jobs.'

'Did you get a psychiatric opinion from Dr Fox?'

'Yes, curious chap isn't he? He gave me a half empty packet of mints and asked to be transferred to Penguin Island. Do you think it was his idea of a joke.'

'Quite possibly,' said Russia.

'Besides, C –'

Russia's face blackened.

'– I mean Sir Mark, won't have a private dining room or butler any more.'

'That makes all the difference of course.'

'Of course. It's a question of prestige.'

'A question of prestige?'

'Yes, it's a question of *prestige*.'

7.6

Ma il mio mistero è chiuso in me,
il nome mio nessun saprà!

TURANDOT -
GIACOMO PUCCINI & FRANCO ALFANO

*H*ouston's crash induction into the CIA immediately proved her exceptional aptitude for science and her athletic abilities. She also scored in the top one percent of marksmen in all the weapons they tested her with. As De Leon stated (much to Blanka's annoyance), 'She was born to be an OhZone.'

Blanka didn't know whether to congratulate Will on being right or be furious with him for getting Admiral De Leon involved. But there was no turning back now. It was also soon obvious that Houston was naively determined to 'help Apollo' in any way she could. For the moment, however, De Leon decided to keep the fact that her blood group matched Blanka's under wraps, confiding only in Hart and Drox who were only too glad to have a potential kidney donor on the OhZone waiting list. Russia and the NATO Secretary General, trusting in De Leon's judgement, quickly signed off on Houston as OhZone 9-elect.

★

*T*he following morning when Russia knocked on the door of his corner office on floor 11, Arms knew what was coming – even though he'd done exactly what the former Prime Minister, Mr Corduroy, had asked and *Macbeth* had been an astounding success, musically.

Behind Russia was the tea lady, Ethyl Lynn, with the old fashioned tea trolley. 'A nice cup of PG Tips for Mr York,' she said as she set the second cup and saucer down with a smile. She was the only person out of three thousand staff not to call him 'Russia.'

'And may I say,' she said to Arms, 'how much my husband, Kingsley, and I enjoyed the opera you officers wery kindly put on. "I ain't never seen nothing like it in my whole life." That's what my Kingsley says. He didn't want a postal ballot, he went out and voted for Mr Corduroy the very next day.'

Arms nodded and sipped his tea.

'And we had smashing seats, wery comfortable. Next to Dr Fox and the new transgender officer that you people named, "Wednesday." I don't know, such names you come up with!'

Russia smiled back at her and nodded.

'Mints or biscuits for you, gentlemen?' Ethyl said, offering plates of Glacier Mints and McVities chocolate digestives. 'I find Glacier Mints a little strong. Although Kingsley has taken a liking to them since the opera.'

'Digestives please,' chipped in Arms.

'I told Miss Miles [Bio] she was a natural as Lady Macbeth,' Ethyl continued, as she handed round the biscuits. 'I hope she took it the right way.'

'I'm sure she did,' said Russia. As he watched Arms nibble his biscuit, he wondered if Bio had also been having Arms practice.

When the tea trolley had rolled on its way down Floor 11, Russia closed

the door and broke the news in one casual choreographed motion.
'You'll be keeping your Grade 9 salary and Crown Pension package, of
course. It's not really a demotion. In a way, you're just being *restored* – to
your former duties.'
'*Restored*. Ever the diplomat, Phil,' replied Arms.
Russia gestured to the phone on the desk, 'May I?'
Arms nodded. Russia dialled four digits.
'Miss Banks,' answered Miss Banks.
'Post the change of Arms, please,' said Russia.
'Yes, Sir,' said Miss Banks.
Russia put the phone down and gave Arms a blank diplomatic stare. 'We
appreciate your loyalty, Charlie. Unfortunately the people you are loyal
to, occasionally shift, and your loyalty has to…'
– take on new forms?'
'Exactly,' said Russia, pleased. 'Or return to even older forms.'

*A*fter leaving his office, Arms took the elevator fourteen floors
down to the firing range. What did I want with an office high up there
anyway? In his old office on floor -3 separated from the range by a
triple glazed armored glass window, he logged into his old computer
and checked his internal mail. He stopped momentarily at a memo on
ordnance.

From Acting Chief York (Russia)
RE. DEPLETED URANIUM ROUNDS (ALL CALIBRES).
*Banned for use by MI6 officers inside and outside the UK,
with effect from Monday May 11, 2015.*

Further down, a staff change memo caught his eye, together with a CIA
mugshot of Houston.

From Human Resources
STAFF CHANGE.
*New officer on secondment from CIA (equivalent MI6 Grade 2),
with effect from Monday June 1, 2015.* **Nightingale, H.J. Miss,**
dob Oct 23, 1995. Reports to Maguire, B.V., NATO OhZone Div.

He hit the print button and his printer whirred.
Further down he saw the official post of C's return.

> *From Human Resources*
> **STAFF CHANGE.**
> *Returning from leave of absence, to Director QC Desk (Grade 9), with effect from Monday June 1, 2015.*
> **Loveless, M.R. Sir**, *Reports to Directors.*

Every dog has it's day, he reflected. I guess this wasn't mine.
He smiled. At least C's gone *down* a pay grade. He's had to give up his private dining room and his *butler*.
Then he spoke out loud with particular satisfaction. 'And he's lost *Miss Banks*.'

Remembering a Cuban cigar C had given him, Arms took the Cohiba Lancero from his drawer, cut the end and lit it.
He puffed on it in a satisfied away and then, just as he returned to his computer, the computer failed followed by the office lighting. Then the emergency lighting in his office and in the firing range failed too. He fumbled the switch on his desk lamp on, but nothing happened. Taking the cigar lighter from his pocket, he struck a light. He took a Maglite from his drawer, switched it on and picked up the phone. But there was no tone. All cell phones were deposited at lobby security.
'Some 'bugger must've pressed the red nuclear fire button,' he snorted. He crossed the room to an old FM radio by the printer. He switched it on and, through an unusual hiss, could hear BBC Radio 4's *Desert Island Discs*. He listened as the guest picked Pucinni's *Nessun Dorma*, which erupted in the key of G major, drowning out the silence of the power outage.

> *Nessun dorma! Nessun dorma!*
> *Tu pure, o, Principessa,*
> *nella tua fredda stanza*

Surprisingly, the guest hadn't chosen Luciano Pavarotti, but the long dead master tenor, Enrico Caruso. The great tenor had the same birthday as Arms: February 25th, and he hummed along with him.

He knew what the words of the aria meant.

> Nobody shall sleep! Nobody shall sleep!
> Even you, oh Princess,
> in your cold room

Lost in the world of opera, he turned the volume up to full.

> *Guardi le stelle*
> *che tremano d'amore*
> *e di speranza*

He puffed aggressively on his cigar and amused himself by whispering the English words.

> Look at the stars,
> that tremble with love
> and with hope

Suddenly cheerful and energetic, Arms took the printout off the printer and sat down with it to study the photo of Houston Nightingale, the latest recruit, by torchlight.

> *Ma il mio mistero è chiuso in me,*
> *il nome mio nessun saprà!*
> *No... no...*

Even by flashlight, her eyes seemed to sparkle, as did her mischievous smile. Arms didn't have children.
If I had a daughter, he mused, I'd want her to look like you, my dear.

> But my secret is hidden within me,
> my name no one shall know...
> No...No...

Just then a woman arms officer ran in with another flashlight.
'The elevators –'
'Shhh,' hissed Arms. The woman stood and waited. When the excerpt ended and chatter returned, Arms turned the radio off.
'The elevators are disabled! Sir. None of the radios work, not even *red*.'
Arms nodded.
The woman, a Hungarian recruit called Erica, coughed in the fog of cigar smoke.

'Want to see the next OhZone? asked Arms, holding out Houston's CIA mugshot. Erica took it eagerly and considered Houston.

'May I state my opinion, Sir?' she asked.

'Please,' said Arms.

'It seems to me we've suddenly gone from having no OhZones, to getting through them rather fast.'

'Yes, it does look like that doesn't it?' said Arms.

7.7

*T*he mysterious power outage all over London S.E.1 ended as suddenly as it had begun. As Drox flew back from New York to Paris in his jet, dropping Blanka and Houston in London on the way, he was occupied in discussions with colleagues at CERN and Fermilab. Forty or so similar unexplained outages – now described by astrophysicists as 'U.P.S. protuberances – had been reported worldwide over the last three months.

At the same time, C was making the first stage of his journey from Cuba back home to MI6 – via Australia – where he was to meet Jude.

*B*lanka returned to MI6 Headquarters to face row after row of sombre faces. She briefed Sokol on Houston but was careful to say nothing about Fox's involvement or the premonition her brother Will had had about Houston's appearance.

At lunchtime, Blanka punched the day's ten digit code into a pad and emerged from the MI6 Headquarters building into the garden on the south west corner. She wanted to go down to the sandy strand where she often ate her vegetarian sandwich, losing herself in the waves of the Thames and feeding the ducks with her crumbs.

Seeing Arms eating a ham baguette on a bench in the garden, she approached.

'Please sit down, won't you?' said Arms. 'I haven't seen you since... Felicity-fast-track ran amok.'

'You seem to have been on quite a roller coaster ride yourself.'

'Yes, indeed,' said Arms.

Blanka unwrapped her sandwich, and they both ate. Blanka was itching to ask Arms about Felicity. After a couple of minutes she turned to him. 'I didn't think Felicity was your type.'

'Don't think badly of me. It was stupid, I know.'

'I have always held you in the highest regard, Charlie.'

'There's no fool like an old fool, Blanka. Do you remember that old joke about the man who suddenly stripped off all his clothes and jumped into a cactus patch?'

'No,' Blanka said.

'Well, they asked him, "What in the world possessed you to jump into a cactus patch butt naked?" Know what he said?'

Blanka waited.

'He said, "It seemed like a good idea at the time."'

Blanka smiled and Arms chuckled to himself.

'You know, I offered them my resignation,' he said. 'Instead they promoted me. Our dearly departed Mr Corduroy was exceedingly fond of opera.'

'I hear MacBeth was a great success.'

'Yes, but those damned terrorists came along. And Verdi got the blame.'

'Those damned terrorists. They spoil all the fun,' joked Blanka.

'And what did Shakespeare tell us?"' said Arms, biting deep into his ham baguette: 'All the world's a stage.' And even though it's a farce, sometimes the exits are quite brutal. I was lucky they wanted to keep an old dog around at all.

'But Shakespeare also said that "every dog shall have his day," ' Blanka said.

'You know.' Arms started chuckling again. 'That's exactly what I was thinking a little while ago. That's exactly what I was thinking.'

Nightingale, H.J. Sings

All the world's a stage,
And all the men and women merely players;
They have their exits and their entrances;
And one man in his time plays many parts.

WILLIAM SHAKESPEARE – AS YOU LIKE IT

8.0

Wednesday May 20, 2015

9 WEEKS AFTER THE KILLINGS The woman formerly known as 'Leila Muhic from Bosnia' had changed names – changed continents twice – and changed worlds…
And now found herself – Nightingale, H.J. Miss – the Girl-who-fell-to-Earth – or just 'Houston' – in London.

But Blanka was so busy trying to get OhZone back on an even keel, she left the job of orienting her to Nearby, who took her to many of the famous sights such as Trafalgar Square.

After visiting Sherlock Holmes' house at 221B Baker Street, Houston used part of her first CIA pay check to buy Nearby coffee at a Café Nero opposite. In the back, they were joined by a tourist-like man who seemed to appear out of nowhere. He was Ma Baker (the sixty-year-old London bureau chief of the CIA) who was based down the road.
'As a CIA debutante and hopefully our new recruit to OhZone,' he told Houston, 'I'll be keeping a close eye on you. I hear you're a fan of Sherlock Holmes.'
'Yes, when I stayed at Professor Hart's loft in Manhattan, it was the first thing I watched… the first thing I can remember from t.v.'
'The first thing?' Ma Baker asked and looked at Nearby.

Before Nearby could say anything, Houston volunteered, 'I've got total amnesia.'

Ma Baker frowned. 'Yes, I've read the medical report.'

'Shall I tell her about the *honey wagon*?' said Nearby, giggling slightly.

'A crude analogy, but it has some truth in it,' Ma Baker said. 'Someone has to clean up the debris that democracy creates.'

'Around the villages in Ireland where I was raised,' said Nearby, taking Houston's hand. 'The truck that picks up the shit is called the "honey wagon." Intelligence agents like to think of themselves as driving the honey wagon, dear.'

'So in a way we envy your amnesia,' Ma Baker added. 'In the world of spying, most of us would like to forget *most things*.'

Houston took her time pulling the novel *The Hound of the Baskervilles* from her bag and handing it to Ma Baker. 'Nearby lent it to me. She doesn't *ever* watch t.v.!'

'I like books too,' said Ma Baker. 'And I wrote the book on staying safe in London.' He caught Nearby's eye, and Nearby shook her head at him. 'The last Brit MI6 put into OhZone went rogue, a woman by name of Robinson.'

Houston recited the OhZones she was aware of: 'Apollo's four, Sokol's five, David (who I haven't met yet) is six.'

'Yeah, she was seven,' said Ma Baker.

'You'll hear the name Felicity-fast-track around,' said Nearby.

'So, before we move you forward into OhZone,' Ma Baker said, 'the ranking officer of the sponsoring agency – that's me – has to make very sure that you really want to be part AI. That you fully understand what becoming an OhZone AI – means to you as a human.'

Houston could feel the two pairs of eyes trying to read her. 'You want to be sure that you won't have another Felicity-fast-track,' she said calmly.

'You got it. And while we've no reason to believe she'd come after you...'

'After *me*?' Houston exclaimed.

'We want you to be safe and secure. You'll probably never cross her tracks, but it's just as well you know to keep clear of her. Then smiling he said, 'Now what's after Sherlock Holmes' house?'

★

*A*t Madame Tussauds wax works, the manikins of the rock music idols fascinated Houston, especially knowing that Blanka had her own band. How strange that music should have been excluded from her amnesia.

Nearby warned Houston that when it came to Blanka's band, Blanka's kind demeanor went out the window; she became an egocentric artiste and control freak like the best of them.

When Houston came to the manikins of Sherlock Holmes and Dr Watson, a question about Felicity-fast-track popped into her head. She turned to Nearby.

'What did FTT do that's so bad?'

Nearby's face turned stony. With a cold detached look, she stared at a group of pre-school children running around the wax manikins.

'Nearby?' she asked again. 'What did Felicity-fast-track do?'

'C-C-Collateral d-damage,' Nearby managed to get out. 'It's classified. Blanka will brief you.'

With her brain like a clean slate, Houston easily grasped what Nearby couldn't or wouldn't tell her. The former OhZone agent had killed children.

At the Tower of London, Houston was further upset when Nearby told her the story of the princes in the tower.

'Sure it's not true,' said Nearby, 'it was only made up by Shakespeare.' When she saw the concerned look on Houston's face, she added, 'He's a very popular playwright from that time.'

'Shake-spear,' repeated Houston.

'It's in the bible too,' said Nearby light heartedly. 'King Herod murdered the new born boys.'

Houston looked at her and said, 'What's the "bible?" '

At Hyde Park, before Nearby returned Houston to Blanka's house, they walked by a series of little waterfalls laid out in a granite oval sixty by ninety yards long. One side of the oval was turbulent rapids, the other placid steps with children walking in the shallow water. They stopped by a sign reading, 'Diana, Princess of Wales Memorial Fountain.'

Houston hopped up into the fountain and walked along the Cornish granite.

'Who's Diana?' she said.

'A prin-c-cess they k-kil – I mean a prin-c-cess who d-died,' said Nearby, biting her lip. Getting control of herself, she went on. 'Sure two sides of

the fountain show the two sides of Diana's life: happy times, and turmoil.'
'Was she murdered?' Houston asked, 'Like the "princes in the Tower"?'
'No!' said Nearby, panicking and laughing nervously. 'No, no,' she jab-
bered. 'Not at all, n-not at all like that. She died in a car wreck that's all.'
Houston jumped down onto the grass and studied Nearby's face. Is that
true? she thought. Or is this innocent-looking Irish woman lying to me?
'It was just an accident?' she asked. 'Nobody's fault?'
'Yes,' Nearby said firmly. But the words of The Monster, in a play she'd
recently seen based on Mary Shelley's *Frankenstein*, stung in her ears

> *At the feet of my master*
> *I learnt the highest of human skills,*
> *the skill no other creature owns:*
> *I finally learnt how to lie.*

Nearby hurried away from the memorial, taking a handkerchief from
her pocket and blowing her nose. 'Come on now, Blanka will be expecting you,' was what she said.

*B*efore becoming entangled in MI6, Nearby had lived in the
Oxfordshire town of Banbury. Her brother, Mike, farmed an organic
smallholding there and supplemented his income running stables.
When Blanka learned about them, she boarded some of her horses
there and occasionally went up with Caesar for a ride in what she
called 'the true English countryside'. On the forthcoming Friday night
Mike was celebrating his 30th birthday with a pirate party. It involved
moving the horses to the surrounding fields for the weekend and
converting his barn beside his narrow boat on the Oxford canal to a
giant pirate ship. He had also paid for a fully set up bar, complete with
barrels of real ale and two cocktail bartenders.
'Do you really need two bartenders?' Nearby asked him.
'You left behind Irish drinking when you left behind your Irish roots,' he
teased her. 'The locals in Banbury can easily keep up!'
Her brother was eager for Nearby to bring her friends along. They
decided Blanka could drive out on Friday afternoon with Houston,
Sokol and Drox.

8.1

Casa Blanka, 10 Buckingham Mews, S.W.1

*A*fter sightseeing, Houston returned to find Blanka just home from MI6, and making tea in her cute kitchen. Her pink kettle whistled in her wall-to-wall rainforest, and she poured the water into the China teapot. Taking their teas upstairs (in matching Libra insignia cups and saucers) they chatted about music while Blanka prepared her dialysis machine. Houston had learned from Will that Blanka's all-time favourite song was *The Night They Drove Old Dixie Down* and she proceeded to play it to her on one of her harps. Blanka smiled and complimented her, and put on a Youtube of The Band performing it. Being politically correct, Blanka went to pains to explain to her young black friend that the song was penned by a half-Jewish Canadian – half-Mohawk Indian and was not racist, but an anti-war anthem, and part of 'Roots Rock.' 'It's about the end of a world,' Blanka had said.

Houston went out to explore and, when she returned, it was real foggy and the gas-fired lamps in Blanka's Mews softly reflected from the cobblestones. Inside, the house seemed very quiet. She recalled Blanka's words: 'The end of a world.'
'*My old world* ended, didn't it?' she said aloud, setting a few groceries down in the kitchen. 'I've been to New York, I've been to Washington. I've been to Camp Swampy and now London town.' She looked out at the fog – glowing strangely in that way it had – in Blanka's beloved cottage garden. This is my new life.
Stepping into the hall, she hollered, 'Rise and shine, Apollo.' In the corner she saw utility bills that had come in the mail, and underneath the face of the Statue of Liberty peeping out from a postcard. She popped the card in her bag, beside a gift for Blanka, and bounded up the stairs.

After the dialysis, Blanka had fallen asleep on her bed. In her dream the motif of Rose alba and cattle car trains to Auschwitz had given way to a train song *The Night They Drove Old Dixie Down* forming the soundtrack to her dream. The little white rabbit from Notre Dame in Paris was being baptized. He was a 'he' and was being immersed in an old canal by a group of pirate-Baptists in pirate costume. Houston was the pirate captain and she called out

White Rabbit, I baptize you,
I name you 'Virgil Caine.'
May Lord Allah help us all.

Blanka started awake, her cat Luna jumped, and a black dress she'd been checking out for the party slid onto the floor.
'I got you a present,' she heard Houston say.
Blanka looked up and smiled, 'Hello, Girl-who-fell-to-Earth.'
Houston handed her a paper bag and Blanka opened it, laughing when she saw a sign showing a cartoon bank robbery with the slogan:
'Put the chocolate in the bag and nobody gets hurt!'
Then Houston lifted a packet of Lindor chocolate balls from the bag.
'Saving my life already,' Blanka sighed.
'Essentials,' Houston laughed, opening the packet and popping one into Blanka's mouth.
'Yummy,' Blanka responded as the taste exploded. 'Your turn,' she said, taking the bag.

*B*lanka pulled a red dress from her closet and slipped it on, while Houston studied the manikin beside the closet.
'It's like the manikins at Madame Tussaud's but better.'
'That's my cousin Valentina. It was made when she became the first woman in space. She was twenty-four, she's much older now.'
Having gotten into the red dress, Blanka twisted in front of the mirror and smiled at Luna, who only yawned.
'She's Russian,' Blanka went on to explain. 'A general in the KGB. She gave it to me as a joke when I joined the CIA.
"Be sure to have your friends at The Company check it for bugs," she told me.'
Houston laughed. 'I bet they did.'
'They sure did,' Blanka said. 'But they didn't find any. My cousin Valentina is a good woman. She wouldn't trick me.'

Blanka flicked her hair from side to side, adding volume, while Houston played a few chords on Blanka's Gibson Hummingbird. 'Can we try *The Night They Drove Old Dixie Down* when the band rehearses?' she asked.
Then she saw Blanka's less than enthusiastic face and hit some discords.

This was too much for Luna who put back her ears and ran off. 'Oh dear, my guitar playing doesn't rate with her.' Remembering the postcard from New York, she pulled it from her bag and handed it to Blanka. 'This was on the mat with some bills.' Blanka looked at the picture of the Statue of Liberty then flipped it over and read

> Dearest Blanka,
> Sorry to miss you in Manhattan. See you on your next trip!
> Love, Danny.
>
> *"Love resembles death in that it annihilates*
> *snobbery, vulgarity, and all distinctions."*
> *—The sayings of Shri Meher Baba*

Blanka smiled, set the card on her dresser and turned to Houston. 'Harmonica could add some punch. Do you play anything else?'
'No, but I've got a great set of pipes!'
'Well, I sing already… Nearby's backing vocals… Sokol sings if she feels like it. But we can try you out.'
'Awesome, Apollo.'

★

*H*ouston, trying on dresses too, adjusted her hair and frowned at her reflection. 'Do you like my hair?'
Blanka moved to look at it in the mirror. She gestured, 'perfect,' and said, 'I love your hair!'
'It's just not how I remember it,' said Houston in a far-away voice.
Itgnoring her remark, Blanka took another look at her dress in the mirror and frowned. 'Maybe red's not my color. Would you mind unzipping me?'
Houston unzipped the dress and Blanka slipped out it.
'Zips are amazing,' Houston declared.
Blanka, held a sky blue dress up to herself. 'You must have had zips in Bosnia, you know.'
Houston looked between the Valentina manikin and Blanka – they were both clothed in sky blue – and smiled like the good Libran she was.
'Apollo, you're beautiful in the blue dress and beautiful in the red dress.'
Blanka was so pleased.

Glancing at a pile of letters lying at the manikin's feet, Houston picked up an invitation that had a skull and crossbones in the corner. 'Look, Apollo,' she said. 'The party is – a *pirate* party!'

'Fuck!' said Blanka. 'I forgot. We'll have to get costumes tomorrow. I'll leave Wonderland early.'

'Like Alice?'

'Yes.' Blanka furrowed the lines on her forehead jokingly. 'How come you know about *Alice In Wonderland* but you can't remember t.v.?'

In response she dumped the contents of her Iceni bag and proudly produced the book, *The Annotated Alice: Alice's Adventures in Wonderland and Through the Looking-Glass.*

'When I started reading it in English,' said Houston, 'I remembered I'd read it when I was a child!'

'One Bosnian memory retrieved. Well done,' said Blanka.

'Nearby gave it to me. She said I'd like these stories, and they'd help me understand why MI6 is called *Wonderland*.'

8.2

Friday, May 22
Stockleigh Pomeroy Farm, Banbury, Oxfordshire

*F*ox, who Nearby had introduced to Mike, was already there for the weekend indulging his sideline of 'horse whispering' on a colt Mike was having trouble with. Nearby and Paddington had gone on ahead with Fox to help Mike set up. When Blanka, Houston, Sokol, and Drox arrived at the farm early evening, the music was already blaring, and small groups of local girls high heels were mincing their way towards the barn.

The barn lay beside the Oxford canal. Together with Mike's narrow boat moored there, it been converted into a pirate hideaway. Curved wooden boards lined up at the front to make the bow of a ship, with a gangplank to the side. On the front of the hull hung a blue EU flag with stars on it, and above that a giant Jolly Roger. Hanging from the bow was a cage containing a skeleton armed with a cutlass. The gangplank was surrounded on both sides by water; two small trenches had been dug especially for the occasion.

As Blanka pulled up in her silver Mini Cooper, Fox, who was at the entrance to the hull admiring the handiwork, waved.

He had dyed his beard black and wore a loose red jacket, black waistcoat, and a wide red hat with a black feather. Looking like an older Captain Jack Sparrow, he even had a sash with a real cutlass held in it.

'Don!' Blanka shouted, jumping out of her car. 'Sorry we're late.'

'You're never late,' Fox replied. 'Like a true Libran, you arrive exactly when you want to. Let me look at you. What have you done with yourself?'

Blanka was dressed in a skeletal pirate costume, with a tattered white lace dress and a pearl-colored corset with marks of age. Her face was painted white with black eyes. A white bandana with ends fell down past her blonde hair; and, in a loop she'd sewn into her skirt, she had tucked a real cutlass. She drew it and cried, 'En garde,' at Fox in a pirate voice. As the others climbed out, Fox and Blanka fenced with their cutlasses. Sparks flew through the air, making Houston gasp with surprise while Sokol just rolled her eyes.

In marked contrast to Blanka, Houston was dressed in a black corset that gradually became less tightly laced to reveal some of her bust. On top of her head a black pirate cap rested atop a red bandanna. Her lower half was covered by a shawl covered in sparkling sequins, tied around by a deep purple scarf, in which a blunderbuss was tucked.

'You'd dare to challenge Blackbeard would you, you land lubbers,' shouted Fox, chasing Houston together with Blanka.

Suddenly Drox's voice thundered as he levelled an old-fashioned pistol at Fox. Drox was dressed as an 18th century British navy captain, with blue coat and collar complete with ruffles and tails, with his tricorne hat laying smartly on his silver hair. 'Surrender or die, Blackbeard,' he roared.

'Never,' Fox shouted back, turning to face him and brandishing his cutlass. Drox pulled the trigger and smoke burst out the barrel along with a flag that read

Bang, bang

When the laughing stopped, Blanka took Houston's hand and led her over to Fox. But all Houston did was stare at him shyly. As everyone gathered round, Fox handed them pirate eye patches. As he handed one to Houston, he smiled and said, 'I see you're quite the pirate. How's the new job?'

Houston had no memory of the aged soldier and stared at him in complete amazement.

Blanka spoke quickly. 'In case you don't know each other; Houston, this is Doctor Don Fox, MI6's token Canadian.'

'I take care of OhZone bodies,' Drox explained. 'And he takes care of their souls.'

'You seem very familiar...' Houston said, uncertainly.

'We *have* met,' said Fox. 'But you probably don't remember. Everyone tells me you have amnesia. I had my Lieutenant Colonel's hat on, and you were lost in the mountains.'

'I don't remember,' Houston said, feeling faint.

'It must be all the attention,' said Sokol sarcastically. 'Give her some air, won't you?'

Fox produced a chair and sat Houston on it.

Drox turned to Sokol, who was in a highwayman costume. Her make-up failed to hide the bruising around one eye socket, and her aquiline nose was still dark blue and crooked under the tape.

'What kind of pirate are you?' he asked her.

'Queen Boudica didn't tell me it was *pirate* fancy dress. But,' said Sokol, pulling her mask down to cover her swollen eye socket, 'I am dark and mysterious and full of allure. I could pass for a pirate.'

Houston, still a little confused, smiled up at her from her chair. 'You make a very tough pirate,' she said.

'No Diana?' Fox asked Sokol.

Sokol shook her head, 'She's visiting friends in Zürich.'

*L*ater, as Nearby finished showing her brother's farm to Houston, they passed Fox. 'I forgot to ask,' he shouted over the music, 'What kind of pirate are you, pray tell?'

'I'm a Russian pirate, in a ball gown,' Nearby shouted back as she and Houston headed into the barn. A light show illumined the inside of it. A big screen showed the opening titles of *Kill Bill* while Nancy Sinatra sang the title track *Bang Bang* over the speakers. Houston watched in alarm as a dance group, dressed as the ship's captain and pirate crew, performed a choreographed interpretation of the song. The women pirates surrounded the captain firing their flintlock pistols at him and blowing the smoke clear in time with the music. Nearby burst out laughing, but Houston was suddenly frantic.

'Didn't something horrible like this happen to Robinson Crusoe and two little girls? Weren't they shot down? Why is everyone laughing?'

From behind them a voice answered: 'There is a time to laugh and a time to cry. If we didn't laugh sometimes, we'd never *stop* crying.' It was Dr. Fox.

Houston burst into tears, thrusting her head on to Nearby's shoulder. 'Am I the only person with any feelings left?' she sobbed. In a surge of recognition, she pointed accusingly at Fox, 'You took my memories from me! Did you mean to take my feelings?'

Looking between them, Nearby swallowed hard and went pale. Reminded of her own teenage arguments with her father, she slunk off to a quiet corner.

Fox remained silent. When he spoke, it was in a measured tone. 'I haven't taken anything away from you that isn't being replaced with something better.'

'According to who?!' snapped Houston.

Just then the song's refrain blared out over the speakers

> Bang bang.
> My baby shot me down.

'And don't think,' he added, 'That every agent here hasn't had what happened to Olga and Emma seared into their minds. If they laugh, it's because they're trying to escape it.'

Houston was silent for a moment. Then she whispered, 'I don't even know what I'm escaping from.'

Drox came to her rescue. 'Ah, but what you're *escaping to* is a new life,' he said, scooping her off to the bar. 'I'm an American in Paris and you're a Bosnian in the CIA,' he said, making her laugh. 'Let me buy you a drink in Oxfordshire.'

The music changed to Bon Jovi's *It's My Life*. Blanka was first on the floor, stealing Fox from where he was standing. Blanka danced low in a breathtaking display and the aged Fox tried to match her move for move, as a crowd of locals and Mike's friends surged on to the dance floor around them.

At the bar Houston answered Drox's question about where she was staying. 'At Blanka's house,' she said and added, 'What exactly's wrong with her kidneys?'
'Ah, the dialysis machine,' said Drox sipping his French wine as the track ended with

It's my life.

Blanka stopped dancing and helped Fox (who had a stiff back) to his feet. They headed to the bar followed by Sokol and Paddington. 'I'm no Grinin, eh,' Fox declared sheepishly.
Paddington got Nearby's attention and made a sad face at her, persuading her to join the group.

Drox quickly explained to Houston, 'Both her kidneys are damaged. We don't know why. The left kidney has completely failed. The machine takes out her blood, and cleans it. She hates it being talked about…'
Once again the bar was crowded: Houston, Drox, Blanka, Fox, Sokol, Paddington and Nearby. In front of one of the horse stalls were real ale pumps, including one with an 'alien' logo and the name, 'Area 51.'
'Seven pints of Area 51, please barman,' Houston shouted.
'No, no,' said Drox holding up his wine. 'Make that six pints.'
'Six pints please, barman,' said Houston.
'Make mine "shandy," ' added Nearby.
Dr Fox held up his hand. 'Just a half, thank you, Houston. It's ten ounces this side of the Atlantic which is quite enough for me. I'm not as young as I used to be.'
The barman smiled and Houston smiled back. 'Five and a half *British* pints, please. One of them *shandy.*'
'One hundred and ten ounces coming up, Madam,' said the barman, hand pulling the ale into beer mugs with handles.
'A volume equal to seven US pints,' smiled Houston.
'Spot on,' laughed Drox. 'We have a new science-friendly recruit.'
'Of course, you can leave these things to Blanka,' said Fox, lifting his mug in the air. The last mug was handed to Nearby who 'didn't drink alcohol.' She sipped the shandy nervously.
'To the Iceni,' Fox toasted.
'The Iceni,' said the other six, and drank.
'I swam naked at Area 51,' Blanka confided to Houston.

'Before the aliens abducted you?' Sokol added, 'or afterwards?'

Nearby giggled and Fox turned to her, 'How's your shandygaff?'

'Oh yes, the old name for it,' said Drox.

'Fine, fine, grand. Thank you,' said Nearby drinking more and getting the head on her nose.

Fox downed his mug of beer, laughed and winked at Houston, who was sipping hers.

'How do you like Area 51?' Fox asked.

'I'm not sure,' said Houston.

'How are you getting on with everything else?'

'Like what?'

Nearby broke out in anxious giggles, while Paddington whispered to Drox, 'Why's she snapping at Don?'

'Beats me,' Drox whispered back.

'The passport names? The hair?' Fox said lightly.

'They don't match,' Houston said, determined to be sulky.

There was a loud murmur from Drox and Paddington.

'It's the best thing about you,' Sokol insisted.

'You can change your hair color,' laughed Fox. 'The gods know I've tried...'

Everyone except Houston laughed at his joke.

'Or your name,' Fox continued. 'Or both! You have options!'

'What I have is *amnesia*,' Houston shot back, angrily.

Drox looked at Blanka, who rolled her eyes, and was about to wade in when Fox took his leave.

'Enjoy it while you can. Glad to see you're making friends. Good night, all!'

As Fox left, Drox hurried after him.

Houston watched the pair disappear and downed half her ale. Putting her pirate eye patch over one eye, she turned back to the women around her. 'So, I have *options*?' she shouted.

The women cheered her conspiratorially. Sokol moved her eye patch over her good eye, giving her a truly frightening demeanour, and cheered after everyone else.

'Let me get this right then, shipmates. You don't have to marry the men to...'

The women shook their heads, the discussion a mutiny concocted between female desperados.

'Drox is hot,' Houston said, turning to Blanka, 'Can I invite him back? Paddington sputtered her drink while Nearby downed the rest of her shandy.

'He plays for the *other side*,' Blanka struggled to explain.

'The other side? What do you mean? A sorcerer playing for the dead?' Sokol, Paddington and Nearby pulled faces.

'The Russians?' Houston asked. 'Aren't they the other side.'

Sokol glowered. The others shrieked with laughter.

'He doesn't have sex with women,' Blanka finally said.

'Saves his energy for karate,' Paddington added. 'He's 9th Dan and teaches the Icenis –'

Sokol raised her bandaged finger. 'Unarmed combat,' she said, and everyone laughed. 'Colonel Doctor Fox, whom you should treat with more respect, young lady, teaches sword. Devices gadgets, Blanka psychic-mumbo-jumbo.'

'Don't get started on that,' Blanka shot back and abruptly headed to the floor to dance.

'There's too much going on around here,' Houston said and turned to Nearby, 'I don't see how I'll ever figure it out. Can you at least tell me where the restrooms are?'

'I'll do better than that,' Nearby replied. 'I'll show you.'

Houston followed Nearby out of the barn and past a porta-John with a queue by it. 'Come in the house,' said Nearby.

Inside the two-hundred-year-old farmhouse Nearby opened the cloak-room door. A pair of girls were finishing up after snorting charlie. 'Hey, cuz!' they said to Nearby.

'Hey, you two,' Nearby replied.

'This john is blocked,' said one of them, giggling, 'and there's a queue up-stairs. You been drinking Rae?'

The other kissed Nearby on the cheek as she passed, 'Got a girlfriend have you?' then cocked a smile at Houston, 'You looking for any gear, hon?'

'No, she's not,' snapped Nearby, pulling Houston away and out the farm house door. She led her the other way around the house, and behind the pirate ship. On the Oxford canal was Mike's Gypsy narrow boat with yellow lights twinkling over it and a Jolly Roger fluttering from its stumpy mast. Houston followed Nearby down the steep steps. Their heads brushed brass bells and sent them tinkling; then they took a turn into the galley. She watched as Nearby opened the cover to the ship-loo. 'The boat's not very grand but at least you won't be sold drugs,' Nearby said and ushered Houston in with a slight flourish. 'Go on now.'

As Houston peed, Nearby gazed out of a porthole at the nightscape across the fields – to the misty spires of Oxford. 'What did you think of London?'

'Big. Very big,' Houston said.

Is that all you can say? Nearby thought. But then again she was probably concentrating on other things. 'Wasn't New York big too?'

'Yeah, even bigger. Gigantic cloudscrapers.'

Used to saving water, Houston wiped herself but didn't flush.

'I guess you're a country girl,' Nearby said. 'Horses and goats. I mean… You come from a village then?'

'I'm more used to playing hide and seek with goats than dancing with men, that's true. But I don't really remember. Lieutenant Colonel Fox seems to think that's a good thing.'

Nearby looked down at her nails. They were green with silver specks. Olga had cooed over how pretty they were. A lump came to her throat as she recalled Olga and Emma's birthday party. Grinin's voice reverberated in her head

> Come on Olga, come on Emma,
> let's play the hiding game.

Houston's voice brought her back. 'I said, I love your nails.'

When Nearby looked up, Houston was checking her make-up in the mirror. 'Thank you,' Nearby said, pulling up her ball gown and sitting on the john. After peeing and changing her tampon, she held up the tampons pack. 'OhZones can *mind-control their periods*!' she said.

Houston's eyes opened wide. 'And you'll never guess what they use *tampons* for!' Nearby concluded, excitedly.

'What?'

'H–High – oh dear – it's classified. Blanka will brief you.' She changed the subject. 'I'm from a village too, you know. A village in Ireland.'

'I don't think I'm at all Irish,' Houston said. 'But I've got an Irish passport.'

'I know, Nightingale's a grand name,' said Nearby. 'London frightened me when I came here. It seemed so "big" to me too.'

Houston looked into Nearby's brown eyes, and took her hands. They would be friends. Close friends; they would share confidences. But all Houston said was, 'I'd *love nails* like yours.'

Nearby looked at Houston's long fingers covered in rings. 'Your wish is my command,' she chanted. 'Green or red? Let's have a look.'

Nearby led Houston out of the galley and through a door into the main cabin. Nail paint bottles were arranged on a stool beside a narrow four-poster bed. 'I'm the kid sister, so I'm sleeping here, it's quieter than the house,' said Nearby holding up three bottles. 'Which one?'

'Crimson, please,' said Houston eagerly, 'to match my shawl.'

'Come on, then,' said Nearby, sitting her on the bed, 'You can chose sparkly bits later if you want.'

★

Houston sat on the bed under the light, while Nearby completed the crimson nail paint. 'Do you mind if I tell you a dream I had last night?' Houston asked. 'It was kind of silly.'

'The sillier the better,' Nearby said.

'Well, I was sitting somewhere in a small room, just like this cabin, and I had my book *Brave New World* open on my knees. Somehow the book was my old life, but it was also my new life. I thought to myself, "What benefit would I gain clinging on to my old life?" Then it gets silly.' Houston stopped. 'Are you sure you want to hear it?'

'If it's *too* silly,' Nearby said, 'I just won't listen. How's that?'

'Okay. The book started shaking and, all of a sudden, the pages flew open and out popped Johnny Depp as Captain Jack.

'Isn't Johnny Depp popping out a good thing?' she asked, as she checked if the paint was dry.

'Yes,' Houston laughed. 'Then the pages flew back and forth and other men popped out from different places! Professor Hart, Will Hart and Drox. They danced around me and with me. But then a fourth man popped out. He looked like a grown-up Will, dressed in a red-and-white striped T-shirt like a big cabin boy.'

Nearby lifted up Houston's hands and blew on her nails. She knew about dreams as well as about astrology. But she wouldn't tell Houston the meaning of the 'the four men.' Not now. 'Stage one complete. Sparkle?'

'Thank you *soo* much. May I have gold specks, please?'

'Then what happened?' she said, starting to apply the gold speck paint.

'The fourth man was the one who took me home. Then I woke up. What do you think it means?'

'I think it means you will meet a mysterious stranger who will look more like Will than Johnny Depp. And you'll probably start fucking like rabbits.'

They both started laughing and Nearby herself was surprised by what she had said. When they had calmed down, she added wistfully, 'It makes me wish Will could have come to the party. Unfortunately, New York is across the pond and Will's stuck in school.'

'Do you know New York very well?' asked Houston.

'I've not been to the U.S. yet,' said Nearby. 'I'm MI6, not CIA like you and Blanka.'

'Well, Langley's massive. Her friend, the Admiral, is Director. Camp Swampy's a massive blur. New York is where I met Apollo, I mean Blanka. I call her *Apollo*.'

'I know, said Nearby, 'it's sweet.

'I don't want to be sweet, said Houston. 'I want to be a badass like Blanka.'

Nearby nodded, blowing on Houston's nails again. 'With the Russia Desk I go to Moscow, Petersburg, Kiev, Warsaw.'

'Blanka said the OhZone office is next to the Russia Desk.'

'Yes, it is,' said Nearby, lifting Houston's hands and displaying the completed nails.

Houston issued an excited purr and kissed Nearby on the cheek. 'Awesome. Thank you, they're beautiful!

'This is how we do it on the Russia Desk,' laughed Nearby kissing her on both cheeks, Russian-style. They laughed and then Houston became serious.

'I'm tired of trying to dredge up old memories, trying to figure out who I was. This is my *new* life and I want to create *new* memories…'

Nearby listened intently.

'I'm nearly twenty and I'm still a *virgin,* Houston lamented.

Nearby giggled. 'If you can't remember anything, how d'you know?'

'I know.'

'Sure you do, silly of me.' Nearby held up Houston's completed hands.

'How exiting then! Your nails are perfect and there are so many men to choose from!'

They laughed again. 'Why aren't you an OhZone?' Houston suddenly asked.

'I applied. F-F-Felicity-f-fast-track beat me.'

'You're stuttering again,' said Houston, puzzled.

'I don't usually,' Nearby said, looking down.

Suddenly, Houston set her jaw, and a look of fiery resolve appeared in her eyes. 'It's Felicity, isn't it. She scares you. If I become an OhZone, I won't be afraid of her. I will be like Mr Sherlock Holmes: I will catch and punish her for killing the prince and princess.'

'They were twin girls...' said Nearby.

'Whatever,' said Houston. 'You were going to be the next OhZone. How did she beat you?'

'I'd never held a gun,' said Nearby. 'It went against me.'

Houston stood. She was slight and barely five feet four, but she had a fire burning within her. Nearby had seen it in her own childhood, in the I.R.A. men. Houston reached out and pulled Nearby to her feet, the ceiling of the cabin making her bend slightly.

'You're so tall!' said Houston.

'Felicity's half an inch taller, and she looks just like me.'

'She looks like you, how terrible for you!'

Houston regarded the older woman. Suddenly, out of nowhere, a powerful intuition came to her. Not only would they share confidences. They would share a man. And Nearby would raise Houston's daughter. As quickly as it came, it was gone – like the mist in the morning, even – leaving behind a feeling of kinship.

'When I'm an OhZone I'll kick Felicity's ass,' was what Houston said. 'I won't let Blanka put me off.'

Outside, an owl hooted and Nearby smiled, 'They can hear like owls, and see through clothes and bags and doors.'

'Awesome,' repeated Houston, turning to the mirror with a gleam in her eye. She checked her makeup and put her pirate eyepatch back on. 'Now let's *see* about the *boys*.'

Nearby laughed and took her arm in hers, 'Sure, you're good to go. If you get carried away by a pirate – you can use my cabin.'

'Thank you,' Houston said, kissing her again. 'I'm not really sure –'

'Oh, there's music' said Nearby, showing her. '*CDs*! My brother's totally retro. Here's a t.v. and DVD. And you'll need these.' Nearby took a pack of Trojan condoms from her Iceni bag. Houston stared, transfixed by the Trojan design.

'Haven't you seen one before?' Nearby asked.

'I don't know,' Houston said.

'Better safe,' said Nearby popping the condoms into Houston's Iceni bag. She held up her own bag beside it. 'Look we match, we're Apollo's girls.'

'Yes,' cheered Houston at the top of her voice, '*Apollo's girls!*'

Nearby locked the door, placed the key in Houston's hand and led her on to the deck. It was a beautiful night and they looked at the stars. Houston pointed, 'There's Orion the sword fighter!'

'So it is,' said Nearby. 'Amazing. The things you know – and don't know. Now all you need is a swordsman in *this realm*.'

Nearby led the giggling Houston back inside the pirate-ship-barn. The most exotic cake imaginable had been placed upon a blue cloth with patterns imitating waves rolling across the sea; model islands with palm trees and sand dotted this sea, and pyres lit with giant candles shone over the display. The cake itself was a 'ship-rigged' pirate ship four foot long, made of chocolate and covered in icing. The hull was intricately decorated and a marzipan Jolly Roger flew from the middle mast. Rows of cannons, fifteen on each side, consisted of a chocolate straw (cigarello), inside of which was a sparkler.

A crowd of two hundred guests pressed around Mike and the cake. Mike was spectacularly turned out as an Irish pirate with an orange beard and green and white stripe, a stuffed parrot on his shoulder, and a wooden leg. He loudly called out, 'Sis,' and got the crowd to part for Nearby, who nervously tugged Houston along by the hand.

Nearby shied away from the limelight, but it was Houston who was at the real centre of attention. She quickly realized she was the object of keen attention for at least fifty male pirates, and several pirate women!

Mike gestured to the big clock (showing midnight) and whispered to Nearby, 'You're cutting it fine.'

'It's all right. Remember, you weren't born til half past.'

'And who is your gorgeous pirate-friend?' Mike asked.

'Her name is Houston,' said Nearby, 'she'll be starting work with me in a

week or so.' Mike gave Houston a big hug. Then he turned to the crowd and raised his stuffed parrot in the air for silence. 'Ahoy there shipmates!'
'Ahoy there Captain!' the crowd replied.
'Let's hear it for Banbury.' (Big cheer).
'Oxfordshire!' (Huge cheer)
'Ireland.' (Cheer from Nearby and Mike's sprawling family members).
'Now, as we all know, Banbury always had it's own time zone ten minutes behind Greenwich, so we'll ask our resident astrologer, my sister, in astrology-pirate costume...'
As the crowd laughed, Houston noticed the dark brown eyes of a young man dressed as a cabin boy who was intently trying to make eye contact with her.
'...ably assisted by her beautiful co-pirate from Houston Texas, to confirm whether it is indeed the correct time for my birthday.'
Houston nudged Nearby. 'The cabin boy from my dream,' she whispered.
Nearby lifted up her eye patch for a quick look; she whispered to Houston to watch out as Sokol had her eyes on him, but it was drowned out by more cheering.

Checking her watch and then looking out at the moon, she turned to her brother and intoned, 'Yes it is your birthday, it has been *foretold!*'
Everyone laughed and cheered. A small team lit the thirty sparklers which let off their canon charge, and the cake was cut and handed round.

Saturday, May 23

*T*he OhZone crowd had set up camp at a large table and, as the night progressed, Sokol and Paddington took turns tempting Nearby with drinks. 'What?' Paddington had declared. 'You've only had two of the beloved English sparkling-pear-ciders? It's an institution second only to the monarchy. A third, you must have!'

So Nearby sat watching the couples dance together whilst sipping her third *Babycham*. Sokol covered her bruised eye socket with the pirate eyepatch, softening her appearance, and took to the dance floor. She danced with the 'cabin boy,' a local Jewish lad of Nearby's age, nicknamed 'Big Ben.' He danced close, kissing Sokol who – Nearby recalled – had got off with him at the last party here. When the song changed, Sokol went back to the bar to get them cocktails. There she found Houston also enthusiastically ordering cocktails (Professor Hart had first introduced her to them two weeks earlier in New York).

Carrying a tray with three Snowballs on it, and now somewhat tipsy, Houston stumbled in the dark. She was only saved from falling by Big Ben. To express her 'gratitude,' Houston dragged him back to the OhZone table where he joined her in polishing off the first Snowball through two straws, while she talked excitedly to Blanka.

Paddington glared at Houston as Sokol approached with two Margaritas. Innocently, Houston tried to make introductions: 'This is a *Snowball*' (pointing to Ben), 'and this is *Ben*' (pointing to her drink).

Before Sokol could correct the mistake, Nearby burst out laughing and knocked her Babycham over Sokol's new Prada shoes. Nearby tried to mop them with napkins, helped by Blanka, while Sokol fumed.

This gave Big Ben an opportunity to lean close to Houston and say, 'Snowball here. I'm curious, you're obviously not from Texas, where exactly are you from?'

'The real question is,' she said, grinning, 'Where am I *going to*?'

As suddenly as she'd arrived, Houston jumped up, grabbed the other two Snowballs and waltzed Big Ben off towards the door, waving goodbye as she went.

Sitting down and rolling her eyes, Sokol grudgingly slid one Margarita across the table to Blanka, who sucked it delicately through the straw. 'I guess Big Ben's loss is my gain,' she said quietly.

Sokol threw her straw onto the ground, grunted and knocked back her drink.

'Careful,' Nearby gently warned Sokol. 'Even with your contacts in, I can tell your jealous OhZone eyes are washing over violet.'

'Listen, Irish Eyes,' Sokol replied. 'Actually, even I *wouldn't sleep with me*.' She lifted off her eye patch and Blanka and Nearby gasped. Her bruised eye socket was red and angry from the effect of the alcohol and the dancing. 'But, I won't forgive Houston in a hurry.'

The next song came on, The Weather Girls 1980s hit *It's Raining Men*, encouraging Sokol to bitch more. 'Five hundred years of democracy and peace – the only good thing to come out of Switzerland is our Swiss sniper rifles.'

'What a very odd thing to say,' teased Blanka. 'There's Swiss cheese, Swiss gold, cuckoo clocks –'

'Don's Omega watch,' chipped in Nearby.

'– and *Lindt chocolate*!' purred Blanka.

'The Large Hadron Collider,' added Drox who had just rejoined them.

Blanka looked surprised, 'Adrian Crider?'

Nearby burped then giggled, 'It's broken.'

The others looked at her. 'A weasel ate through the wiring,' she explained. Everyone looked even more puzzled.

'I mean the Collider, not Adrian Crider,' Nearby added, breaking wind.

'Jesus, Joseph and Mary, the Babycham.'

Drox nodded his confirmation. 'Quite true. In both cases.'

'Well,' Blanka concluded, 'Although Houston came with her own Swiss Army Knife, she's not using her Swiss name. She's *officially Irish*.'

'Yes, we'll have her,' said Nearby. 'We need everyone we can get.'

Trying to cheer Sokol up, Blanka started talking about the men on the dance floor and assured her that, 'there's no shortage of men out there.' But Sokol harped back to Houston and Big Ben as the song reached its chorus

It's Raining Men

'I don't know where she's going to have sex anyway, unless it's on the canal path,' she said, smugly. 'Half of Oxford is here. I brought a tent.'

It's Raining Men

'Alleluia,' shouted Nearby at the song, descending into drunken giggles.

It's Raining Men

⭐

*O*nce safely in Nearby's cabin, with her own t.v. for the first time, Houston put on a children's cartoon pirate show DVD, *Captain Pugwash*. She danced round the four-poster with Big Ben to the theme music (an accordion version of the *Trumpet Hornpipe*) while trying to play along on her harmonica.

'Look,' she shouted, pointing to the cartoon cabin boy on the t.v. 'It's you. Take the shirt off. Off, off...' she chanted, trying to catch Big Ben. On the show, Captain Pugwash said: 'We are alone in the midst of a hostile ocean.'

And a pirate replied: 'We're at the mercy of the sharks and the she-monsters.'

'*He*-monsters, Pirate Barnabas,' Pugwash corrected, 'most of them are masculine.'

Big Ben laughed as Houston pulled his T-shirt over his head. Her black corset had come largely undone, and Ben skilfully removed it. Houston screamed and then jumped into his arms sending him toppling on to the bed.

★

When Nearby went down to her cabin at two o'clock that night, she heard the sound of music coming from inside. She paused a second and recognised the voice of the great-big-bad lady of rock 'n' roll, Patti Smith, coming through the door rocking out *Because the Night*. I bet Ben picked that one, Nearby thought. She could also make out the sound of Houston singing.

Nightingale, H.J. Miss

she told herself. 'This nightingale will be chirping tonight.'

She smiled a big smile, turned on her heels and went back up the ladder. As she reached the deck, a rhyme came into her head

Ride a cock horse to Banbury Cross,
To see a fine lady upon a white horse;
Rings on her fingers and bells on her toes,
She shall have music wherever she goes.

Nearby couldn't resist. She stood on the deck, facing London, and solemnly intoned:

'And so it comes to pass, Great Britannia, in the God-fearing Christian county of Oxfordshire, that a young Muslim and a young Jew celebrate the communion of the flesh, giving new meaning to the '70s hippy slogan of our parents' generation, "Make love not war." God bless us all, each and every one of us.'

★

*A*s she wandered back toward the party, Nearby drifted into the farmhouse kitchen where she found Sokol, who had removed her contact lenses and was sitting alone sulking.

'I should have brought Puppy for company,' she said looking up.

'What you need is a nice cup of tea,' said Nearby.

'English tea is rubbish.'

'Yes, but look what I've got!' Nearby held up a packet of Russian imported tea, called 'Rasputin.'

Sokol jumped to her feet, kissed Nearby on both cheeks and raised her fist in the air. '*Fuck Houston*. We have *Russian tea*.'

"Oh, I think Houston will get all the fucking she needs tonight,' Nearby mumbled under her breath.

But as she poured Sokol the thick black tea, she commented gently, 'Nightingale's a sweet name and all that.'

Sokol put a Russian cigarette in her mouth and lit it with her Zippo lighter. She added a little milk and tried the tea. Then she nodded. 'It's good. Did you learn this in Moscow?'

'Yes, I did,' Nearby said. She paused before continuing. 'Our Nightingale already hates Felicity.'

'Ah…' said Sokol, drinking the tea. 'Nightingale, H.J. …Well, it doesn't take a genius to hate Felicity. But my enemy's enemy is my friend? Is that what you're saying?'

'Why not? Perhaps it's a new dawn,' said Nearby. 'Felicity and C are gone.'

'Really?!' she said with satisfaction. 'Blanka obviously hasn't told you yet.'

'Told me what?'

'About C's miraculous comeback? I'm afraid it's more of "same old, same old",' Sokol said, and caught Nearby up on the latest MI6 office politics.

★

*A*round 3:40 a.m. Nearby checked her cabin again. All was quiet. Deciding they must have left, she opened the door and was greeted by a full frontal display of Houston's lithe naked body gliding slowly up and down on top of Big Ben's manhood.

'Sorry,' said Nearby, backing out of the cabin. 'Lock the door,' she shouted through it. 'And if you're going to keep on doing it, make more noise so's people will know not to barge in on you.'

'Okay,' came Houston's answer a couple of seconds later, followed by peals of laughter. 'We'll do our best.'

8.3

*T*he party continued throughout the night unabated, though in the early morning hours the music wasn't quite as loud. Yet the biggest surprise, at least for Nearby, was still to come. As the moon was setting and the big currant bun of a sun was thinking about rising, she made her way out of the barn and heard the distant noise of a car engine. Nearby had trained as a car mechanic when she was a teenager and her hobby was rebuilding classic engines. She didn't have OhZone hearing, but she knew the sound of a Chevy small block V8 engine anywhere. She stuck her head back in the barn and yelled over the music, 'Listen everyone! Here's Jude!'

A few moments later Jude – who had returned that night from visiting with his parents and laying his brother to rest in Australia – roared into the farmyard in his red '69 Chevy Camaro. Blanka, Sokol and Paddington rushed from the barn, and ran out after Nearby to greet him.

★

*L*ater that morning a campfire burned. Everyone cooked English breakfasts outside and Mike's disco filled the morning air. The four Iceni danced arm-in-arm with Jude giving him their love and emotional support, but then Blanka started crying. Nobody said anything but they all knew.

Blanka's mother had been a woman who lived in and for the moment. Unexpectedly, her all-time favourite recording came on – carried over the fields and the canal by Natalie Merchant's voice – the 10,000 Maniacs *mtv unplugged* version of *Because the Night*. It had been made at the point in Kitty's life half way between her dream of The Goldheart, out at the Piper Alpha oil platform disaster, and her brutal murder in Rome.

Once she had started, Blanka couldn't stop. Not even when the song ended, the cock crowed and another song came on. Soon none of them were dancing. Silently, they escorted Blanka off the dance floor, leaving behind only the most diehard dancers.

⭐

*H*ouston and Ben brought the rising sun out with them. They reappeared, hand in hand, the ingenuous smile on Houston's face saying it all. Nearby's brother, Mike, got between them and slapped them both on the shoulder.

'So, Pirate Houston,' he said. 'You're new to England, but you've at least seen Big Ben now!' The locals laughed, more at the young lovers embarrassment than at the joke itself. Even Sokol smiled a little, secretly convinced she would have her turn at Ben again.

Nearby, who was consoling Blanka, watched Ben and Houston follow Mike up to the music consul and Ben take over the disco. 'Let's have some '70s,' Ben said as he cued a CD of '70s movie soundtracks, Houston at his side.

'Sure,' she said, 'who doesn't love '70s music?' The new song, *Everybody's Talkin'*, plunged Blanka back into her emotional reverie. She realised a part of her had never stopped crying for Kitty, and for all the other victims

All the human sacrifices to the god democracy.

And what about her own victims? It was as if suddenly she could feel the pain of them all. Ashamed, Blanka ran away from the crowd and found a room alone in the farmhouse. And there she started crying again, tears like raging seas, tears to wash away a thousand ships. She cried for the whole world of pain and separation, for all those lost in their worlds of games and lies. It seemed like nothing would make the pain stop.

⭐

*O*nce the sun was high enough to burst forth from behind the trees, Mike served the English breakfasts. Having seen Blanka enter the house and finally emerge from it, Nearby carried two plates to the canal where Blanka sat by the narrow boat playing the bass tag from *Everybody's Talkin'* on her 4-string acoustic bass. Nearby sat down next to her and sang the chorus.

Blanka set down her guitar and started to eat.

'Thank you for lending Houston your cabin,' she said as she bit thoughtfully into her English sausage. 'We need all the comfort we can get.'

A look of mischief that Nearby rarely saw appeared on Blanka's face. 'She's probably sore if Big Ben kept ringing all night.'

Nearby giggled, 'She can hardly walk.'

Blanka stared at her breakfast muffin. The look had disappeared.

'Is she set on being an OhZone?'

'She's heard about Felicity.'

'And she's going to bring her to justice? Set the world right? Being part AI doesn't make it any easier. Doesn't wipe away the tears,' Blanka said.

Nearby opened her mouth to speak, then stopped.

'Remember when we met?' Blanka said. 'The day I found you in the tree out here?'

'Go on, course I remember,' said Nearby.

'The man MI6 killed. The man we killed...' Blanka paused and looked Nearby straight in the eyes. Nearby stared back. Without the contacts to hide it, Blanka's eyes were obviously washing over purple. 'You spoke to him?' Blanka asked.

'He was a grand old gentleman. We talked about fruit trees. And I told him the four planet conjunction in Pisces was over his great pear tree.'

Blanka forced a smile. 'What did he say?

'He said, "I'll give you a leg up. Hide before MI6 find you. And don't come down 'til they're gone." So he gave me a leg up into the pear tree.'

'But you came down.

'You sang to me, your sweet voice called to me.'

'Come down, come down whoever you are,' sang Blanka.

Nearby laughed. 'At that moment, your horoscope showed Pisces entering your first house,' she said.

On an impulse, Nearby leaned forward, put her arms around Blanka and kissed her on the mouth.

Blanka didn't stop her, but she didn't really kiss back. Nearby didn't expect her to.

'Sorry,' said Nearby. 'Sometimes you're just so – '

'Depressed?'

'Among other things. Sometimes I think if I could really get inside you, close enough to comfort you. You're probably thinking about that poor man, aren't you? Doctor –'

Blanka set her finger over Nearby's lips. 'Follow the script – don't *ever* say his name! You were never there!'

Nearby nodded wearily, 'His only crime was writing a book.'

⭐

*H*ouston and Ben came giggling and shrieking, running around the walkway of the narrow boat.

Houston was in her swimsuit and Ben, back in cabin boy outfit, was trying to catch her.

Just as Ben caught hold of her, Houston dove off the end of the boat.

Ben proceeded to pull his clothes off as fast as he could, as Blanka's AI vision followed the girl as she swam underwater.

'She's hard to catch,' said Blanka.

'Quite *the catch*, don't you mean?' said Nearby.

'Well, Don somehow managed to catch her in the Dinaric Alps – and now we have her,' Blanka concluded, as Ben dove from the side of the boat.

From the canal came more shrieks as Ben caught Houston and tickled her. Houston leapt on him and ducked him under the water.

'I don't know what to make of all that,' Blanka suddenly said.

She felt distracted; her mind – her analog mind, her intuition – was flooding with something new. She didn't know what exactly, but she knew it was important.

She thought of Major Grinin, and the Grinin of her mind – with two arms – was giving her a double thumbs up.

Go, Blanka, go, he was saying to her.

At that point, Sokol came swinging along the tow path with her Fender Stratocaster in her good hand and a Russian cigarette in the other. Behind her ran Paddington, carrying a keyboard, thrilled to be standing in for Fox.

'Hoist the flag, Pirate Roadie,' Sokol called out to Nearby.

Nearby jumped aboard the boat and lowered the Jolly Roger at the mast.

'You taking it down? asked Paddington.

'Hell no,' said Nearby, unfolding another flag which she fixed above the Roger.

As Paddington set up her keyboard, Sokol plugged her Strat into the Marshall amp and tuned, using a plectrum and nursing the bandaged finger on her right hand. Meanwhile, Nearby raised the two black and white flags:

> the Jolly Roger with the Point-Blanka-target-logo flag
> fluttering above it

'Band practice,' said Blanka, jumping aboard, her OhZone weight setting the boat rocking. She looked at groups of partygoers appearing from the camping field and heading for the boat and, in an effort to conciliate Sokol's good will, approached her. 'What will be easiest on your hand, Sol? Probably not one of my songs. How about *Born To Be Wild*? or *Smoke on the Water*?'

Sokol looked across the water to Jude approaching on the tow path. She tossed her hair out of her eyes and flicked the cigarette into the canal where it hissed.

'*Sweet Home? Africa?*'

'I don't see any drums. And I don't see any Don,' said Sokol.

'We can still practice, Paddington's standing in for him,' Blanka cooed, smiling at Paddington.

Sokol raised her eyebrows. As Paddington started the synthesized keyboard track for *Africa*, Blanka came in on her electric bass.

A few bars later, Sokol tentatively came in on her Strat, observing Jude with the peripheral vision of her AI eyes.

But as Blanka sang the first line about drums echoing, Sokol shook her head and looked fixedly at the place where the drums should be.

Houston, recognising the melody, turned to Big Ben, 'My mother was from Africa,' she said.

'Wow, that's suitably exotic,' laughed Ben.

From the depths of her Iceni handbag, Houston produced her journal. In it were the postcard of the Alex Tower in Berlin, and the two Polaroids. Her goats, Cassie and Naughty, in the mountains, and the photo of her, aged seven, with her black mother Fatima.

Tentatively, Houston showed the Polaroid of her mother to Ben.

'Oh my, your Mum's so beautiful! Just like you. But you don't have her eyes,' he laughed.

'My dad was white. He was murdered in the Bosnian war,' Houston said, holding her head high. 'I was told. I don't remember. Before I was born. Well, I don't remember anything...'
Ben put his arm around Houston and kissed her.
'...Before last night,' she went on, kissing him back.

As Blanka sang the words, 'rains down in Africa,' Sokol looked straight at Houston, shook her head, and stopped playing, unhanding her Strat. 'I'm not playing this Africa now.'
Then she turned to Paddington. 'No offence intended,' she added.
'None taken,' replied Paddington, switching the synthesized drum track off.
Blanka looked at Houston who, now joshing around with Ben, was oblivious to the slight. Then she turned to Sokol, trying to avert a band war and trying really hard not to swear.
'Whiskey November, Bravo?' [What now, bitch?]
Sokol smiled. 'Let's try *Sweet*, Queen B,' she said.
'Hell yeah,' joked Nearby, and then wished she hadn't because the partygoers all watched her as she walked up to the second mic to do backing vocals.

Jude climbed aboard the boat, rocking it too, and smiled at Sokol (who shrugged back). He sat down by Houston and Ben as Point Blanka launched into their cover of Lynyrd Skynyrd's *Sweet Home Alabama*.

'One, two, three,' called Blanka.
The Southern rock song was different sung by two Catholic convent girls with a grumpy Russian on lead guitar.
'Turn it up,' said Blanka before she sang the first verse.

Mike and quite a crowd had gathered when, four minutes in, Blanka and Nearby sang

> *Sweet home Alabama*
> *Sweet home*

Abruptly, the power plug was pulled, cutting Paddington dead on the keyboard and leaving their voices trailing off to nothing.
'Now what the fuck already!' swore Blanka.

Jude stood with the power plug in one hand, and his Samsung cellphone in the other.

He crossed the deck to Blanka and addressed her:

'We've traced Felicity.'

'Da!' shouted Sokol, her AI hearing catching his words. She punched the air, unstrapped her Strat and threw it across the deck to Nearby, who scrambled to catch it.

Blanka nodded, quietly assimilating the information.

'To a bullion dealer in Rio,' continued Jude. 'I'm heading to Brazil right now.'

Houston jumped to her feet and opened her mouth to speak.

Still looking the other way at Jude, Sokol shoved her – gently – off the side of the boat and into the water. 'No you don't,' Sokol said. 'This one's for me.'

Although Mike and the crowd couldn't hear the conversation, people knew something of great significance was transpiring, and watched Blanka as she quietly unstrung her Fender and stood it on its guitar stand.

A lone voice from the water cheered, 'Apollo!'

Blanka smiled at Houston, and then turned back to Jude and Sokol.

'I think Jude will need an OhZone,' Sokol said. 'May I go?'

'Yes of course he will. Felicity is still an OhZone in all but name,' Blanka said, smiling at the pair of them. 'She even has a captured OhZone Scanner.'

Sokol nodded gravely.

'You go on,' Blanka said, 'I'll catch up with you there. Report in on your new Scanner, Sol.'

'Wilco,' said Sokol as she jumped off the boat and headed for the car, followed by Jude ☡

Lava Jato (Car Wash)

Stille Nacht, heilige Nacht,
Silent night, holy night,
Hirten erst kundgemacht
Shepherds quake at the sight;
Durch der Engel Halleluja,
Heavenly hosts sing Alleluia!
Tönt es laut von fern und nah:
Glories stream from heaven afar,
Christ, der Retter ist da!
Christ the Saviour is born,
Christ, der Retter ist da!
Christ the Saviour is born!

JOSEPH MOHR & FRANZ XAVER GRUBER -
FOUR GENUINE TYROLEAN SONGS -
TRANSLATED BY JOHN FREEMAN YOUNG

9.0

Flamengo Município, Rio de Janeiro, Brazil

9 WEEKS AFTER THE KILLINGS On Wednesday May 20, 2015, Felicity finally tracked down the man *she* had been searching for in Rio. Jim Evans was known by a lot of names, but in the surveillance business he was referred to as Bob Blog. Felicity had never met him, but the rumours of what he had done for rogue agents were legion at MI6. The most chilling, and damning, was that he had helped agent OhZone 1 vanish off the grid after the celebrity assassination.

Bob Blog liked to keep a low profile. When, wearing a black wig and disguised as an Amazonian peasant, she found him, he was working as janitor at a rundown joint called Hotel João Severino. As she watched Blog mop a third floor corridor, her vision told her he was unarmed. Despite the fact she was an OhZone and a few inches taller than him, he somehow loomed. Damn, he's built like a brick shithouse. Adopting polite Portuguese and holding out her hand, she started, '*Boa tarde, Senhor.*'

Blog ignored her hand and said, '*Senhor está no céu,*'(the Lord is in heaven).

'*Eu estou olhando,*' she continued

'Whiskey Tango Foxtrot,' he spat at her, swearing under his breath in Portuguese. Catching her by surprise, he pushed her against the wall.

'*Eu sou –*'

'Know who you are,' he growled. 'Heavy for your size, ain't you?' Fingering her left ear tip with fat grubby fingers, he whispered, 'Lose your helix to Grigori before you killed him?'

'If you know who I am, you know I could kill you with one hand,' she hissed back.

'You won't, you got other business.'

He was right: she hadn't come to kill him. It'd be the end of Rio as a hideout and she'd never get Sokol's Scanner unlocked. She turned her face away: his breath stank, what had he been eating? Hera, she said internally, cut adrenalin by 90 percent; override all emotions. 'Keep your hands to yourself,' was what she said as she gently but firmly freed herself from his grip.

'Got the music box?' he asked.

'Not here,' said Felicity.

'You notice anybody stopping and staring at you on the way?' he asked.

'I'm a good looking woman, hard to hide that.'

'You're foxtrot five ten, hard to hide that,' was Blog's response. 'Your average campesina is five one. You couldn't pass for one in a million years. Get out, come downstairs at 22:00. And dress in man's clothes.'

Felicity returned that evening, as Dr Casadevall carrying her doctor's bag. She looked around for Blog in the basement for several minutes, before he suddenly appeared from behind her. Carefully checking the street, he conducted her inside the janitor's office and locked the door behind them. Unlocking a closet he switched on a consul and took out a harness of wires. 'Put down the bag, take off your jacket and shoes,' he ordered,

Felicity complied and Blog spent a good two minutes sweeping her for bugs and G-tracking devices. 'Hands in the air, turn around slowly.'

The consul picked up her AI vision and hearing and internal GPS but otherwise nothing.

'So you're Francisco's swallow?' he said, locking the closet. Felicity was shocked he knew this, but didn't let it show.

'He always had impeccable taste,' he said, smiling for the first time.

'You know him? Have you seen him?' she blurted out.

'I know everyone, I seen nothing,' Blog laughed, holding out his hand. Felicity opened her doctor's bag and handed Sokol's ℧Scanner over to him.

'Stay there,' he said, walking to the far end of the office and unlocking another closet which had a lead lined door. He stepped inside and placed the Scanner into a portable X-ray machine. He punched a green button, stepped back and closed the door. When he heard a beep, he opened the door and studied the digital X-ray image on a screen.

He returned to Felicity and examined the outside of the Scanner through a loupe. 'Sokol's all right,' he mumbled. He squinted through the other eye at Felicity. 'Presume FFT don't want to call home.'

'I thought a working Scanner might be useful.'

Blog laughed, 'A working one, yes. And lucrative, worth a fortune on the black market. My price is a million to crack it.'

'Reals? said Felicity

Blog's face darkened again. 'Fuck with the boys an' girls in Wonderland, hon. Don't fuck with me.'

'A million dollars? You're kidding. I'll just keep it,' she said, taking it back from him.

'You need money, I'll give you three million.'

'It's worth twenty times that.'

'*Workin'* it is.' Blog shrugged, 'Got a better offer to crack and unlock it from OhZone, take it.'

A check with Hera confirmed what Felicity already knew: there was no one else. How could she get the money? She couldn't access her UK or US accounts, but she had six figure savings in a Swiss bank account she'd opened many years ago in a male identity. It had never been compromised. And there was her income as a doctor at the Rio childrens hospital. That would add up quickly if she started 'collecting' and 'selling't again.

'Half now, half as a loan,' she said.

'How does ten percent interest sound?'

'A bit high,' said Felicity

'Per month,' Blog continued.

'How about a night with me,' said Felicity undoing the belt of her pants and tugging them down a little to reveal her French waxed 'landing strip'.

'FFT,' laughed Blog, '*Felicity-fast-track*, wondered when that celebrity was coming out... Wonderland's wonderpussy! Take off five hundred not five hundred thousand.'

Felicity resisted the temptation to slap him. Her OhZone slaps, no matter how much she restrained herself, seemed to leave a mess. 'Five per cent,' she said.

'Okay, because I admire balls in a woman. Balance over two years.'

Felicity grinned.

'I'll always be able to trace you,' he continued. 'If you don't pay on time,' he continued, 'I'll lock it again.'

'Deal.'

'Come back this time Saturday with the half million in bullion.'

'Gold bullion?' exclaimed Felicity.

'Oh baby it's a wild world, catch up,' he joked as he did the math. 'That's thirteen kilos.'

First thing the next morning, disguised as Andreas Casadevall again, Felicity visited Lima S.A. bullion dealers in Downtown.

'I need the bullion Saturday,' she said.

'That's okay,' the dealer replied. 'We're open.'

Then she wired the money to Lima S.A. from the Credit Suisse account in Zurich.

That was her mistake.

9.1

Thursday, May 21
Zürich, Switzerland

*F*elicity didn't have aircraft passenger list surveillance, a team behind her, or even Francisco watching her back. But she trusted in her wits, her disguises, her cunning, and what, for some reason, she felt to be the homeyness and safety of Brazil. And also in her luck. Nobody, least of all Felicity, was expecting anything from Diana, the numbed and grieving widow.

But Felicity's luck had just run out. Credit Suisse had received a tip off from the UNHCR that she had an account with them under a false name. They'd flagged it

> **— GESUCHT WEGEN KINDESMORD**
> **— WANTED FOR CHILD MURDER**
>
> *Robinson, Felicity Mrs / aka Furness, Felicity Miss*

In Zürich, one of the Grinin's friends who worked inside a bank had been hacking the system each day looking for large transfers from suspect accounts. Within seconds he was able to tell Diana the amount of the transfer and the city. Four hours after the wire transfer was made, she was in Zürich. Diana had been grieving the massacre of her family. But with typical Russian passion, her silent resolve was nothing less than to have Felicity cut up into small pieces and fed to her late husband's tropical fish. Those who knew her best were chilled by the fierceness of her need, not just for revenge, but for some impeccable form of justice beyond what the law could offer. This was not the Diana they knew. She had changed. But they also understood the horror of what she had been put through by Felicity.

When her friends met her at the Zürich-Kloten airport, Diana was full of ideas. At first she insisted on going to Rio herself. But her friends persuaded her against it. 'You are not a professional assassin,' they said.

'She is. And this woman is no Blanka, she won't play fair. You'll end up like Grigori.'

That gave Diana pause for thought. They also told her they had contacted a unique hitman, one who really did exemplify 'honour among thieves.' The invisible, and invincible, German

J.T. Wenders

known in the criminal and Intelligence worlds as, '*Stille Nacht*' – meaning Silent Night, but pronounced '*Stiller*' – because of his habit of distilling elaborate poisons to kill his victims, and a preference for killing them during the hours of darkness.

In fine Swiss sunshine, Diana strolled down Bahnhofstrasse and turned into number 9 again. After the usual formalities she took the hundred and twenty thousand dollars from the safety deposit box in Zürcher Kantonalbank (Stille Nacht's fee and an additional twenty thousand for expenses). She put the expenses in an envelope and tucked it inside her coat. Putting the bulk of the cash in a knapsack, she left with it on her back. As she crossed the River Limmat on foot at Rathausbrücke, she passed a children's merry-go-round, and swallowed hard.

Her friends waited discretely for her at a restaurant on the east side of the river, half way to the rendezvous. They completed the journey to the Zoological Museum at the University on foot. At the aquatic exhibit on whales Diana walked past a small middle aged man wearing coke-bottle eyeglasses. Her friends turned her around, and they returned to sit with the man who had a pockmarked face and a big nose. Stille Nacht turned to Diana and bowed politely, 'Sočuvstvuju Vašej utrate,' he said in Russian. 'Pust' zemlja budet puhom.'

Diana smiled, surprised.

'My Russian is very limited,' he continued in German. 'But I thought as curator of mammals you would like this. Whales care very affectionately for their children.'

Diana thought to herself, what can a paid assassin possibly know about a mother's love for her children? Or a wife's love for her husband? Switching to English, she said, 'My German is also limited, but I thank you for your expression of sympathy in my native tongue. What I want from you is to kill this Robinson creature so she tastes her own medicine.'

Stille Nacht, expressionless on the outside, laughed on the inside. He liked this woman! Her body; so pretty and yet so fierce – like a leopard or a jaguar. He would call the operation in Brazil 'Car Wash.' Yes, Car Wash, *Lava Jato*. And he would brush up on his Portuguese on the plane.

He took a minute before he replied to Diana. 'I understand. …Please know there is *no recall*. Are we clear? You cannot text to abort the hit.'
'We are clear,' said Diana. 'Jan has told me how you work.' She handed him the knapsack and took the envelope from her coat pocket.
At this point Diana's friend, Jan, injected himself into the conversation. 'You have the wire transfer details and photographs of this Felicity-fast-track?' he said in German. 'It's a favour, at ninety percent discount, we're all agreed? That's a hundred thousand there.'
'Now I meet the widow, I'm changing the arrangement,' Stille said. Jan looked at Diana, confused.
Jan's wife squeezed his arm: a sign to be quiet.
'I'll work for expenses,' continued Stille, turning to Diana and smiling for the first time, showing his gold fillings. He handed her back the knapsack and took the envelope from her hand.
'I know some of the history of this killer. Large birthmark on her right shoulder blade, date of birth December 31st, 1983.'
'I thought she was twenty-four,' said Diana.
'No, she's older, no time to explain now. My plane leaves in two hours,' Stille said, standing. 'But understand, I want justice done too.'
Diana jumped to her feet, 'Let her know *who's sent you* before she dies. And report back to me… I won't change my mind!' She had tears in her eyes as she kissed him goodbye, Russian-style, on both cheeks.
'I understand,' he said. And then he vanished into the crowd at the museum.

Stille Nacht woke up in First Class, as Houston had a few weeks before. The Felicity-fast-track assignment was a new challenge. His associate, who would be paid his normal rate, had already arrived in Rio. And he had just the poison to deal with an OhZone. Like Stille himself, it was derived from a descendent of the Second World War: Zyklon B, the infamous chemical weapon developed for genocide at Auschwitz. Stille's Jewish mother, Eve, had been one of the few to be found alive when the Red Army reached the complex of death and work camps on its westward march on Berlin. The date January 27, his mother's birthday, was branded on his soul by the Auschwitz furnaces.

She had turned nineteen the day the Russians liberated Auschwitz. The Soviet Union was forgiven for every inhuman act it had subsequently committed, by that one supreme act of Grace: freeing the unknown and seemingly forgotten ones –including his mother – who had avoided being turned into soap and candles in the showers of death. He *never* accepted an assignment to close-the-file on a Russian national or anyone born on January 27th.

'The whole world's in Auschwitz,' a t.v. documentary maker, a woman as fierce as Diana Grinin, had told him in the '90s and he had never forgotten. That woman was Kitty Maguire. He knew much of her subsequent history, including the fact that Kitty's daughter, Blanka, had tried so hard to protect Diana's husband and children. Kitty had made a deep impression on him. As Stille looked out of the aircraft window down at the sea of indigo, he thought

Who killed Kitty?

After the Second World War ended, his Mother had returned to Germany, married and given birth to him, before she and his father emigrated to Israel. Stille had a successful career as a chemist (he ran a large chemical works) before becoming a garbage cleaner determined to eradicate as much evil from the world as possible. It was his way of righting the balance. He was known as the best in the world for poisons and he'd distilled a new poison in his chemical laboratory. He had longed for an opportunity to try it out. Racist, anti-semite and child murderers got priority on his waiting list. Felicity-fast-track was all three. His 'Plan A' for her was to spray molecular acid on her contacts. That would melt them onto her AI eyes and the human tissue underneath, blinding her, so that he could then execute her. Whenever he prepared for a new job, Stille would meditate and repeat a sutra from the *Anguttara Kikaya*, 'Given to the Dying' that his mother had taught him to recite as a boy. It ended with these words

> *Birth and death are only a door through which we go in and out.*
> *Birth and death are only a game of hide-and-seek.*
> *So smile to me and take my hand and wave good-bye.*

9.2

Saturday, May 23
Rio de Janeiro, Brazil

*B*y the time the MI6 station in Rio put out an A.P.B. for Felicity, Sokol and Jude were flying southwest over the Cape Verde islands en route there.

At Lima S.A. in Downtown, Felicity packed her thirteen kilo bars of gold into a hard-tshelled Samsonite. Locking it and lifting it with ease, she shook hands with the man, stepped out of the bullion dealer into the street, and flagged down a yellow-cab.

Looking like a thousand other Rio yellow-cab drivers, Stille's timing was so good that his cab was the one that Felicity flagged, driving her the first stage of her journey home. Later, he watched her at Ipenema beach, not so crowded in winter, with the temperature a mere 75 Fahrenheit. He didn't know what she was doing with the gold, but he guessed she would take it to its destination after dark. He was correct. The shortage of OhZones, their illnesses, their vulnerabilities had been his reading matter in the last two days. He thought of David and Goliath. An OhZone a full six inches taller than him was certainly a Goliath. But she's sloppy, he thought, as he watched her promenade down to the beach and pop into the English bookshop. It will be like taking wool from a kitten.

Fifteen minutes later Stille Nacht sat in his yellow cab as it went through a Petrobras car wash on Avenida Ayrton Senna. The name he'd given the Op, *Lavo Jato*, was most appropriate he'd decided. He was, in his own way, a car wash. The garbage collector, the honey wagon for evil. As the giant green soapy brush rolled up his windshield he thought, MI6 had been really scraping the barrel to employ her. But to make Felicity suffer and give a name to that suffering? As the soap was rinsed off his taxi, Stille decided he would prolong her death by using just a low dose of his Zyklon F. She drank bottled water, six bottles a day, but the poison would go through her skin when she showered. Not enough to kill her, but enough to considerably slow her reflexes.

Later that day, as Sokol and Jude touched down at Galeão International

Airport, Stille overrode the security systems at Felicity's house and easily cracked her safe. He didn't see the Scanner because Bob Blog had it, but he did find Sokol's ΩArmor and the bullion, and he placed a minute tracking device inside one of the gold bars. He soldered the surface gold back in place and waxed the mark invisible. It didn't even cross his mind to take the gold. That wasn't his job. Stille was an ethical assassin. Only one other person like him in the world. He saw her once in a blue moon. Kitty's daughter, Blanka.

★

*T*he ghost of Major Grigori Grinin had been following Stille and he laughed to himself as he saw the little man crawl into Felicity's roof space to install the small pump to inject his Zyklon F into Felicity's water supply. 'Come on Olga, come on Emma / Come on Johannes Stille,' he chanted to himself using Stille's first name. 'Let's play the hiding game.'

Grinin had been watching Felicity too, without making himself visible: he had learnt how to control that. At 5 p.m. Felicity was in a bar on Mojitos, watching the sun set over Ipanema beach, for the last time.

He laughed to himself as he watched her skimming through the paperback she had bought, Cormac McCarthy's *No Country For Old Men*. He even helped the breeze ruffle the pages to the end. He'd been instrumental in delaying Francisco, with mishaps like his passport disappearing and his cell phone falling in the john. He hadn't wanted to hurt the man. Why would he want to hurt the man who'd first translated the Fatima Secret from Lucia's original Portuguese handwriting?

But Felicity was quite another matter. Knowing what Stille Nacht was doing, Grinin's original plan had been to sit in Felicity's overstuffed easy chair projecting thoughts of water falls in oases in vast deserts to her in the shower. His projections would induce an urgent thirst so great that she would foolishly gulp down mouthfuls of the water.

At 6 p.m. Felicity was back at her house and showering. Grinin's ghost relaxed as he saw her brushing her teeth in the shower water, something even Stille had not foreseen. The woman was obsessed with cleaning her teeth.

*A*fter the shower, Felicity dried herself and dressed up for her evening meeting. Under the shirt, slacks and jacket of her Dr Andreas Casadevall disguise, she donned the thin liquid Armor. She carried a 321 with ℧Nightsight and clip of six standard .45 rounds in a high holster, and the P238 micro-compact she had stolen from Sokol in her jacket pocket. She was surprised when she staggered slightly as she lifted the case of bullion. It wasn't heavy for her, but she was sweating. It was quite dark when she got out of the second taxi and made her way along Rua Paissandu. She had been feeling good about her new life that day, and her thoughts had kept turning to Francisco. Why hadn't she heard from him? she thought as she flagged down a third cab.

Sitting in it, she was gripped by a sudden bout of nausea she was barely able to control. Had she got a fever? She knew OhZones were prone to dehydration, so she got the cab to drop her at Bar N, on Praia do Flamengo. She ordered a Caipirinha; while the bartender made it, she drank half a quart bottle of mineral water. But it didn't really make her feel better. As she stood outside at a table in the cool evening breeze and sipped the Caipirinha, she felt slightly better: she was living the life.

She took out her iPhone for the third time but didn't notice that there was zero signal. Catching herself, she checked the time in her head. It was 21:00:99. That's very strange, she thought.

*N*o Scanner, no link to Bob Blog. It didn't matter though. Stille knew Blog's reputation, and knew he was in Brazil. The trace in the gold bar was more than enough for him to track Felicity. As he continued to follow her route, he sat in his yellow cab oiling his garrotte wire inside his doctor's bag. The garrotte was a nice touch, he'd do it for Diana; but for an OhZone he needed to have a range of options. When she stopped at Bar N, he parked the yellow cab a block past her. He reviewed the extensive armoury in his two doctor's bags, knapsack and a case marked 'transplant blood.' He undid the case and packed the Barrett Model 95 'anti-materiel' rifle in the knapsack. It had a sawn-off barrel with a silencer fitted. The small cylinder marked oxygen looked surprisingly out of place as he lifted it out of one of the bags. It was filled with molecular acid. There were several places where he had attached wall anchors for the Barrett. If, as he had correctly surmised, she would cross Flamengo Park in the direction of the Ascensão favelas (Ascension shantytowns) the .50 BMG (Browning machine gun) rounds would get her attention. Get her to face towards him.

He wouldn't claim to be an expert on killing OhZones (only one was known to have been killed in action: by a depleted uranium round fired by Felicity) but he loved the research. An OhZone's eyes were so sensitive – it was their weak point. A high frequency laser would not only temporarily blind them, but would also confuse their AI (contained largely in the optical system). It would render Felicity's actions uncoordinated, that's if the poison wasn't causing confused and uncoordinated actions already.

As Felicity left Bar N, Stille took time to appreciate her Dr Casadevall disguise. Nice, he thought. MI6 always were good with prosthetics.

★

*B*ob Blog had told Felicity to call when she was half an hour away. Stifling a cramp in her guts, she called him on her number two burner, looking dreamily at the lights on Sugar Loaf Mountain. While she waited for him to pick up, she finished the quart of water.
'Hello,' she said when he answered.
'You got the payment?' he asked.
'Yes,' replied Felicity. 'I'm just shooting the breeze.'
'Okay,' laughed Bob Blog. 'It's ready. Careful you don't overshoot,' and hung up.

Felicity had two ways of getting to Hotel João Severino: one was across the deserted end of Flamengo Park, the other route went around on the highway but was better lit. Her AI Vision suddenly flickered. About to put her drink down, she gasped. Along Praia do Flamengo she saw a Rasputin-like man in an ornate Russian housecoat leave a building, stare at her and wave – with both arms. Felicity's head spun and her AI mind blimped out. The glass tumbled and smashed on the sidewalk. She looked down nauseously, 'Bugger.'

When she looked up again the highway was empty. That decides it, she thought drunkenly. Not the 'highroad'; I'll take the 'low road.'
Most of Flamengo Park was frequented by tourists who flocked there for the many museums and art galleries. But, after dark, the south end (being smartened up for the Rio 2016 Olympic Games the following year) was neglected because the police force were so short of petrol. The anti-corruption investigation *Lava Jato* or 'Car Wash' – to clean up the state of Rio – was yet to really kick in. Just inside the gate, Felicity retched, not at the sight of the dealers and small-time gangs sitting around a towering Nativity statue and fountain, but at the stink of her own breath. Something was wrong, seriously wrong. But she still managed to put on an act and walk with the confidence of a hit woman. Not only was she armed and dangerous, she told herself, but she had OhZone armor underneath her man-clothes. The dealers leered at her, but she was particularly struck by a small man with a pockmarked face and a big nose. He looked familiar.

Only her training kept her walking on autopilot. Slowly it dawned on her where she had seen him before. In the movies and in her dreams – he looked just like Dustin Hoffman's Rizzo out of *Midnight Cowboy*. This would make a great movie, she thought: *Return of the Midnight Cowboy*. The man was artistically backlit, by the half-moon which was starting to set. She looked at the soft moon shadow which he cast, and laughed at it.

(This Rizzo had more dirty tricks than the movie version, including jamming Felicity's Brazilian iPhone. 'Killing this OhZone is going to be easier than I thought,' Stille told himself, as he watched her.)

As the poison took effect, Felicity burped and recoiled at the stench of stomach acid rising up her throat. To distract herself she put the iPhone earphones in her ears and tried to find the theme from *Midnight Cowboy*. For some reason she couldn't find it. Instead she played a live cover by Stephen Stills. It went

> *Everybody's talkin' at me*

Not nearly as good as Nielsen, she thought, heading for the alley that would cut through to Hotel João Severino. She didn't notice that Stille had marked the back of her jacket electronically. If she hadn't been bored in Paris and skipped the training, she'd have recognized the warning signs. If she hadn't been playing her iTunes she'd have heard a text come in on her number one burner. She also didn't register one other important thing: her AI sensors picking up that a man had just parked a truck at the end of the alley, blocking the exit.

That man was Stille's associate.

⭐

*T*he alley was lined by high buildings on either side. A fire escape from a building opened out half way along it. Just behind the door Stille screwed the sawn-off barrel onto the Barrett. With one step into the alley, he could click it into the wall mount and empty the magazine of five .50 BMGs into her back. Then, if the ΩArmor held out, she'd turn to face him. He would then fire the laser in her sensitive OhZone eyes, followed by the high pressure molecular acid. Finally, when she was helpless, he would walk up and whisper in her ear, 'From Major Grigori Grinin, Emma, Olga and Diana.' And finish her off with the garrotte. That was his plan. He visualized it carefully, so when it came time to act, he could act quickly, without thinking.

⭐

*O*h bugger, I have to pee, thought Felicity, I can't wait. She clutched her bladder and glanced up and down the alley – tall buildings, a fire escape, a truck at the end. Could she squeeze through? Probably not. She'd have to go back around. The buildings seemed to bend and melt and then fall in on her

Everybody's talkin' at me

The song talked about going where the sun kept shining. But she was already there. Wasn't she? She was in Rio already! she laughed inanely. Then Felicity tasted undigested food in her mouth. I'm gonna chuck, she thought. AI lights flashed in her eyes; her weak right leg gave way. She stumbled, spun right around, and ended up facing the truck blocking her exit.

(Activating the laser and pressurizing the acid gun, Stille prepared to step into the alley.)

I'm peeing myself! thought Felicity in alarm. She squatted forgetting she wasn't in a dress and toppled over onto the ground. 'Shit,' she groaned. She struggled up on to her legs, tugged her slacks down, squatted again and peed in a fast spray on to the littered floor of the alley. The urine was pale blue and she retched at the smell of it, spitting out the sick from her mouth.

She stared at her pee as it formed a rivulet, ran across the alley and trickled into a drain. Then her bowel heaved at the same time as her stomach. 'Oh, God,' she said aloud.
At that moment Stille stepped into the alley and pointed the Barrett Model 95.
'I don't think God's going to help you,' he shouted.
Felicity's eyes washed over violet – silver – purple –

> *Everybody's talkin' at me*

and never before seen turquoise and green. The music in her head changed to the martial *Ride of the Valkyries* from Wagner's *Ring Cycle*.

Felicity saw Major Grinin floating face up in his aquarium. There were red and orange and white fish. Clotted blood was dissolving from his beard into the water. His big brown eyes glowed. Then she heard his voice

> *I was expecting you tomorrow, could we reschedule?*

She felt her nipples go suddenly erect at the memory. Heard herself say, 'Sorry, I don't reschedule appointments.'
Then she lurched forward and upchucked the quart of water.

Hallucinations – visions – kept coming, obliterating the reality of the filthy alley she was in and what was happening to her body. She heard children's voices mixed in with the Wagner. Mothers' screams. Children's cries. Is hell like this? she thought as she jerked forward and hurled again, this time lunch.

She saw an SS officer with a white doctor's coat over his uniform and a gap in his teeth. He was whistling Mozart. There were horrific train wheels, screeching on rails, train whistles. Children's screams again. She saw her lookalike – Nearby.

Then twin girls, naked, howling, tied to a bare wooden operating table. The *Ride of the Valkyries* echoed around her, inside her…

'Jesus I'm gonna shit myself,' moaned Felicity just as the five .50 BMG rounds powered into the Armor on her back – thrusting her flat on her face into the pool of her own vomit. Her AI mind spun wildly out of control to a random line she remembered from the movie *No Country For Old Men*.

The man, the killer from the movie, was sitting in the overstuffed easy chair at her house – but he looked like Rizzo from *Midnight Cowboy*. The man's words echoed in her static-filled mind

> *When I came into your life your life was over.*
> *It had a beginning, a middle, and an end.*
> *This is the end.*

HG

End of Book 2

The Hiding Game

Dear Reader,
If you are enjoying the saga so far, please tell
your friends, and you might like to:

★ Give the books a star rating or review on Amazon,
goodreads and your bookstore's site

★ Follow or message me for updates
Twitter — Instagram — Facebook

★ Pre-order the next book

And remember, "help is just around the corner."

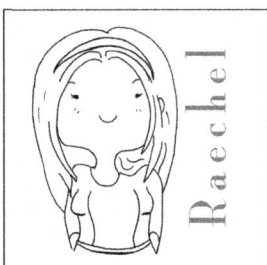

Raechel

THE
HIDING GAME
SAGA

Other Hiding Game Books by Raechel Sands

Lightning Source UK Ltd.
Milton Keynes UK
UKOW04f0307251117
313273UK00001B/47/P